ZULU DAWN

is a novel of imperial adventure set against the sweeping landscapes of southern Africa.

ZULU DAWN

is Cy Endfield's powerful sequel to his celebrated epic *Zulu*.

ZULU DAWN

is shortly to be released as a blockbuster film starring Peter O'Toole, Burt Lancaster, John Mills and Simon Ward, produced by Nate Kohn and directed by Douglas Hickox.

Cy Endfield

SEVERN HOUSE

First British hardcover edition published 1979 by
SEVERN HOUSE PUBLISHERS LTD
of 144–146 New Bond Street, London W1Y 9FD
with grateful acknowledgement to Arrow Books Ltd

ISBN 0 7278 0479 0

Endfield, Cy
  Zulu dawn.
  I. Title
  823'.9'1F   PS3555.N/

  ISBN 0-7278-0479-0

Printed in Great Britain by The Anchor Press Ltd
and bound by Wm Brendon & Son Ltd
both of Tiptree, Essex

I dedicate this book
to a great man
and a dear friend
CHIEF GATSHA BUTHELEZI

Prologue

By the final morning of the umKhosi, the great ingathering, all the soldiers of King Cetshwayo's warrior Impis, full 50,000, were encamped on the slopes beyond the spiked palings that encircled the royal Kraal. These men, each a pledged full-time Zulu warrior, were to be the audience in the gigantic natural amphitheatre, scooped in the hills, while within the great Kraal itself the leading performers prepared: the King, his own royal regiments and royal medicine men, supported by the hundreds, if not thousands, of royal servants and retainers, and the hundreds, certainly, of the royal wives; and, not least in importance, the choicest cattle from the King's royal herds, which numbered 100,000.

On the still dark slopes, the pulsations of collective excitement were palpable in the dawn air almost as soon as the encamped warriors arose from their sleeping mats. Indeed, the inDunas, the Zulu officers, made certain that all their charges would be aroused in time for the ceremonies, generously lashing out with kicks or uninhibited swipes of their deadly knobkerries. None of those awakened, however rudely, were allowed a protest, but some laughed raucously and dodged or joked or made mock aggressive responses. Finally all moved with purpose into their ranked formations.

In the cooking areas of the encampment, torches of bound kindling were applied to piles of dried thorn tree branches, and there were flaring bursts of flame which lighted the many dark shapes of Zulu faces. Pots of earthenware, or in some instances of iron, staked over the now-smoking fires, started to

7

steam fragrantly while the heavier smoke of the fires twisted erratically in the fresh-blowing morning air.

Then, all in an instant and everywhere, there was a cessation of casual movement. A contagion of anticipation spread in moments across the vast throng suddenly grown silent. The trigger for this was sight of the Royal Guard emerging from the royal enclosure to take up positions in two well-dressed lines flanking the surprisingly low exit of the outsize twenty-foot high royal hut itself. These superb men, the Royal Guard, were selected for bearing, for muscularity and, of course, for their warrior's skills; for instance, they were required to fight with shields much too massive for the ordinary warrior even to hold, let alone to maintain in a guard position, during combat. Their gleaming-bladed assegais were held at thrust position. They stood rigid, but the tail-and-paw tassels of their royal leopard skins danced to the morning swirlets of air. Following on, the courtiers of Cetshwayo's Inner Council emerged from the low entrance, positioned themselves flanking inside the line of Royal Guards.

The tension of waiting increased. Now a single high-calling voice enunciated the great name – a fantastic ululation that reached the hills beyond the Kraal and returned as a multiplying echo. An answering chant of 50,000 voices rumbled, grew in volume: Hail, all praise, our great King now come amongst us. At last, magnificently haunched and girded, but crouched low of necessity, the form of the great King Cetshwayo emerged from the low exit; then unfolding, bellying outward, he stood up to his full, overpowering height. Immediately body attendants crowded about him, straightening and fussing, arranging his most magnificent leopard skins, extending ready bowls of water, scents, liquids and unguents for the many ablutions and anointments of the royal awakening. The ritual actions were executed with a precisely balanced mixture of profound reverence and courtly finesse, while the volume and reverberations of the massed chanting increased.

Then, ready, the King turned, his royal hand stretched out to the first amongst the royal medicine men. The venerable ancient in fantastic garb handed the King a bowl of flecked-brown liquid. Cetshwayo clasped the bowl, raised it, tilted it to his lips, filled his mouth until his cheeks were distended to their full. Thus holding the liquid contained in his mouth, he turned again, lifted his face to the rising sun and in a mighty spray squirted out the medicine at the curruscant fire-ball and, at the same time, thrust his assegai *skyward. Three times he filled his mouth and spat upward. Squirting of medicine at the dawn sun was the magic act by which the King of the Zulus could command the all powerful sun itself – surely the Great Chief of the heavens – to bring destruction and confusion upon all the would-be enemies of the Children of Heaven, the Zulus. In fact, was that not the very meaning of the word Zulu – 'Children of Heaven'? Did Lord Chelmsford have a magic to equal this – on behalf of a world Empire upon which the sun was supposed never to set? Surely not.*

The King's assegai *thrusting at the sun became the cue for all those in the royal* Kraal *and surrounding it: 50,000 massed blades tightly held in black fists thrust skyward in unison to the accompaniment of the single-voiced roar, 'Bay–ed–e!' Then again and again the mighty chorus of 50,000 warrior throats, shields and spears stabbing repeatedly in unison to the heaven, giving fearsome expression to the armed will of the Zulu nation.*

'Zu ... Zu–u–u! ... Bayede! ... Bayede!'

The First Fruits Ceremony had begun in good order.

1

Being the third-born male offspring of the Viscount Gort
had secured for Standish William Prendergast Vereker an
Oxford education and the inconsequential title, 'Honourable', but no money and no idea of what he might do with
his life – most of it still before him. Deprived of any
income by the unequal custom of primogeniture, he was
left only with the option of marrying into it – not at all
difficult for a young man so blondly handsome, so stur-
dily expert with gun and horse, so well endowed with
most of what are deemed to be the aristocratic graces. But
neither the prospect of arranged marriage nor the limited
careers open to him – military, ecclesiastical, legal –
sparked in Vereker any fire at all. There remained for
him, therefore, as with other nineteenth-century youth in
similar plight betwixt good birth and no position, the
'faraway places', the many pink-coloured areas of the
world maps where Queen Victoria's Imperial armies held
sway, and which held promise of adventure, possibility of
achievement and even, ultimately, establishment of one's
own independent identity. From the planet-wide
Empire, the Hon. Standish Vereker chose the south of
Africa, possibly because that was where his eye first lit, if
for any reason at all.

His wayward search for satisfactory activity in a congenial location landed him first at the Cape province, and
over the next few years took him north into the Transvaal
where he tried to master growing. His crops failed in two

11

successive seasons, ravaged by blight and insects. He sold out at a loss and then, after a brief, dissatisfying stay in the expanding Natal port of Durban and thereafter in the increasingly sophisticated capital at Pietermaritzburg, he moved again – and found by chance his first taste of peace.

Seventy-five miles further inland, a fair distance from anything recognizable as the outer edges of civilization, he farmed an acreage just this side of the Buffalo River on the border of Zululand. The kind of peace that he found waiting for him there was not, to be sure, one of those dramatically profound or relevatory experiences – rather more simply, it was a cessation of restlessness, a feeling that he need search no further for a place to settle. It was never a thriving enterprise. He tried crops such as red yams, tobacco, sugar cane, and more cotton, yielding a pittance of financial rewards for much fatiguing labour. The products – the ones that survived the voracious insects, the virulent moulds, the thieving baboon – he delivered some miles downriver to the store at the mission station, established at a place called Rorke's Drift, which had only a few years earlier been taken over by the Rev. Otto Witt and his dour Swedish family. Ultimately that produce went by wagons to an export agent in Durban and cash was returned. It was never very much ... enough to settle for what he purchased at the mission store. Any small surplus he paid to the Zulu hands who helped him work his acreage. It was this money, and the European manufactured goods it could buy at the store, that linked Vereker's Zulus to the white economy and differentiated them from the warrior Zulus of the great *Kraals* in the hinterlands beyond the Buffalo River, beyond the peaks of the Nqutu range of mountains which now formed the young Honourable's permanent eastern horizon.

There were no more than twenty of these immigrant Zulu families who had built their thatched mud huts on

12

young Vereker's land, worked for him – and called him *ņKhosa* with the reverential bowing, clasped hands and averted eyes which they would use for their chief whatever his skin colour. A warmth of feeling, and respect, grew between them quite early on. Indeed he came to realize that it was the very nature of these black people with whom he had chosen to live that was the fount of the peace he had found here, and kept him here. They were completely themselves, he could be completely himself – and that was the end of it.

He lived full long days from sunrise to nightfall, full of hard physical work when such was required, full of silence when that need prevailed. He worked *with* his Zulus, he felt, not *over* them, though their ingrained habits of unquestioning response to leadership gave him status without force.

He frequently rode off, at first guided but often, later, alone, to hunt the local antelope or crop-stealing baboons or marauding leopards, though these were becoming less common. Hunting in this mode he regarded as real hunting: not mere sport. He learned to speak Zulu quickly enough, and enjoyed its picture-forming richness. Zulus invariably gave to whites, with whom they had frequent contact, Zulu names, not always flattering, but piquant and unexpectedly accurate. Vereker's Zulu name translated as 'the tall tree with yellow leaves in which the winter birds nest before they migrate northwards'. It amused him and also helped him see himself with their eyes.

These people were unselfconscious performers of surprising excellence, and when he learned through observation their dances and rituals it was very natural that he became a participant. There was a typical dance, a male dance called the *ameGaga*, which consisted of whirling and charging, thrusting stabbing-spears (*assegais*) at imaginary enemies, making patterned movements with cowhide shields, then repeatedly rocking the solid earth

13

with the unique Zulu stamping action. Zulu stamping was executed with the awe-inspiring – it would seem leg-shattering – violence, the legs alternately lifted head high (and higher), then propelled downwards with earth-shaking force, right and then left, time after time with furious rapidity. Rythmic sledge hammer-like blows were repeated unendingly to the pounding accompaniment of spear shafts beating on the taut hide surfaces of their war shields. Vereker's own first tries at this were enthusiastic and uninhibited rather than expert; but a space was cleared for him, he danced as they clapped and drummed and beat shields, and he was much hailed and cheered and encouraged to continue when exhaustion brought him to pause, panting, perspiring, and stimulated. He had been enticed into drinking more and more of their fermented mealie beer, and thus liberated by the alcohol, by the companionship and the community of participation in song and uninhibited movement, he ended up having – there was no doubt about this – the best times of his life.

His last obstacle to contentment vanished at a later time when he was invited to a local Zulu wedding, where he watched the graceful dancing of the unmarried girls who escorted the bride forward. He was enthralled by the natural demeanour and noble posture of these growing women, who easily carried gallon-sized earthenware water jugs on their heads, twice each day, to fetch drinking water for the farm from a fresh stream a mile away. There was one of the young girls in particular ... his thought hovered, captivated by a certain quality of image, then he consciously shifted it. But further on in the ceremonies, after the betrothal, the bridesmaids, who included this girl, danced again, this time a dance called *umKlazo*, shrilly sung, the sound and movement imitating the swarming clatter of a horde of locusts, amusing,

14

full of laughter and play, and insect-like teasing of the newlyweds. Then the nubile youngsters, pout-breasted, lithe, glistening golden-skinned in the sun, danced yet another dance, the *umShikilewana*, a provocative and sexually daring dance, turning buttocks to one another; then, as she might be moved by the spirit of the moment, one or another of the girls whould emerge from the line to turn that particular feature of her anatomy for a flaunting instant to a young man she favoured, then scamper back laughing to the security of the line of her sister dancers.

Among them danced this fifteen-year-old girl called Thola, the one who had provoked that stray, disconcerting thought for the Hon. Standish Vereker earlier on; he dallied on the word 'Honourable', smiled, and decided not to censor any further his natural masculine admiration for the subtle richness of this young lady's feminine characteristics, such as – the adjectives fell into place – the quite perfect ripening fullness of her breasts, the sexual precision of the curvature of hip into stomach into the delicate delightful convolution of navel, the supple and again, sexual, architecture of her thighs and arms and calves and ... the demureness of her downcast eyes which, looking up, revealed brief pools of such limpid ... but enough, enough. Look at the others, all lovely seductive dancers. He felt flushed, embarrassed. He was now staring, he felt, only at her, but her gaze did not turn downward quite so quickly as earlier – was there a sprightliness and flirtatious daring he had not earlier guessed at? The glance that held his started a further curious churning within him. No, he decided, not curious, most familiar and recognizable. But now she turned away, she and another dancer bumped buttocks again, tantalizing moons revealed by the swaying beads of the tiny G-string moochies she and her sister dancers wore. And then she was dancing out of line, past several young Zulu swains who were calling and reaching for her show of favour – but she passed them by, to where *nKhosa*

15

Vereker sat on a low stool, turned as she reached him to expose her delightful rear with a fluting back movement. Her head turned over her smooth shoulder, her eyes meeting his were full of laughter and acceptance. The Zulu audience laughed at the girl's jest, but Vereker knew then with complete certainty of body, soul and mind that she would be his, and himself hers. And soon.

Soon it was. The *lobola* (the dowry, which at home he would have received, not paid) was rich beyond her parents highest expectations. There was a more than generous moeity of the usual cattle, utensils, and some money ... but he had added an elaborately padded silken counterpane with the Gort crest emblazoned in gold and silver thread: *Con Mortuus sui agressevesi*. It was a wonderously rich if not wholly comprehensible item surely never before seen in the history of Zulu *lobola* giving. There were other similar items which his mother had lovingly packed, trying to ensure that her prodigal would maintain expected family standards in whatever alien clime he might fare; but most of these had been shed or lost in his travels. The most valuable of these, the counterpane, went now to his bride's family.

Thus, without undue delay, the girl Thola and the English Honourable were married within a traditional Zulu wedding ceremony. The singing bridesmaids of the *inTanga* formed lines between which the lovely bride danced; next the older women joined their voices to sing phrases which proclaimed Thola's immaculate grace, poise and beauty; then they turned on the uncertain bridegroom, wailing and cursing him for his possible intentions to travesty or to not respect, in some loathsome male way, all of her golden qualities. Although he knew it to be only ritual, this assault on the groom was conducted with a certain passion which might just reflect how these older women estimated the meaning of marriage in their own lives. Vereker certainly did not see

16

himself ever taking the Zulu male preogatives of polygamy, or arrogation of so many of the more strenuous agricultural tasks to the distaff. Not with Thola, ever. She would be his one true companion forever, he had no other thought.

Although it went on quite long enough, much of the usual ceremony was necessarily omitted because of the absence of the groom's family. (Vereker amused himself imagining his parents, the Viscount and Viscountess, and his brothers during the *amaviyo ayo shobinga*, 'the interval for going to relieve nature', when the excitement of the jeering and challenge between the wedding parties could lead to a fair amount of blood-letting, or wielding of sticks.) But absent his family unquestionably were; so there was not the usual requirement that the bride amalgamate herself with her new in-laws, asking for their patience with her inexperience or possible periods of unhealth, for consideration of her inadequacies should such be revealed, and hoping, particularly, that she would be acceptable to the groom's family's ancestral spirits. Contemplating those venerable corpses so confronted, Vereker found himself in a fit of giggling that lasted quite some time.

The *lobola* he'd paid was publicly counted and displayed – the huge ornamental counterpane, when waved glinting in the sunlight like a silken ocean, brought gasps of awe from the guests. The fattened cattle were patted and appreciated. Then all were given beer and delicious hot crackling meat from a choice bullock killed and spitted and roasted whole for the occasion. Speeches and invocations to a vast assortment of controlling spirits, delivered in clicking staccato and with mouth-sucking fluidity, far too complex in theme and language for the young man to follow except in skimpiest detail, went on and on while the voluptuous feasting and copious drinking increased. The atmosphere thickened: the conterminity of young persons of both sexes in so emotional a cli-

17

mate, the essential nakedness and availability of person led to the inevitable physical contact, the reaching and grappling of hands to easily accessible body parts, writhing embraces and rubbings together. Thus, as the afternoon waned, more and more of the impassioned younger couples disappeared from the centre of festivities into the concealing surround of bushes and trees. Love begat love – with no notice or reprimand from elders who drank and ate and sang or danced or quarrelled or reeled or sank into languorous torpor. At some point unnoted by the white odd-man-out, the bride was protectively spirited away from all this. But he remained at the centre of the revelry, was pawed, embraced, plied with drink, involved in the unending dancing and guzzling and rowdy proclamation of the pleasures of the night forthcoming. There were the same nudges and leers and lewd flauntings he had seen at weddings at his English homeland (where the couples were of more expected mixture.) He was quite drunk and enjoyed it fully without loss of stamina. Surely no man could have a better wedding.

Dusk arrived as the sun, disappearing below the west horizon tipped the mountains of the Nqutu range with fiery orange which crept upwards to the peaks then slid away. Drama intruded when an amorous couple, in their threshing, inadvertently upturned a stone and disturbed a black scorpion family thereunder, one of whose members uncoiled a lashing, poisonously barbed tail at the offending rump – the girl's. Anguished and frightened, she came screaming for help. The young man followed, carrying the crushed body of the venomous super insect. It was excitedly examined and discussed. Expert opinion was that it was the least poisonous of the region's varieties, but that the sobbing girl would have a few quite unhappy days before she recovered. A poultice of bruised herbs of curative powers was applied. Nothing more could be done. She was led off, but the party was sobered by the event; it became a cue for general retirement. The guests bade him well, then departed. Vereker, on his own, went to his quarters.

The young man waited wakefully in the dark on his sleeping mat. From out of the night, he heard feminine whimpering, which he presumed to come from the scorpion-poisoned girl. He wondered in what way his Lady mother's crested counterpane might be put to use now? He waited. He had learned a new Zulu word this day – *ukungenisa*. It was a term denoting the moment when a bride stole out into the night from the care of her family to enter the dwelling place of her husband. *U-kun-gen-isa-* a melodic word. He whispered it. The sound that came back to him from the doorway was Thola's sound. There was no light to see. But his sense of sight had had glory enough. The touch of her and feel of her as she lowered herself into his embrace confirmed all those wondrous visions. Her warmth pierced him. Then closeness merged, became oneness.

In the weeks following it seemed to Standish Vereker, not that he dwelt on such matters, that his life was wholly perfect now; if he could control its course he would never allow it to significantly change. He was twenty-five years old. But it is given to very few men to exert real control over their destiny; the peace and perfection of his new life was to last hardly at all. In fact he had been given the vital clue to his destiny but had misjudged it. Africa was full of such caprice. Some days before the wedding he had seen, or thought he had seen, a momentary slither of green amidst the yellow weave of the roof thatching above their sleeping quarters. Mamba, deadly green mamba! But if it really had been there, it failed to show itself during the beating-out he had ordered, and in due course the incident was forgotten. Perhaps the grim reptile did depart,

19

and quite a different one had arrived those weeks later. Vereker had been away for two days on a hunt. When he returned to his farm, his servants brought him terrible news. Thola had been found dead from two fanged punctures on the inside of her bruised purpling wrist. They had been married hardly a month.

2

Later that year, in a close, humid December, what had been numb acceptance of God's will, or Nature's inscrutable ways, began to transform itself into feelings of anger against the place where the terrible event had occurred. Some of the old restlessness returned, and he began to count days to decision, but feeling a need to decide gave no clue as to what such decision might be; only that some change must re-enter his life grown sullen and dull.

Just then, news arrived of the appearance at Rorke's Drift of a contingent of red-coated Imperial soldiers. It was a reconaissance group, he was told, one of several such from Pietermaritzburg charged with exploring the defensibility of the Natal-Zululand borderlines should the King of the Zulus decide to launch an attack across the Buffalo. Vereker was puzzled – why ever would King Cetshwayo make that decision? It appeared that Sir Bartle Frere himself, High Commissioner of Natal, thought it a most likely possibility. Furthermore, Lt. Gen. Frederic Augustus Theisiger, the second Baron Chelmsford, had been charged with mustering an army to secure the royal colony from any such barbaric incursion *when*, not *if*, an attacked was launched.

In the hope of receiving more news from the uniformed visitors, Vereker had ridden into the mission station to pick up supplies which were not really immediately necessary. Although there was no sign of the army on his arrival, he did not have long to wait. As the afternoon faded into the evening, the military party rode back in from their reconnaissance. Four officers, and a dozen men. The officers went into the mission station. To Vereker's relief, he was invited to join them by the missionary Otto Van Witt.

Vereker found himself enlivened by the sudden presence of men of his own age. Hearing of his background, the officers were most interested in him, and in what he might know of the Zulus across the river. In turn their leader, Brig. Henry Evelyn Wood, a well-known Zulu expert, revealed the background to their mission. He said that he had his own spies out amongst some of the minor chieftains of Zululand, and was here now at the Upper Drift to obtain and evaluate first-hand information about King Cetshwayo's intentions. Both Sir Bartle Frere, the High Commissioner, and Lord Chelmsford, reasoning from what might be called a geopolitical basis, were convinced of the inevitability of the Zulus' need to secure their own land requirements as against the colony's. In spite of nineteenth-century Africa's unoccupied vastness, good grazing land was at premium. Cetshwayo's intensive programme of remilitarization along the lines of his warrior ancestor, the great conqueror Shaka, was positive evidence that the Zulu *need* would be implemented by Zulu *action*, eventually if not sooner. The young subalterns chimed in agreement. Damned arrogant, this black barbarous chief, this so called Great King.... Cited were numerous raids and other illegal crossings of the river to exact Zulu punishment from Zulu offenders who fled to the Natal side. And when the invasion happened it would be atrocity, it would be rape, it would be pillage, it would be ... a damned cheek; they all agreed.

To Vereker almost everything these young officers said about the Zulus was either foolish and misinformed, or mischievously and dangerously wrong. What misconceptions, what arrogant ignorance reinforced by stupid pre-

22

judice. He bridled internally, but none the less replied to the aggravating statements quite mildly. To his continued surprise his hunger for conversational exchange, in a familiar idiom, was now so strong that he didn't wish to antagonize more than necessary, or at all really. He listened more than answered, he dallied, giving the weak excuse that he wanted to oversee the reloading of the crops he had brought on to Witt's larger wagons, which would go to the coast; even then he waited, deciding to send his own two Zulu cart-drivers back, saying he would follow on.

Walking with the younger officers to where the tents of the soldiers were pitched alongside the mission's stone cattle *Kraal*, Vereker listened as one sardonic young lieutenant, by the name of Teignmouth Melvill, disdainfully compared the Zulus' *assegai* weaponry to the sophisticated Martini-Henry rifle.

'Very well,' Vereker agreed, 'your bullets will get to them a damn lot faster than their spears to you. But wait until you see them keep on coming, dear fellow, forty, fifty thousand of them, trained a lifetime for this moment; eventually, some get through, one of them yours! You're there with just your bayonet against his *assegai*. It's a snake, it's a scorpion's tail! You never see it, slithering under your guard, ten inches of flattened sharpened iron blade backed by muscles of the same material and a frenzy of hate – dear fellow, it's *their* country and *their* King. . . .'

'Wait,' said Melvill, 'You've made my point. Damn barbarians, if we don't get there first, they come after us. Not content to kill a chap – have to rip him up and down the gut afterwards, mutilation. And no exception for women and children. No damn manners. If we don't go in there and teach them our ways, they'll come out and show us theirs.'

Melvill's companion officer, Coghill, a born enthusiast who believed that all Her Majesties armies were engaged by Destiny itself to participate in these great foreign adventures for God, Queen and Empire, cut in:

'Absolutely. We have no choice! It's a question of stopping them before they get us, as you just said!'

Listening to these young officers, so arrogant, so sure and so determined to have their war, Vereker felt a grim sense of foreboding at the inevitability of it all.

He glanced at Helga Witt, the missionary's eldest daughter, arrived only recently from Sweden, her mouth compressing and pursing in a quite odd way as she listened to the conversation, which she wasn't at all certain was for a young (well, not quite *that* young) Christian lady's ears to hear. The overwhelming maleness of the soldiers' presence at the mission added to a nervousness that she had felt on arrival in Africa and which had increased daily since then. Time was not helping her get used to this savage continent. Now it was talk of an invasion by an even more dangerous and wilder, and probably black and more naked, kind of Zulu than she had already encountered; huge muscular men, they were describing, with disembowelling stabbing spears, who might arrive any moment from across the river on a night dark as this. Stabbing, stabbing! She felt Vereker's momentary glance, turned her eyes to see her father whispering in a corner with the General called Wood. Men, all men.

Helga notwithstanding, Vereker felt he had to retort to Melvill, at least explain why Zulu warriors mutilated, or seemed to mutilate fallen enemies. He hoped he wouldn't sound pedantic. He rose to his feet as if to stretch, to hold back a yawn.

'Tell you what, old fellow, from the Zulu point of view, he's doing his enemy a bit of a favour disembowelling him.'

Melvill sniffed disdainfully, looked at his friend Coghill, arched one of his devil's eyebrows. ' ... must remember to dash off a thank-you note after some damned Fuzzie's mutilated you, Coghill – doing you a favour old boy, you see.'

Vereker jabbed his forefinger towards Coghill's second Warwickshire belt-emblem buckling his patent leather webbing at his waist. 'Behind that belt there in your tummy resides a warrior's soul – that's what a Zulu warrior believes – just like his. And if after you've fallen in combat, the victor didn't bother to cut you open, the poor lonely warrior spirit might never, never be freed to wing its way up to heaven where the great God Unkulunkulu is waiting to receive it into an eternal paradise of many pleasures for having died nobly, in combat.' Vereker leaned in closely, direly, 'Do you, Lieutenant, want your immortal soul to be trapped forever miserable in its putrefying corpse, when a few neat slashes with a stabbing spear . . .!'

Laughing, they went through to supper. They ate coarse fare, and conversation switched to Zulu marriage customs. Helga returned, to clear the dishes ostensibly, but in the midst of this task she ventured a tight-lipped opinion of how dreadful it was that King Cetshwayo could force as many as a thousand young girls into marriage with veteran warriors, like so many cattle, in a single ceremony, as payment for war service.

'Young girls, old men', she said with distaste.

Melvill remarked in answer that a few of the lads in his command might well deem such compensation as worth a lot more than the Queen's shilling. Coghill laughed, and she started to get angry again; surprisingly Witt counselled his daughter to tolerance in this domain of alternate custom.

'In Europe,' he said sagely, 'marriages are arranged with wealthy men. Perhaps the Zulu girls are luckier getting brave ones.'

Vereker decided to refrain – there was always too much to explain. He recalled once trying to communicate differences in romantic ritual to Thola, how it was amongst

25

the British. Lovely, eager-to-learn Thola. But most of the things he had said made her giggle, or exclaim in amazement or, quite often, in disgust. And if he couldn't lead Thola across the divide of understanding, what was the use of making more effort with these people. The evening was over, really; he now had a surfeit of the conversation he had hungered for earlier. Time to bed down. The officers would retire soon to their bivouac and he, with borrowed bedding, to the storeroom off the chapel. Remembering Thola had initiated in him a brief erotic reverie, replaying the fleshy ecstasy of their union. He looked about. There was nothing left here in this corner of the world where he had known peace briefly and where, inevitably, war and killing would soon arrive – but where else was there to go?

The following morning he rode down to the river with the soldiers to inspect the fordable shallows of silt known as the Drift. The river was in spate – the unrelenting spring rains, which had ruined all possibilities of early harvest, were still running off. It was not safe to cross at the moment, but not typical either. Under orders, some of the soldiers tested the crossing. Having ridden hazardously through the swollen river, then back, most of the time swimming their horses, they decided that if even slightly less in flood, the river here was fordable for heavy military traffic. With luck, with no repetition of the rains, it was viable as an entry into the enemy country.

Then they all rode north along the west bank, that is, the Natal side of the Buffalo, until they came to Vereker's farm with its wretched rained-out crops, the jerry-built central house with most of its doors opening directly on to the outside, and the perimeter of the farm dotted with individual *Kraals* of Vereker's own Zulus.

Vereker was instantly alarmed by what he saw: the older men and women were waiting for him, eager to come forward to speak matters of urgency, but were clearly deterred by the presence of the mounted soldiers who were themselves at that moment probing Vereker with questions and evidently not in the least interested in this motley of hovering natives. But Vereker was sensitive to the urgencies that his folk felt and, turning from his questioners, addressed the waiting Zulus in their own language. Then they crowded around, jabbering, miming, thrusting hands and pointing fingers eastward in the direction of Nqutu mountains beyond the river, towards the peak known to them as Isandhlwana. Eyes of the soldiers, sheltered by the short peaks of their white helmets, now turned to glance in the direction of the pointing – not understanding what was being said and certainly not suspecting that the odd-shaped sentinel peak would soon be, too soon, the sole marker of their many graves.

Vereker covered his own eyes briefly to reflect on all that had been chattered out to him by his Zulus. He had to explain to his escort but did not want to convey the full sense of foreboding gloom that seized him at the news which had been told him.

Why were there only the elders here, Vereker asked the group. The young men, he was told, had sat in council the evening before, taking advantage of *nKhosa* Vereker's absence; they had decided as a group to return across the Buffalo to seek out and rejoin the warrior *Impis* in which they had trained as younger men. All gone? Yes, came the answer, all of them.

Explaining the position to the soldiers, Vereker told them that his Zulus had emigrated from across the river only three years ago, in a year of bad crops and military inactivity. The young men came then with their families, but many were not really satisfied with farming as a principal mode of existing. Like every young Zulu, they had been brought up as warriors, removed at an early age from their home village *Kraals* to huge, miles-in-diameter, military *Kraals* for many years of indoctrination and training in the unique forms of Zulu war. In these military *Kraals* they learned the running formations in the shape of the buffalo: the head, loins and the horns which surrounded and destroyed the enemies. They learned the supreme art of man-to-man and hand-to-hand engagement with the stabbing spear; the unique balanced Zulu *assegai* supported by the shield; the incredible disciplines of endurance and the ultimate development of the body's muscular structure as a fighting machine. Now, news had come from across the river of a huge ingathering of all the *Impis*, the Zulus' super regiments. Fifty thousand warriors were marching from all parts of Zululand, converging at King Cetshwayo's command, to the mighty royal *Kraal* at the centre of the nation – at Ulundi.

Perhaps with more emphasis and gruesome detail than necessary, Vereker dwelt on the intricate refinement and deadliness of that military machine *par excellence* – the Zulu army. It did not displease him at all to note several uncomfortable swallows and perspiring brows as these arrogant young conquerors were forced, if only momentarily, to re-evaluate the nature of the war in which they were next to engage.

The Redcoats demanded to know the reason for the Zulu ingathering. Was this the prelude to the feared invasion? If so, then what foresight Sir Henry Bartle Frere, High Commissioner of Natal, and Lord Chelmsford, their commander, had shown in ordering preparations for it, even this late in the day.

A Zulu invasion – *now?* Vereker was doubtful. Yes, war was in the air, no doubt – that was why his own young men had deserted. The desertion even included many of the pubescent boys who, aspiring to be soldiers for their King, would march with the *Impi* of boys and women. They formed the supply and cooking *Impis* which followed each warrior *Impi* at a respectful distance, the boys herding the cattle, the women carrying the utensils, preparing the food as well as spare weapons, shields

28

and *assengais*, and whatever other supplies were necessary but not carried directly by the warriors themselves. However, the war, if it were to be, was not necessarily Cetshwayo's war. To Vereker's mind, the atmosphere for it had been created by the British military presence, including the presence of those who sat here alongside him on their horses now at this very moment. The war atmosphere had been created by Lord Chelmsford's recent ultimatums and demands that the Zulus suddenly stop acting like Zulus, but remould their laws and lives to suit British concepts of what decent national behaviour should be. As for the ingathering, that was an annual occasion anyhow. The Ceremony of the First Fruits went far back into Zulu history, and it was custom that all the nation collected at the royal *Kraal* prior to each harvest to celebrate with their King the bounty of nature which had rewarded their year's work with the sustenance for living. The King, as Vereker knew, was responsible for arranging with heaven for the days of sunshine and the fall of rain on the whole of Zululand and for all the other conditions of fruitfulness that had been required during the year just past; it was death to anyone who partook of the new growth of green crops before the King did.

This year, the excess of rain, for which the spirits were scolded very sharply indeed, had delayed the crops. The Great King had decided that the *umKhosi*, the ingathering of the warriors for the First Fruits Ceremony, would not be delayed because of nature's intransigence.

Hearing this news of the gathering of the *Impis* at the royal *Kraal* had made Brigadier General Wood immediately unhappy. He knew that the tempo of His Lordship's preparation had been based to some degree, on the presumption that the *Impis* would not be assembled until there was full crop growth sufficient to justify the First Fruits Ceremony. The general had now to ask himself, was Cetshwayo's decision to call his troops together before full harvest merely a lucky caprice, or was it a calculated military strategy, or perhaps even a sure warrior instinct that the ingathering of the *umKhosi* could not afford to wait either for heaven or for a spiritual beneficence with these threatening British elements showing up on Zulu borders?

'Whatever Cetshwayo's reasons,' remarked the general to the young officers around him, 'what now has to be ascertained is the true purpose of the ingathering – is it aggressive, or only defensive?'

There was spirited discussion and expression of opinion as to this choice. Aggressive! – was the soldiers' dominant opinion it seemed, but they argued all the possibilities. Vereker sat there wondering what the difference was. There would be war and it would spill across these very borders here, into his sheltered haven. Here they were, so interested in his little section of the world just at the moment when it was becoming blurred and unimportant to him. He watched as Brigadier General Wood and Lieutenant Melvill and Lieutenant Coghill and the others of the party of soldiers bade him farewell, spurred and rode away, back towards the Drift.

He considered his immediate future.

'I'll go to Durban first,' he thought with sudden determination, 'and settle outstanding matters with my shipping agent.' After that – well, one's chances of finding congenial activity were probably best at Pietermaritzburg. The charmingly eccentric Bishop Colenso, Bishop of Natal, a family friend from the early days, had been particularly welcoming when three years ago the young Vereker had been through the capital on his way out to here. And the Colenso daughters – he smiled briefly – were delightful. The eldest – ah, yes, Fanny – well, her age was exactly the same as his, so she'd be twenty-five years old now also. When he looked up again, the soldiers were well distant, and in the next few moments they vanished beyond a hillock on their path back towards Rorke's Drift. Vereker turned to his remaining folk – could he leave them to their chancy fate if, not *if* but *when*, war came? Firm intention about departing faltered, fled; no, of course he could not. Well, he would just have to sleep on the problem. He would decide all on the morrow.

But he wasn't to have even a full night of postponement. Sounds came to awaken him before next dawn. Emerging from his sleeping quarters, he found that now all but half a handful of his remaining Zulus had departed; and even these few faithful ones remaining advised that staying would become increasingly unsafe. They were, he realized, as worried about him as he was for them. They wanted to try their luck to the south-east, coastward, in fact, away from their own sons who had returned to join their *Impis* in Zululand. Vereker was relieved of decision. And why shouldn't he go coastward also? Once in Durban, he mused, perhaps he could locate old Harding, the manservant who had travelled with him from England, but who had remained on the coast when his young master had insisted on going further inland. It would be an excellent starting point for picking up on the old life.

He looked around at the surroundings that had become so familiar and, smelling the damp, cold air of the early morning, was seized with angry regret. Damn this river, damn the crops, and damn all poisonous green mambas, damn them all – for some minutes now the red suffusion of pre-dawn light had been limning the horizon, separating the solid black of night into red sky and a silhouette of mountains. Suddenly his eyes screwed against the harsh blinding-white halations as the sun came up from behind the peak of Isandhlwana. And damn all warrior Zulus, thought Vereker, let them come over those mountains – the Hon. Standish William Predergast Vereker will be far, far away. He embraced each of the remaining Zulus, waiting for his decision, paid them what he could in kind, and duly they fled southward too.

31

He re-entered his living quarters, dressed himself in tweedy garb he hadn't taken out in these years and, in spite of the rising temperature, donned a matching Inverness cape. The soft-brimmed stitched hat that went with the outfit refused to fit over the knot of long untrimmed hair at the back of his head. He skimmed the useless thing away. No hat then. He collected his ivory set, comb and brush, shoe hook and boot horn, his chased-silver-backed mirror and his silver picture frame with the daguerreotype of mother, the Viscountess. Then he went outside again and caught and saddled Dandy, the all-white stallion. He fetched a water bag, filled it, took his various possessions, hung them onto the back of the all-black mare, which the Zulus had inappropriately named amaJimu. He tethered her to the back of Dandy's saddle. Then riding on the white, leading the black, he rode southward, abandoning all he had built in three years. He did, briefly however, turn to watch again the east horizon he knew so well. This would become his last lingering memory before he faced his new direction.

Just fifty miles north-east, if Standish Vereker's line of vision could carry past the intervening Nqutu range, the same sub-red of dawn that first separated his firmament into earth and sky lighted the awe-inspiring grandeur of King Cetshwayo's royal Kraal at Ulundi; revealed to daylight its three and a half mile circumference of spiked palings, and more than a thousand huts set in perfect inscribed circles, which themselves were circumscribed by the encampment of Cetshwayo's 50,000 warriors of the *umKhosi* gathered, or still gathering.

3

A half century earlier, the first British *arrivés* of the Fair-well Trading Company encountered the Zulus in their habitat of the 20,000 square miles that would include the present Natal. They reported their astonishment at finding that the domain contained not simple or primitive tribal groups but a single people who had in fact reached quantitative and qualitative nationhood. It was, they said, a nation that controlled a vast territory and a large population by means of an original and complex – yet wholly integrated – military-political overstructure. These Zulus said the members of the Fairwell Trading Company, lived their daily lives in an interweave that formed an existence tapestry hardly less rich than that which the explorers could claim for their own world.

The Farewell Traders' awed description of the Emperor Shaka's capital at amaBulawayo, both for its vast circular majesty and social-organizational complex-ity, would have to be exceeded to do justice to the royal *Kraal* of the 1870s now evolved here at Ulundi under the reign of the great Shaka's descendant, the great King Cetshwayo, wearer of his ancestor's mantle.

This present King believed intensely that the several Zulu rulers, including his own father, who had succeeded Shaka upon his death fifty years earlier, had allowed the fibre of that mantle to soften. The rigorous laws and customs instigated by Shaka had been eased or forgotten, and the nation had lost much of its will and unity. But he,

Cetshwayo, the Great King, since his coronation a decade earlier, had restored it – by the simple expedient of re-imposing the ways of Shaka that had created Zulu greatness. Now the greatness was returning. Zulu pride was reborn. The world of the spirits approved, and blessed the strivings of the Zulu nation with great bounty. This celebration of the Ceremony of the First Fruits was being conducted in the manner and breadth of spirit of olden days. The King was one with that spirit world. His people wanted him to be a god, and god, on this day, he was.

The law of Shaka commanded that the King, having been hailed by his worshipping subjects, now tasted the first food. This he did. He approved. It was the signal that all could now fall to with festival gusto. It was a celebrant breakfast of rare proportions. Whole spitted cattle turning brown, dripping hot fat on to the early morning fires, were cut precisely into long strips of meat by each partaker; each strip of hot meat was held dangling over a gaping, upturned mouth, so it could be seized with the eater's teeth, then expertly sliced with the keen blade in his other hand, rapidly, into chewable portions, each one quickly masticated and swallowed. Hugh quantities of meat disappeared with astounding rapidity. Then came the platters of fruit and of grain; even with the harvest of many of the available crops not yet completed there were available nonetheless a rich and varied selection for the feasters. There were whole boiled mealie grains and pumpkin slices cooked whole and cooled, then a variety of underground beans and several varieties of sweet potato, and of spinach like leaves. These and many more items all bearing Zulu names rich in description – names like *uQoomo*, *iziNndluba*, *umHlaya*, foods as succulent in taste as in pronounciation. And, too, on this day in particular, the potent ferment of mealie-mash beer was being quaffed even at this early hour. The ceremonial dancing and the troop reviews would follow on after the

34

breakfast, but there was already entertainment in progress for the morning feasters.

A detachment of fifty warriors from the *inGobamakhosi*, the name of a military *Kraal* and of its regiment of young warriors, required shields from the King. This was not an uncommon request to present to the great King, because while the military *Kraals* fashioned most of their own weapons, it was the royal *Kraal*, with its huge surplus of hides of cattle slaughtered each day, that specialized in the making of the shields. The ceremony of 'begging' for these shields required that the young warriors convince the Great Chief that they would use them with the greatest courage and ferocity, as required from a Zulu warrior in service of his King. The King and all of his royal attendants sat eating behind a special enclosure, fenced in by narrow palings, decorated by the branches of trees in a variety of red and purple blossoms. The youthful contingent that required the shields from the King was brought forward; then, brandishing their *assegais*, the young warriors charged forward towards the King's eating enclosure shouting fervent war-calls, whirling, stabbing furiously, executing acts of mock combat with the utmost violence. Individuals from amongst them emerged to forward positions and frenziedly dance-mimed their horrendous intentions against the King's enemies, whoever and wherever they were, and especially if they were white-skinned, red-coated, gun-bearing. They would war for his victory in their thousands, aided by the gift of the shields now being begged.

For a while there was no response from the enclosure – but then the King's head appeared, to look out over the palings. When he was seen, the masses stood up from their eating, again roaring his name and the word, *Bayede*. And upon the appearance of the King the young supplicants for shields immediately hurled themselves belly-flat, faces into the dirt. All was silence as Cetshwayo

35

deliberated, then finally spoke his will. As he pronounced each phrase, the callers echoed it in singing, piercing tones so that all within the giant circle of the royal *Kraal*, as well as the *Impis* encamped on the slopes beyond, were appraised of what was to take place.

Instead of accepting the promise of future performance, Cetshwayo challenged the young supplicants for the shields to earn them there and then. The challenge was one of wicked humour, and this fact was immediately understood.

It was known by all that the young warriors of the *inGobamakhosi* regiment, which was an *Impi* formed by Cetshwayo himself, had been at odds with certain members of the *uThuluwana*, Cetshwayo's own personal *Impi* of veterans, that is, wearers of the *isi-Coco*, the Zulu head-ring. Only such wearers of the *isi-Coco* could *iKhela*, which is to say, take brides of their own choice as a reward for 'washing their spears' in the blood of the King's enemies. And when the King permitted the *uThuluwana* veterans to *iKhela*, many of the young warriors of the *inGobamakhosi* had to yield their long-term affianced sweethearts to those thus favoured to choose. The consequent hatred between the two groups flared into violence of some scale and lives were lost. The marrying of older men to choice young brides was a prize of war initiated by Shaka. Now Cetshwayo directed that the supplicants for shields, the young men of the *inGobamakhosi*, choose a champion who would be given one of these great warrior shields, and that this champion should therewith prove his ability, and by implication that of his comrades, to use the King's shields properly be taking on in battle the warrior whom the *uThuluwana* would elect as *their* champion. The contest was ostensibly about shields, but symbolically it would confer honour to one side or the other whilst bypassing group conflict at a time when division coul not be tolerated.

There seemed to be little doubt among the younger

36

men as to who would represent them. It was a lithe-limbed youth whom his companions called 'Bayele'. He was thrust foward by his comrades, although he seemed to protest the selection. Bayele's *assegai* was removed from his hand. It was replaced by a long black ebony-wood stick – a full one-inch thick, four feet in length, carved from the hardest of hard woods. He was then handed a great shield covered with a patterned black and white hide, the black dominant. This shield had been hurled down from the King's enclosure. Bayele picked it up, tested its heft, thrust his powerful left arm into the carrying strap, seized the fighting stick in his right fist, then stood erectly, proud, prepared for whatever eventuality the combat might bring. Bayele stood an ebony sculpture of perfectly disposed muscularity, balanced on oil-rubbed carved calves and thighs, bare feet planted wide. He waited without a tremor of movement for the selection of his unnamed, as yet unknown, opponent. Perhaps ground breezes stirred the decorations of monkey fur at his ankles and wrists. The great shield was balanced steadily on his left arm, his teeth were slightly bared between wide, curled black lips.

It was plain that this young man had no doubts at all about his destiny or the nature of his service. He was still five years younger than Standish William Prendergast Vereker, with whom his destiny was soon to clash, but he would never share that other young man's uncertainties. Nor did a single quaver agitate him even when a sigh of awe arose from the amassed audience of his tribal fellows when the selected champion of the *uThulwana* stepped forward, then shed the leopard skin that signified him as a Royal Guard. Bayele was now facing the legendary warrior, Nomzaza, twice as broad and as old, thews and biceps of hard black granite, the incarnation of experience and confidence and implacability and earned fame that spread the breadth of Zululand. His awesome reputation was the invisible weapon that Nomzaza carried, in addition to his great white shield and the headless hardwood *assegai* that he would use for this stick-fight. The ceremonial acknowledgements which were his due were made to the great King, then passed between the two combatants. The royal command was a gesture with the royal trident. The contestants circled at a respectful distance, studying the nature of each other's movement and balance, then closed warily. A pervasive silence of anticipation had taken control of the giant amphitheatre both within and outside the *Kraal* palings.

To the main body of Bayele's fellow *inGobamakhosi*, encamped on the slopes surrounding the *Kraal* palings, the figure of their champion appeared tiny, discernable from his formidable opponent only because Nomzaza carried the almost pure white shield of a Royal Veteran. The youthful watchers squatted, riveted by the circling opponents while eating gustily from wooden platters of steaming food. Mouths full, they spat out gristle, bits of bone and expert comments on the abilities of the combatants. All were certain that it would be a classic of stick-fighting (in performance of which, as in knowledge, all Zulus excelled). Bayele's considerable skills many of these young warriors knew from painful personal experience. Nomzaza's abilities were legendary in all departments of warriorhood. Though stick-fighting was regarded merely as training for truly mortal contest with the flat-bladed, stabbing *assegai*, as well as to test courage under duress of pain, at this level of skill and antagonism it could easily cripple, or damage permanently or, with some frequency, end fatally unless Cetshwayo in his wisdom declared a victor before such dire ends came to pass. What all agreed was that voluntary capitulation by either combatant, fighting before the king and all the armies of the nation, was inconceivable.

None of the watchers believed the acquisition of the added regimental shields actually to be at stake – the few hundred required could be purchased if necessary by a tribute of cattle paid to the royal *Kraal*. The combat was understood to be the wise King's method of symbolically defusing the long-term and sporadically violent antagonism between two of his important regiments at a time of approaching national crisis, when common Zulu purpose must prevail. The stakes were regimental honour. Only the King's intervention could terminate this battle short of the total incapacitation of one of the combatants.

The chief *inDuna* of the *inGobamakhosi* youth *Impi*, Uhama, himself a veteran warrior and skilled leader, deep-lined of visage and quite grey, but not much less powerfully structured than the mighty Nomzaza, stood erect at the near, front end of the squatting line of Bayele's cohorts. He shouted with the others, urging and coaching the young champion so tiny below, though amongst the roar of supporting shouts at this distance no one voice could possibly be heard.

The combatants circled cautiously, tense as hunting lions ready to charge, no feinting or false moves yet. Then, in a moment, the opponents had clashed and made first contact. The first blows from each were parried with the same flickering rapidity of dextrous shield moves. Not one of the massed expert watchers quite detected the flashing thrust from the veteran's long stick, which caught the young man across the side of his shoulder to send him whirling askew, stumbling to one knee, stunned, wavering. There was an excited roar as the great Nomzaza descended on the dazed youth to terminate the battle hardly a moment after it had actually began.

Incredibly, the boy managed to twist with some incomprehensible acrobatic finesse, avoiding with a snaking movement the first two strikes. Then, somehow back-somersaulting from a third to come up to a half-crouch and to parry the fourth and fifth mighty flails, angling his shield above his head, he simultaneously counter-attacked at ground level with a deftly thrust foot which caught the advancing giant at his monkey-skin-clad ankles. This unexpected saving manoeuvre worked. Nomzaza tottered, fighting for balance. The shouting thousands, already prepared for Bayele's instant demise, reacted. Their partisan roar of encouragement for the underdog reached Bayele's consciousness, although it did not interfere with the superb reflex sequence that launched his follow-up. His stick started forward below the wavering guard of the momentarily unbalanced Nomzaza. Even off-balance, Nomzaza thrust to counter the strike, but it too was only a feint – Bayele's real blow was an off-side shield smash which caught his surprised opponent's unguarded left flank. Incredulous, the crowd saw the great Nomzaza fall. Above him, Bayele swung down with the long hard stick at the centre of the veteran's head-ring. Bayele alone knew that the blow could be parried by one of Nomzaza's skill and strength, even though he was half-fallen; the great shield swung up covering Bayele's exposed head. Bayele had counted on that reaction, and the swing of his stick in fact became leverage for an unsupported airborne cartwheel which took him spinning over Nomzaza's head. The parrying shield protecting the giant's head also blocked his view. When the expected blow did not descend, the massive warrior looked up from below his shield in amazement to see that his young opponent had apparently vanished. Instantly he realized what must have happened, and instantly he tried to whirl about to meet the attack from the rear – too late! Bayele's rain of blows on the back of Nomzaza's head and neck knocked the big man face-flat and more blows drove him grovelling into the dust. Somehow the big man rolled over and, with stunning strength, despite receiving blow after blow, managed to come staggering to his feet, although completely dazed, disoriented. Bayele in a flame of triumph went in for the kill, the crowd thundering, frenziedly gesticulating, mouths agape screaming, *U-Su-Tu! U-Su-Tu...!* – Kill! ... Kill!' as Nomzaza staggered, unable to mount a defence. His stick, futilely raised to counter just one of the stunning blows, was knocked flying and an instant later Bayele's dark-patterned shield hooked underneath Nomzaza's all-white one, ripping it off his arm. Now the giant stood unweaponed before his youthful vanquisher.

The young warriors of the *inGobamakhosi* led by Uhama exceeded all others in their screams for demolition of the *uThuluwana* champion, but none exceeded the frenzied joy of the twelve-year-old herd-boy who stood with *inGobamakhosi* supply *Impi*.

'He's my brother! He's my brother! – that's my brother, Bayele!' he screamed out, repeatedly. The boy Sizwe echoed with the crowd, *'U-Su-Tu! ... U-Su-Tu!'*

But it was at this moment of maximum opportunity that his brother's attacked faltered – then, stick put aloft, ceased. For several moments, Nomzaza stood defenceless before Bayele, but Bayele still withheld final attack. The shouts of the massed watchers became uncertain, then ceased. A strong wind had been rising, and now only its soughing sounds prevailed as it stirred the thatching of the huts, the floral and leaf decorations of the ceremonial areas. Bayele looked instead to his King. Nomzaza too turned his bloodied head and face blindly to Cetshwayo who looked down from beyond the protection of the royal enclosure.

The King slowly surveyed the combatants – the erect young man, the swaying dethroned Champion of Champions. Then the Great King's glance turned to the quietened throngs, all of his subjects. They watched Cetshwayo's hand as it raised slowly. A mass sigh exhaled. It was the out-turned palm of peace and forgiveness. Bayele slowly lowered his weapons, bowed his head. The swaying Nomzaza could no longer stand; he tottered, came down again to his knees. Then the chant of the throngs began again as the arrogant veterans of the *uThuluwana*, on the King's command, ran among the triumphant contingent of *inGabamakhosi*, giving out the black shields for which they had begged. There were shouts of joy, of congratulations to the victor. The King signalled the end of the matter with a wave of hand, and a return to the eating and drinking. There was a final roar of approval. And the Great King Cetshwayo himself, most pleased with the outcome, stepped out of sight to rejoin his own board. The feastings and celebrations of this splendid day had only begun.

4

Vereker's blonde hair had been further whitened by daily exposure to the high sun that beat down on him as he journeyed south-eastwards to the coast. He cut a conspicuous figure against a country of dark green and rich brown hues, of endless purple distances domed by unflawed ultramarine skies. The few possessions he had chosen to keep hung in saddle-bags. He spent his time mentally enumerating tasks to undertake when he reached the port of Durban, in preparation for the more important return inland to Pietermaritzburg. 'I'll get rid of the beaver and moustache, and have my hair cut to a decent length,' he decided, and, contemplating further, thought that a change of wardrobe to meet current fashion might be in order. Once in Durban, he would find his manservant Harding, and Harding would help him choose – Harding would know exactly what a young gentleman should be wearing at the moment. And, perish any doubts, Harding simply must still be about, and being there, couldn't possibly refuse coming back into his former master's service.

Suddenly he was aware of danger and his hand shot back quickly to the carved-stock rifle protruding from his saddle-holster. But the stirring at the brush edge that had alarmed him turned out to be only local Zulus he had seen before, themselves moving also along the south-east trail to safety, away from the borders of Zululand. He gleaned from them that, the previous day, the petty chief

Mantshonga, a renegade Zulu chieftain who had once had considerable power and independence in Zululand, was travelling towards the Buffalo with a small escort en route to the land of his banishment. He claimed to have important business with the Great Chief Cetshwayo, bearing personal messages from his British masters – at least so Vereker's informants had deduced from what they had heard from some of Mantshonga's coterie.

Vereker was not surprised by this gossip. He knew of the fat old villain Mantshonga, who had been profiting well in this role of intermediary between the British and the Zulus. Could he be bearing a message of reconciliation? Vereker wondered for a moment if he had been too hasty in his decision to leave. His head turned back. The Nqutu range still loomed there undiminished. But Thola would never be there, no matter. He rode on – why try to decipher the mysteries of political or military purpose?

Uhama and his young warriors, still discussing Bayele's glorious win, glanced briefly backwards to see the Mantshonga interlopers emerging from a background clump of thorn trees. Uncertain of their welcome, they paused and stared hungrily at the feasters who were arguing, eating the long strips of hot meat in the Zulu fashion. Mantshonga's dozen-strong party was indeed a motley. The mixture of European items – of which they were inordinately proud – with the more familiar paraphernalia of tribal wear revealed them to the regiment for what they were. Mantshonga was crowned with the veteran *isi-Coco*, not to be gainsaid, and wore the leopard skins of a chieftain, although a fat gold watch chain hallmarked in London swung across his ample middle. He was astride a somewhat scraggly horse, which suffered under its master's great weight. His minions travelled on their own power, armed with *assegais*, shields, and a musket or two. Mantshonga had tethered a long ancient fowling piece to

44

his saddle gear. With an imperious gesture he sent forward two of his retinue, one young man, one older.

The two men paused tentatively a few yards from Uhama and his group, but the Zulus merely continued to eat gustily, discussing details of Bayele's victory. Mantshonga's messengers stood waiting for recognition, unashamedly salivating as they stared at the savoury food being engorged. They were ignored. Uncomfortably they glanced back at Mantshonga, who merely gestured with impatient fury. They had no choice. The elder coughed, and spoke with a show of forthrightness, 'Greetings from the Great Chief Mantshonga! We are fellow Zulus from across the Buffalo River, and we have not found food nor eaten since yesterday morning. Our Great Chief wishes to trade valuable goods with you for a share of your food.'

Very deliberately, Uhama now turned to survey the two men. Then he glanced back at their mounted leader. Instead of replying, however, he conducted a whispered conference with his men. The messengers waited. Mantshonga, astride his horse at the treeline, seemed to stir impatiently. One of Uhama's men crackled with laughter, and finally Uhama, rather indifferently, answered.

'Tell your Chief he can keep his white man's goods – it is our Zulu custom to share our food with needy strangers without requiring payment....'

The messengers nodded, pleased, and turned to convey the good news of free victuals. They were halted by Uhama's well-timed continuation:

' ... but my warriors say, you do not appear as peaceful vistors' – he glanced back at Mantshonga somewhat direly – ' ... they say you and those with you have the look of servants of our enemies. So, run, tell your Chief that I, to whom he sends messengers, am Uhama – Uhama who is sworn to *kill* the enemies of my King – not to *feed* them!'

Uhama turned away. The messengers stood confused, until the elder of the two barked at his junior, who promptly scurried back to Mantshonga. Mantshonga kicked the sides of his reluctant horse to start it plodding forward; his retinue followed. Uhama glanced up as Mantshonga arrived, but did not bother to rise from his squatting position nor to pause in his eating.

Mantshonga was clearly in poor humour, nor was he accustomed to suppress his annoyance when he felt it. 'You are Uhama – who speaks of slaying enemies of Chief Cetshwayo instead of feeding them? Are you he who says this?'

Uhama was not in the least intimidated by the chieftain's aggressive questions. He stared back at the glowering stout figure seated on the tired animal.

'I am he who says you are fortunate to arrive when we Zulus celebrate the Ceremony of First Fruits – an occasion of peace not of war. Otherwise we would not talk of filling your great belly with food but of slitting it open to celebrate the Ceremony of the Vultures ...!' Uhama's young warriors grinned and clicked tongues at their leader's well-chosen words.

Mantshonga's tone became even harsher. 'You speak foolishly, old man. I, Mantshonga, carry a most important message for your great King – and if Mantshonga came to Cetshwayo at this moment, he would gladly share his meat with me and with my followers.'

Of course, both men knew that the Great King's whims in the matter of giving audience made Mantshonga's claim empty – at least if he were counting on such unlikely generosity to quell his very immediate hunger pangs. Cetshwayo was known to have kept men, much more important than Mantshonga, indeed of highest status, waiting many days for an audience. Uhama shrugged, turned away.

Mantshonga pressed his case assertively tapping his head-ring, self-righteously indignant. 'I have earned my *isi-Coco* slaying enemies of Cetshwayo – ask whose stabbing spear was washed in the blood of the Swazi King.'

Uhama turned for another look, his memory prodded. 'Ah ... yes. We have heard of a Mantshonga, the renegade, who lives under the rule of the Redcoat soldiers ....' Mockingly he spoke to the warriors, 'This person says the Great King would invite him to eat at his cooking fire.' Then to Mantshonga he added, in a way that clearly meant the matter was past further discussion, 'Beware, renegade ...! You may end up *over* the Royal cooking fire instead of *at* it'. Sardonically he gestured the turning of a great spit bearing Mantshonga's considerable carcass. His mocking actions elicited braying hoots from the warrior audience.

Mantshonga, whatever he was, was not a coward, nor did he attempt to conceal his cold fury. 'You turn away my request for food with insults?'

'Our repast is meagre.' Uhama grinned evilly, filled his mouth with food to make his point. 'We would not wish to keep you from the pleasures of eating the King's meat, as you say you can.'

Mantshonga stared, his fat mouth spluttering, then wheeled his horse to move downhill, but turned for the last word – spat out with violent rage.

'Uhama! – that is a name that will not be forgotten when new laws come to this land – sooner than you think, old Uhama! On that day, I, Mantshonga, will remember you well!'

Mantshonga and his bedraggled party continued their way down grassy, human-filled slopes to the *Kraal* perimeter. Poor old fat Mantshonga. How could he know that the memorized document, which he was taking such great pains and great risks to deliver, was at this same moment being made obsolete by another document drafted by the same men, in the same place, as the one he was now bringing into this leopard's den.

5

In the long gallery at the mansion of Sir Henry Bartle Frere, the High Commissioner of the Royal Natal Colony, his staff, together with Lt. Gen. Frederic Augustus Thesiger, His Lordship, the second Baron Chelmsford, and his staff, were working on the new document. In its content it presumed Cetshwayo's rejection of the unacceptable terms in the ultimatum which Mantshonga had been commissioned to recite to the Great King. It was in fact the final draft of the official notification that the Imperial British forces had crossed into Zululand. It was justification for the invasion in anticipation of its occurrence, stating that it had been prompted by British concern for the well-being of all the unfortunate Zulu people under the tyrant rule of Cetshwayo. Of course, any and all Zulus who failed to realize that the invasion was for the Zulu good would find themselves dealt with as enemies of HM Imperial Government. The draft was recognition of the impossibility of Cetshwayo's accepting the terms of the existing ultimatum.

Although the morning sun shone palely beyond the windowed doors, the day's warmth had not yet penetrated inside the cooly dark interior of the High Commissioner's mansion. At his elegantly carved desk, Sir Henry Bartle Frere executed the document in an equally elegant cursive script, the steel pen-point of the quill scratching out flaring emphases for the resolute points it made. By the time the hand-written words had been converted into

48

official print, they would become the active description of the reality of a war already begun. Frere, seated at the French *boule* desk, garbed in official dress, re-read the words he had penned, seeking Lord Chelmsford's approval. Chelmsford, tall and aristocratic in his immaculate uniform, nodded, brushed the grey, precisely curled lips of his black beard with his fingertips. The conclusions of the document he doubted not at all, saying firmly to Frere, 'When the war is won we will make the best possible arrangements for good government for all Zulus.' Brevet Lt. Col. John North Crealock, Chelmsford's dutiful military secretary, who stood there ready to serve and agree whatever the conclusions reached by these two great men, also nodded. Thus by the stroke of a pen two men of particular will and inclination decided that a war would be fought.

6

Remarkably, when Mantshonga did manage to get himself announced he was received by the Great King more or less without delay. Although Cetshwayo was enjoying the First Fruits Ceremonies immensely, he had anticipated a message from the British – some modification of the ludicruous mandates of the ultimatum delivered to him, also verbally, by an assembly of minor chiefs and *inDunas* at a meeting held just across the Buffalo a few weeks prior. Perhaps Mantshonga was bringing more satisfactory, at least more negotiable, terms. Mantshonga, on his part, felt that the King would respect his role as intermediary. Still, his was not a coward's errand. He had told the messenger who announced him that he and his party had travelled swiftly and uncomfortably (and ill-fed) to serve the common purpose of avoidance of war, for peace. Now he stood silently under Cetshwayo's fixed stare, again enduring the spectacle of a group of men indulging in platters full of deliciously steaming meat and succulent vegetables. However, the King stopped eating and all with him followed suit. Then Cetshwayo signalled that the fat visitor might speak.

'I am sent here by the English High Chief Frere, whom you know. I carry a message from the great warrior Chelmsford, mighty amongst mighty *inDunas* of the White Queen – she who rules forty lands each forty times greater than all of Zululand!'

The uproar was instant. Mantshonga's clear implication was that there existed greater rulers than the Great King, and of greater lands. And a woman ruler.... To Mantshonga's credit he didn't flinch when the *inDuna* mBlini, who was high in the King's councils and well-known for his heroic rages, sprang forward, *assegai* at thrust, holding it underhand at the drum-tight sweated shine where Mantshonga's belly protruded through his leopard-skin drapes.

mBlini's teeth were bared, a lizard split across a scar-red black face, his voice a dragon-lizard's hiss, 'Should a man speak thus and live, my King!'

The *assegai* trembled towards lunge if the King showed displeasure with Mantshonga's ill-chosen words. The others of the entourage seconded mBlini's sentiments in hissings and clickings of equal ferocity. Mantshonga's eyes flicked downwards, regarded the closeness of the *assegai* point to his mid-region, then turned to Cets-hwayo. His voice was low and hoarse, but did not quaver.

'You will let this rabble kill me ... here? at your board? – before even the words I carry from the great warrior Chelmsford are heard?'

Cetshwayo looked from one to the other. He was a master of suspense when making fateful decisions. The two possibilities were that mBlini's suggestion of instant execution might be taken by the King to mean termi-nation for the renegade – or of mBlini for making the suggestion.

Cetshwayo then stood full height, much taller and grosser than even Mantshonga, although the underlay of muscularity to the King's astonishing girth gave it the quality of enormous physical power rather than of flaccid obesity. The actors in the drama before him were judged. With a few words, Cetshwayo dismissed most of the gathering, a disarray of crowding sycophants who backed away at full speed until out. A few of his retinue remained; one female attendant, who knew the King's favourite morsels to pick and drop into his mouth at the

51

exact instant of desire, remained, as well as mBlini and one other of the King's highest councillors, together with another pair of *umDlunkulu* girls to attend the remaining guests including Mantshonga. With most of the attendants and lesser councillors gone Cetshwayo was instantly gracious, gesturing Mantshonga to seat himself on a low stool at the board bearing food.

'Rest and eat, old warrior ... then you can speak.'

Mantonshonga began a ritual of acceptance, but Cetshwayo waved dismissively, and Mantshonga's sense of ceremonial collapsed. With an audible grunt he fell to, with such voracious lust that Cetshwayo and his two high councillors could not but grin at the sight of such appetite unleashed. The food before the starved fat man disappeared at a truly alarming rate. Cetshwayo watched for a good while, then caught Mantshonga mid-bite with a question:

'Tell me of this great warrior Chelmsford. What are these words he has sent to me?'

Mantshonga's hand froze. He wiped his mouth and tried to swallow quickly. Then, sweating and sucking food fragments from his teeth, he replied as best he could.

'The *inDuna* Chelmsford is angry because you have not sent an answer to his ultimatum; he has heard that you have not dissolved your *Impis* of war – on the contrary, your armies grow larger and larger despite his ultimatum demanding that you disband them. He. ...' Cetshwayo snorted his disdain, stopping Mantshonga with a gesture. The King addressed mBlini. 'Mark the words of this man who was once a Zulu – and the foolish words he brings from his English masters. ...' With an impatient gesture his trident of office lashed out, sending a bowl of fruits scattering across the board. Mantshonga's face for the first time showed frightened alarm – had he so soon exhausted the King's short patience, had he misjudged the royal respect for his important assignment? But Cetshwayo immediately relaxed, merely gesturing for the attendants to regather the spilled items, which they did with alacrity. Cetshwayo then formed his answer carefully. 'Did you ask this great Leader of Warriors, as you claim he is, how he would judge another Leader of Warriors who would disarm his men in the face of war threat? Surely, *inDuna* Chelmsford is not serious? – he expects me to laugh when I hear this! He wishes to amuse me.' He laughed, though how much mirth was in the laughter was difficult to estimate. The others echoed the laughing until he held up his sceptre. He pointed it at Mantshonga.

'Why is it you have not explained to this British warrior chief, and to the Chief Frere, that we Zulus have no quarrel with the British. Our quarrel is with the Dutch. They demand our land from us; surely, also, we will use our armies to fight the Swazis, because they steal our cattle, and graze our good pastures when the red fever disease spoils theirs. But why do the British fear our attack – unless they too secretly wish to take from us what is ours? But they have shown no sign of that, merely fear of us. But why? Tell them what you see here, Mantshonga, a nation celebrating the fruits of its hard work in the fields. Is this the behaviour of a nation seeking war, for no reason? Return to them, tell this Frere and this Chelmsford that my armies will not be used against them – except to defend what is ours, and our right to live on our own land as we choose to live.'

Mantshonga nodded and bowed his consent. 'I will tell him your words, Great Chief.'

Cetshwayo relaxed, accepting that the power of his arguments had persuaded their messenger and hence the British who sent him. Unfortunately Mantshonga then went on speaking: 'But more convincing than my words, I fear, will be the threat of your fifty thousand warriors. The Lord Chelmsford has repeated to me, Mantshonga, many times, "Cetshwayo rules in the old ways, which are wrong." He asked me to say this: that the Great White Queen *herself* cannot order the killing of her lowliest subject, without that subject having a fair trial by others of his own station. He says that you, Cetshwayo, take more power for yourself than does the British Queen for herself. He says that you promised not to kill your own people only on your own orders, only at your own whim. . . .'

Mantshonga winced at the interfering shout from Cetshwayo, who had reached the end of all patience. The King's sceptre, inherited from Shaka, smashed down on to Mantshonga's wooden platter, splintering it, scattering its half-eaten contents. The Great King's outrage at the assertions and demands contained in Mantshonga's message spilled over and destroyed the last vestige of his diplomacy, and Mantshonga noted Cetshwayo's words of outrage carefully. He was to take extreme pleasure in repeating them verbatim to his new masters.

In the morning room, where it had been composed, Frere read and re-read the printed text of the Declaration with the care it would receive when, back home, the Foreign Office would evaluate the action he was initiating on behalf of the nation and in the name of the Queen.

Waiting, Chelmsford sighed deeply, arose, walked to the french windows to gaze out. Let political niceties be Frere's concern, he thought. Chelmsford, at fifty-eight, with a lifelong military career which was not insignificant but yet without a truly notable achievement, found himself quite pleased to contemplate a military foray against so formidable an enemy as the Zulu – an event which he felt must be given significance by future historians. He stood at the windows, contemplating what might be written by those careful academics – about the decisions, about the strategy, and about himself.

He noted that, outside, the mansion's lawns were

being laid out for a luncheon garden party, another of Lady Frere's impeccably conducted social activities. But after the Declaration of Invasion was posted this weekend it might be, he reflected wryly, the last such light-hearted entertainment for a while. For the moment he enjoyed watching the African servants move slowly between the formally laid-out tables, each with its lime green, yellow and pink canopy. The sense of heat from the sun-glare was pervasive, but it was cool indoors from where Chelmsford watched. He studied the banks of scarlet and vividly blue tropical flowers leading to a lower lawn where African gardeners sprinkled grass and flower beds. Very well laid-out, he noted; a pleasing arrangement, although he missed roses and other English blooms one expected in gardens.

Chelmsford's gaze shifted to note his personal guard waiting stiffly atop the verandah steps, while at the bottom of the steps, more casually at ease, but talking together less than usual, were the several subalterns of his horse escort, Lieutenants Raw, Coghill, Melvill and Harford, occasionally minding their tethered horses in the nearby courtyard, but otherwise clearly bored. But then their attention, and His Lordship's shifted suddenly to the lower garden entrance gate, which was swung open by a noisy scatter of children, running, chasing, skipping across the lower lawn, ignoring admonitions and calls from the ladies who followed, carrying pastel-coloured parasols and wearing the finery expected at one of Lady Frere's rather famous church garden parties.

Next through the gate came Bishop Colenso, wearing as was his eccentric wont (thought Chelmsford) the full regalia of his purple ecclesiastical robes. Fanny, his too forthright daughter, cheeks aflame, unnaturally excited (Chelmsford thought) was on her father's arm, but it was damn evident (Chelmsford saw clearly) that the focus of her attention, and cause of her inflamed state, was Colonel Durnford. Damn chap, trust him to take up with this sort of thing on a day's leave. A ladies' 'church do'!

Durnford indeed cut an impressive figure – balding, moustache down to his collar-bones and his war-paralysed left arm slotted into a slit especially tailored into his Colonel's tunic. There was no doubt, the man's long experience in this part of the world – even his known softness for the native populations – all rebounded to the benefit of the task that he had been given and enthusiastically taken on for His Lordship, namely, raising native infantry and mounted contingents. This was a considerable task because of the unusually high proportion of such units to the available Imperial troops, which this war seemed to require. The War Office's stinginess, particularly in the matter of providing Imperial cavalry, was the cause of this disproportion but Durnford's efforts, volunteers seemed to be making up for the deficiency.

In fact, Chelmsford had to admit, he had himself been so enthusiastic about Durnford's first results that he had contemplated making the fellow his second-in-command. But he hadn't won the respect – well, the affection at any rate – of his fellow officers. They were against the suggestion, almost unanimously. On his head, then; he could be damned impetuous, and future records might show ill for one who put a chap like that into a position where his established rashness could lead to serious errors. He watched Durnford and Fanny round the corner of the verandah, out of view. This ill-concealed affection by a man of fifty for a girl half his age – a free-thinking Bishop's daughter to boot, was a case in point – Chelmsford felt pleased that he hadn't reached an over-hasty decision on the order of command. Another group of visitors entered the gate of the lower lawn, coming into His Lordship's view, a vivacious group of the more grown-up daughters of the colonial ladies, in party dresses of bright patterns and lively colours. Chelmsford noted the suddenly brightened interest of the subalterns of his escort as this latest contingent, parasols spinning, stepped out upon the lawns. He turned away from the window and spoke to Frere.

'Your guests arrive, Your Excellency.' Then he addressed his military secretary. 'Colonel Crealock, be good enough to move my escort out of the gardens immediately.'

But Frere quickly intervened. 'On the contrary, Frederic, let them take some refreshment with us. . . .' He paused, smiled. 'And I trust you will have time to join the ladies, also. They – and Lady Frere – would be honoured, and delighted. . . .'

His Lordship reflected for a moment, then shrugged and nodded his agreement, thinking indeed this might be the last occasion for pleasantries of this sort for months ahead – exciting months, but dangerous and fraught ones. He nodded acceptance to Frere's invitation.

He sent Crealock out to instruct the subalterns to be of assistance where they could, sociable if they would, and for God's sake not to offend the locals or to molest their daughters excessively. He returned his attention to the events on the lawn, waiting for Frere to clear the papers on his desk. More guests were arriving in stifling suits – he recognized some of the Afrikaans Herrnvolk of local prominence in this essentially English domain. Fighting your bloody wars for you, mused Chelmsford – but still, an ounce of prevention. . . . None of it my damn concern; the job's the job, stick with it and get it done properly this time. There was glory ahead – if one lived long enough to benefit from it – other than in the pages of a history book when one's dead and gone. But to enjoy one's success *and* also to be remembered by posterity . . . he glowed with the thought that both suddenly seemed within realms of possibility.

Chelmsford noted an English boy in Sunday suit and Eton collar, chased by a Zulu boy in a crisp white shirt and knee-length pants, as they collided with an African gardener holding a sprinkling can. Disaster for the new clothes. Children! The black youngster with his white-toothed grin – from Colenso's congregation, of course. And what on earth is that fool Durnford...? Ah, yes, evidently pacing out a cricket pitch for his young lady, Fanny Colenso; he hammered in the stumps with his one good arm while she held them, whispering covertly, unable to keep the adoration from her demeanour. Such public display. Damned wrong. And, my God, cricket on a scorcher like this. They were gathering the children to play. Durnford would have to be talked to – perhaps Crealock could issue a memorandum on the behaviour of military personnel when with the civilian population....

Frere tucked away the last of his papers, then came alongside Chelmsford. 'Are you up to it, Frederic? The ladies will be....'

Chelmsford continued to look at Durnford and Fanny. 'Tell me, Henry, there *is* a Mrs Durnford, isn't there?'

'She exists, I understand, but Durnford's been here in Africa alone for ... sixteen years? ... Yes....' Frere paused as Fanny handed Durnford the cricket ball; there was an unmistakable lingering of touch as their hands met, not half so discreet as they evidently thought.

'Hm ... mm ... yes, I see....'

Frere felt constrained to justify himself. 'Recommended the chap to you, Frederic, because he knows this continent so well. He's....'

Chelmsford dismissed Frere's suggestion that some apology was required. 'And spot on too, – don't know what we'd have done without all those good fellows he's been bringing to us. Mind you, they'll have to be judged under battle conditions, face to face, so to speak....'

Frere nodded agreement, gestured to the exit. They moved forward. 'Enormous courage – Durnford, I mean. Loyalty beyond question....'

'Personally ambitious ... er ... would you say?' Chelmsford tried to make the question sound casual, but it was an aspect of underlings in which he was very interested. They moved out through the open window on to the verandah, the guard-duty men coming to quick attention. These two considerable men, who were launching a considerable war, went down the steps on to the lawn to join the visitors in the pleasures of Natal's most delightful summer morning.

7

Tired and bedraggled, from their long journey, Mant-shonga's party was only minutes away from the High Commissioner's residence; the thatched roofed mud huts of the native quarters at the far outskirts of Pietermaritz-burg were already behind him. Colonial buildings and wooden walkways appeared flanking the streets on which the traffic of wagons and white-skinned riders, English, Boer, moved in increasing profusion, slowing down progress of the old chief and his retinue. He was rehearsing Cetshwayo's words, in his own translation. He remembered the awesome but controlled rage with which the words were said:

'Tell the warrior Chelmsford that I have not done anything yet in the way of killing ... so why does he start at nothing? It is the custom of all Zulu kings to kill. Without killing my people will not listen, will not obey Zulu law. And the King is that law, he keeps it true to the spirit of Shaka, the founder of the Zulu nation. Do I go to the country of the white man and tell him to change his laws and customs? ... to forget who they are and from where they come? Chelmsford talks to me as to a child. I am not a child! Go back, tell him I am a King, and a King of the Zulu and while I wish to be a friend of the British, I will not give my people over to them, nor will I accept their laws....'

Mantshonga was skilled at remembering words, as most Zulus were. He felt the heat of the morning, licked his heavy dry lips in anticipation of receiving again the long cool drink which it had pleased the High Commissioner and Chelmsford to offer him before he left on this mission from which he now returned. He felt he had been treated as a near equal. He was certain he had a good chance of being reinstalled in power once the Great King was defeated by the mighty arms of His Lordship. He must ask them the name of the drink and its ingredients.

Although Colonel Durnford did not have the advantage of achieving proper counterbalance with an immobile leftarm, his cricket bowling was quite good enough for the children – English, Dutch and African – who faced him from before the stumps and bales. He bowled to an exuberant Zulu youth who managed to tip the ball, to be caught out by Fanny. An argument developed with the twelve-year-old English boy referee. The game went on. At the tables drinks were sipped and the Zulu invasion threat discussed; the subalterns had managed to get within conversational distance of the young ladies, although the constraints set by parental and older officer observation were felt. Indeed, colonial parents usually regarded soliders as of poor marital promise for precious daughters – the military's intrinsic transiency being a strong contributing factor to this low evaluation. Nor had the male population amongst the colonials been particularly responsive to Chelmsford's recruiting calls of the past weeks, although it was for their safety, and that of their women and children, for which Imperial soldiers were expected to meet the dread Zulu in mortal combat. The soldiers were quite aware of this irony and rarely refrained from mentioning it, bitterly often as not.

The precisely trimmed lawn, the decorous flower beds, the informally paced cricket game, Lady Frere's flair for arrangement of tables, service and well-apparelled guests, the stillness of the air and the brightness of the sun, and the most civil passage amongst the parties of white-attired African servitors – how could the encroachments of the forces of destructive carnage and the bloody ruptures of violent death be imagined in a scene such as this – the essence of peace and harmonious self-containment?

On the rolling upper lawn, so as not to interfere with the cricket game, the Bishop of Natal, John William Colenso, had gathered himself a group of the teenagers – both sexes, both races. He had stretched himself full length on the lawn, a familiar pose for this non-conforming churchman, his thin donnish head (thin steel spectacles set on his thin, long nose) propped on his elbow. His sockless, sandalled feet protruded from beneath the full-length ceremonial robe of office which he wore for nearly all occasions. He had collected an assortment of fruits to help illustrate his astronomical lecture on the solar system. His youthful audience sat cross-legged, enthralled, on the sward around him. He held up various items from the bowl of fruits.

'The sun, the centre of the solar system ... we will represent it with ... what?' He waited for a volunteer answer, and an English girl finally found her tongue.

'An orange, Your Grace?'

Colenso always encouraged young learners; he picked the orange from the bowl and said, 'By all means, an excellent choice. Orange, after all, is the colour of the sun, at least in the evening.' He set the orange at the centre of his proposed solar diagram. 'The planet closest to the sun is Mercury....'

An Afrikaner boy cut in with assertive confidence. 'That should be a grape. Because it's the smallest planet....'

'Also the smallest of the fruits we have with us. Very precise, Piet. Well chosen! And what for the planet Venus?'

Colenso had looked hopefully each time at a Zulu

fifteen-year old, who now spoke softly, and with a winning easy smile.

'The pear' – he curved his hands through the air – 'like a beautiful woman.'

All laughed, and Colenso was pleased. He set the pear in position, and inscribed the ellipse it would follow outside the orbit of the grape planet, Mercury.

'It's not quite astronomy, Fanase, but the symbol you have chosen is even better, because it deals with a quality other than mere measurement or mere colour.'

He paused as he saw an adult hand descend into the bowl of fruits. He looked up at the owner. It was Vereker, in morning habit, shaved, trimmed, coiffed, and garbed out of all recognition. He was saying in rather droll accents, 'And may I suggest a slightly rotten apple for the Earth, Your Grace?'. Vereker, bit into the fruit, showed a worm hole, spat out the bite and set the apple in third place around the citrus Sun.

Colenso was delighted, and obviously not unfamiliar with this young man's antics.

'William! I thought.... My gracious, what a welcome sight after all ... in how many years?' The Bishop held up a cautioning finger to his youthful charges, 'I ask you to ignore this gentleman's cynical remarks ... rotten apple indeed.... Where have you come from?'

Indeed, young Vereker had done all the things he had promised himself when he left Rorke's Drift – picked up a bit of money due from the shipping agent, found Harding in Durban and kitted them both out for dramatic re-entry into the social scene in the capital. He had presented his compliments to Lady Frere a few minutes earlier and was delighted to find himself a guest at a most opportune event – 'everybody' was here, as if to welcome his return to Pietermaritzburg. First the Colensos, though Fanny seemed somewhat embarrassed to introduce him to this strange military chap, Durnford. He knew the name well, of course. Durnford had been the leading member of the Boundary Commission that decided in favour of the Zulu claims over those of the Boers, just the past March in fact, and a matter of great concern to all who lived at the border. Most colonials were dismayed by Durnford's report, but not the pro-Zulu Bishop Colenso. Aha, that was it ... Fanny and this chap. There he stood, making some caddish remarks about young men out of uniform in a time of crisis. Wasn't at all amiable when Vereker said he was in Pietermaritzburg only for a cool drink and some amusing conversation.

It appeared that all the officers Vereker had met at Rorke's Drift had made it back safely and were on the spot on escort duty with the Baron Chelmsford – or Freddy Thesiger, as Vereker had known him in England. He reflected with some amusement, and a shade of embarrassment, on what the reaction would be of a slightly down-class snob like that Lieutenant Melvill if it were revealed that an ex-Buffalo River farmer like himself and the second Baron were on Christian-name terms. Well, his father the Viscount had thought 'Uncle Frederic' was more suitable, considering âge differences, but William never could accept that particular nonsense. He always called him 'Frederic' and thought of him as 'Freddy', but perhaps he might now have to switch to 'Your Lordship' if the occasion required.

They all sat around the lawn tables together, the young officers flirting with the local girls, whom Vereker thought not worth a damn; the locals frightening each other with horror stories of Zulus on rampages of rape and slaughter; Frere reminding them all that Cetshwayo had slaughtered 20,000 of his own people during the kingship succession struggle between Cetshwayo and his brother; and Colenso defending Cetshwayo by reminding Frere, to his displeasure, that the Tudor kings were equally bloody a good deal later in English national history than the Zulus were in theirs. Mr Pretorius the Boer

64

snorted, 'And who is that supposed to make feel safer?

Durnford commented that if the people of Natal wished to feel safe let them go forth and persuade husbands, sons and friends to volunteer for His Lordship's army and, looking straight at Vereker, that gentlemen were required as officers *pro tem*.

A Zulu butler garbed in London best approached His Excellency with a whispered message. The quests looked across to the lawn to see a fat elderly Zulu with a motley group of savages bearing spears, firearms and shields, waiting at the courtyard entrance. It was Mantshonga, with his momentous message.

Frere and Chelmsford excused themselves, walked rapidly to the verandah. The guests then saw the Zulu chieftain being led in after the exalted pair. Of course, they couldn't hear Mantshonga mumbling to himself the last words the Great King had uttered, ' . . . tell him, this warrior Chelmsford, that if he does not listen to what I have to say, I, who am King and chief *induna* of all the Zulu nation, then will I kill . . . then will I kill . . .!'

As Mantshonga disappeared within the mansion, Vereker felt a tremor of despair, of internal coldness. There came to him a memory of sound, of the frenzied crescendoing thunder of *assegai* shafts pounding on thousands of drum-tight shields, and of the massed voices of the carriers of those shields and spears, crying in one dread voice of seemingly infinite volume, '*U-Su-Tu* . . .! *U-Su-Tu* . . .! Kill! Kill!'

8

Company C, First Battalion of the Twenty-fourth Regiment of the Warwickshire Foot, 100 strong, was standing at rigid attention waiting for its next command from Company Sergeant-Major Williams. And waited, sweating in high brass-buttoned tunics and steel-shod, knee-high boots – both much too heavy for this climate; red-faced men, exhausted but uncomplaining, eyes set unswervingly forward. Only the eyes of CSM Williams moved, darting along the squad lines; bird-of-prey darting, black obsidian hardness glinting, deeply embedded in pudgy, broken-veined cheeks, eyes closely astraddle his flattened, irregularly shaped, most pugnacious nose, eyes matching the threat of an angry slash of lips set between a bristling, coarse-haired moustache and the choke-tightened chin belt which anchored his white canvas shield-emblazoned helmet.

Past the sentries posted at the camp entrance rode Lieutenants Melvill, Raw, Harford – the first of the Chelmsford garden party escort returning, but now with a sense of urgency in their movements. Durnford had already arrived and was waiting just inside the sentry post, apparently expecting somebody or something to make an appearance from the road beyond. He looked up briefly as a horseman appeared, but returned to his waiting when he noted that the figure approaching was Lieutenant Coghill, being somewhat laggard in this return to HQ.

66

Still CSM Williams kept his men at full attention. He was an expert in the art of making men wait. Waiting was an essential discipline, he believed, for soldiers everywhere, but especially under the God-accursed conditions obtaining in Southern Africa. Then, from beyond the entrance, two huge creaking ox-wagons, hauled by spans of sixteen stolid beasts each, rolled into the company's vision. Each team was led at short rein by a walking African infant. Drovers sat on the wagons flicking long whips at the oxen-span and sometimes at the lead men, shouting at them all in indecipherable man-animal vocabularies of grunts, snorts, and hoo-ees. In fact there seemed to be a general herding of many beasts – horses, certainly, but also oxen, mules and slaughter-beeves, rumbled past the rigidly transfixed drill lines of Company C. The roil of dust and the foul droppings threatened them, at times engulfed them, but failed to move them. Indeed, the encampment was as much an assembly place for lesser animals as for the human beings who involved them in their wars to work and to die alongside them. But at this instant, the beasts were allowed to move; the men not; only the CSM's flickering marble eyes, waiting for an inevitable dereliction.

The beasts passed on to a central inspection area, and then a squad of Basuto infantry marched into position directly in front of C Company – tall, rangy black men, more appropriately dressed for the steaming climate in loincloths and a few neck ornaments – only a red rag of cloth tied around right biceps was badge of their enlistment into Her Majesty's forces. A bawling voice brought the Basutos to a ridiculously ragged, out-of-step halt. Immediately their European NCO screamed foul epithets of rage and despair as the bewildered Basutos jostled and readjusted positions in confusion, trying to satisfy the incomprehensible demands for unobtainable neatness and order. The Basutos wanted desperately to obey and, so trying, compounded their disarray.

To all this clumsy display there was not a muscle twitch of reaction from C Company – except from one soldier, Private Williams. His concentration finally cracked – possibly because for a change he was seeing someone making more foolish errors than he himself. A young man, too thin, gangly and consummately inept, Williams the private peeked at the antics of the Basutos pushing and shoving, stumbling black fellows, one too far forward, one too far back. He tried not to grin, but he did, then giggled and even went so far as to nudge the private next to him. Instantly, Williams the Company Sergeant-Major wheeled round angrily, his third eye, the one in the middle of the rear of his helmet, spotting the dereliction on the part of his unfortunate namesake. Too late, Private Williams tried to correct to full attention as a shadow fell across his face; there was the CSM's purpling face only an inch in front of his, the mouth, slash spitting, open, stained teeth gaping, the uvula at the back of the wide throat vibrating to full volume.

'You moved! ... You moved! Go and tell that NCO with them black apes that you love 'im more than you love me...! Double!'

Private Williams only reaction was to obey, immediately and without error. He shouted 'Suh!' instead of 'Sergeant!' because he was on parade, and double-marched forward – his pack and rifle bouncing and banging out of rhythm. He snapped to strained attention alongside the NCO of the Basutos – who ignored him completely. Staring at nothing, sweating, red-faced, Private Williams shouted, 'I'm to tell you, Sergeant, that I love you more than I do my Company Sergeant-Major!'

The NCO wheeled and shouted back into the young man's face, 'I don't want you! Get out of me bloody sight, man! Run around this field till you fall down dead!'

Young Williams had no options – he started running around the Company drill grounds.

His rifle-stock jarred at each jog forward along his nar-

68

row right shoulder blade; he grabbed at it with his left as it fell off and almost immediately his pack slipped down his back, slapping dangerously lower against his backside at every pace, unquestionably destined to engage his legs and finally send him sprawling. Lieutenant Coghill had come past the sentries into the encampment, looked about and spurred forward to C Company, glancing at Private William's progress. CSM Williams responded to his officer's arrival by shouting, 'Company, Company atten-shun! ... Present ... arms!'

With three crashes in perfect unison the C Company Redcoats of the Twenty-fourth brought their Martini-Henry rifles up to 'present'. Lieutenant Coghill swept a glance across the perfectly aligned ranks, then said curtly, 'Sergeant, at the end of drill, fall them out to hear general movement orders at parade assembly. Understood?'

'Sir', replied the CSM, and then to the Company, 'You heard that officer?'

They had indeed, and understood exactly ... fall out to hear orders! The time for war had come! It was a command devoid of double meanings — there was no outward sign from the rigidly standing men, but then their pulse rates were not visible. Coghill was already spurring towards the Officer's Mess. Quartermaster Bloomfield, leading a squad of a dozen drum and bugler boys, was forced to break his purposeful stride, side-whiskers bristling, swagger stick under arm, as he pulled back to avoid being ridden down by Coghill. He glared at the impetuous rider, then resumed his march in the direction of the band tent, the boys scampering after him. CSM Williams looked at the high sun: 'Company ... order arms. *Dis*miss!'

The men broke rank, crowded towards the Sutler's wagon, which had just come into camp with fresh supplied of gin and cigars. Two strange men on horseback, in civilian dress, were already there making purchases, one elderly, one a boy of no more than sixteen. From their rolled blankets slung behind their saddles, slung rifles, stained broad-brimmed hats, simple corduroys, there was no doubt that they were Boer farmers, part of a trickle of enlistees who were able to settle within themselves a priority of distaste as between the British and the Zulu antagonists. However, most Boers apparently were going to stay out of this fight. These two Boers immediately sensed that they were upsetting the Redcoat soldiers who resented outsiders taking up supplies even though the items were privately sold by the Sutlers. As the two men backed their mounts away to clear for the C Company soldiers, CSM Williams intercepted them, glowering his hostility.

'Just passing through, is that it?'

The elder Boer answered, his Dutch accent thick with rolled r's. 'We're here to fight the Zulu, man. . . .'

The CSM shook his head negatively. 'Left it too late – we're moving out tonight, if you haven't heard.'

The elder Boer patted his rifle confidently, 'We're ready anytime, man.' Williams knew it was true – this breed needed no training to become warriors. They grew up with gun and horse from earliest life, and staked their lives frequently in active combat to hold what they believed was theirs or their right to take. They would have to go into one of Colonel Durnford's irregular units. He pointed to Colonel Durnford, still waiting on his horse near the camp entrance. 'See the officer there?'

The Boers started to move in the direction pointed, but halted when the CSM added, dubiously sizing up the youth, 'You're wasting your time with him – too young.'

The older Boer lost none of his self-assurance. 'He's my nephew . . . he can shoot, track, speak Zulu – and he can fight like hell. He's got *assegai* wounds to prove it!'

The boy pulled up his shirt, neck high. A truly horrendous pink-white scar slashed from the boy's navel to sternum. CSM Williams shrugged. They continued on towards Colonel Durnford. But by this time, CSM Williams noted, the Colonel, who of necessity did all his manoeuvering with his good right arm, was reining his mount about to observe the source of a chorus of male singing first heard faintly, then growing in volume as a mounted troop of natives approached the camp entrance. The chanting horse troopers were escorting a wagon-train of supplies. CSM Williams could see from Durnford's sudden enlivenment that it was for this he had been waiting so long at the entrance. Well, the Boers, then, would have to wait their turn to enlist with the Colonel.

The troop of black singers entered the camp, magnificently rendering an African Christian hymn. Durnford's pleasure in watching them was obvious. His face was lit with the wide-beaming smile of a man who had sought hard and now produced a prize. The Sikali Horse rode like angels, smartly uniformed (their attire purchased by themselves) though bare-legged, their big toes thrusting into rawhide-thong stirrups as they guided their groomed, handsome horses with their bare heels. And they sang joyously, harmoniously:

> 'Fight the good fight with all they might!
> With all thy strength and with they might!
> Lay hold on Christ and thou will see,
> Thy joy and hope, eternally.'

Durnford was so taken up with their arrival that he failed to note that, coming into view behind them, seated with dandified grace on his white stallion, rode Standish Vereker. Behind Vereker rode his English servant on an all-black mount. Vereker's entrance, no matter how dramatic, could not compete with that of the Sikali Horse, who had captured all eyes in the vicinity of the camp's entrance.

The Basuto infantry troops looked up at the mounted newcomers with a certain alarm. Who were these black Africans, so smartly dressed in complete, and perfectly

71

clean, khaki uniforms and, what's more, each carrying in saddle holders a spanking new Martini-Henry rifle? Incredible. It would have been surprising if the near-naked Basuto recruits didn't feel put out. They did, and immediately some taunting shouts and pointing and derisive laughter rose from their ranks.

However, the dignity of the Sikalis was not that easily ruffled. Their mounts had simultaneously halted in a line a good deal straighter than that earlier achieved by the barracking Basutos, unmounted. The Sikalis sat easily, unreacting, eyes front. Their impressive Sergeant-Major, CSM Simeon Kambula, was a handsome figure of piercing gaze, features delineated as if carved of deeply polished mahogany. Was it CSM Kambula who gave an indiscernable signal? – because at a single instant all 100 of the Sikali horses reared, pawed the air together, whinnied. The the 100 fore-hooves crashed to earth, and all the mounts were pointed at the area where the Basutos lounged at ease after their exertions at drill, casting their remarks in their own language.

They looked up at the sound to see the Sikali charging full pelt in their direction. They started uneasily, and a few rose to their feet. At this moment, across their vision Private Williams came running, stumbling, into the path of the Sikali, his rifle trailing in the dust, quite oblivious of the thunder of approaching hooves. It seemed to all the onlookers that he was doomed to be ridden into the earth as in a swirl of dust and wheeling horse legs he became engulfed, lost to sight. CSM Williams briefly closed his eyes in dismay, opened them and saw Private Williams standing motionless, looking about, completely confused. But by now the Sikali horses were almost upon the front line of the thoroughly alarmed Basutos. The horses must stop now. But they didn't! They maintained their gallop straight at the Basutos, who panicked and ran, or froze and cowered, as dust and horses engulfed them as Williams had been moments before. With incredible dextrous twisting and wheeling, jumping over men when necessary, and with great whooping delight at exhibiting their riding skill, the Sikalis rode and careered through the dense picket of human obstacles, not touching a single one.

The NCOs in charge of the Basutos, who were no less threatened by the wild charge, had behaved as badly as their troops. As the Sikalis cleared, the NCOs stood indignant but, for a change, speechless.

Boy-Pullen and the other bugler boys loading ammunition boxes and checking quartermaster Bloomfield's invoices hooted and called out their derision. The men at the Sutler's wagon applauded the Sikalis and laughed. Durnford grinned, while Vereker and his servant, who had pulled up just behind, watched, mildly amused, quite self-contained. Private Williams still stood slack-mouthed, sweating, every part of him drooping, until CSM's dread shout came across the parade.

'Private Williams! You've stopped! You hear me, Private Williams! I'll have you lashed!'

At which Private Williams, using some incredible instinctive reserves managed to draw himself up to attention: 'Yes, Sar'nt-Major, sir! ... you'll have me lashed, sir!' and once more stumbled forward, running, dragging his equipment. The Sikali, now on the far side of the parade grounds, sat on their mounts, entirely motionless, their identity and position fully established.

Moments before this display, Chelmsford and his escort had ridden in and reined to watch from just behind Durnford. Durnford, pleased at the well-timed arrival, waited for and received His Lordship's compliment. It came: 'Splendid horsemanship, Colonel Durnford – they come well-recommended, do they?'

Durnford just about contained his patience. 'My Lord, they rode for me at Bushman's Pass. I know each by first name.'

'Ah, indeed ... ', mused Chelmsford. Durnford's

heroic stand at Bushman's Pass eight years prior was Natal legend – it was at Bushman's Pass that the intrepid Colonel had lost forever the use of his left arm. What was Chelmsford on about, he wondered bitterly, to ask if the Sikali came 'well-recommended'? Didn't the august Commander appreciate the sixteen years of relevant experience that gave a man like Durnford his credentials to carry out this job? Didn't the man realize he would have had no chance of conducting his cherished war without Durnford's unmatchable contribution of 7000 effective native troops raised, trained and equipped in a mere matter of weeks? He must know the scale of effort and the size of the achievement. What had happened to all the enthusiasm and amiability at Durnford's first successes? Durnford had even heard his reward stated by Chelmsford – he would be made second in command! But when would he hear Chelmsford's confirmation? Weeks had elapsed with less and less communication. Now, even with this latest scintillating acquisition of the Sikali he had the taste of ashes in his mouth.

As if reading Durnford's mind Chelmsford turned to Crealock, saying, 'Colonel, you must find a suitable officer for Colonel Durnford's new riders. . . .' Did he hear correctly – to pass that over as a responsibility to anyone but Durnford himself? Surely Crealock knew what was happening. . . . Was it perhaps his connivance?

Crealock suggested a subaltern of the Twenty-fourth, then pointed out that the Sikali had been issued individual rifles, contrary to the policy of maintaining a proportion of only one rifle for every ten Natal natives or, in the best cases, one to five as with the Basuto riders. The local white population wouldn't be at all happy with a war that ended leaving an extensively armed native population.

But Crealock knew damn well that the rifle issue had been made on Durnford's orders. Chelmsford mused on the problem. If the man said something else as stupid as his earlier comments Durnford felt he might not be able to contain himself.

Chelmsford looked from Crealock to Durnford. 'The question, gentlemen, is will they make good use of them?'

Durnford spoke before Crealock could: 'There's no question, sir, they are Christians all ... and as good marksmen as horsemen. That's why I ordered the issue. . . .'

Chelmsford nodded, weighing Durnford's statements. The adopted Christianity of the Sikali should take care of the colonists' qualms; the marksmanship was a soldierly criterion. His horse was moving about nervously, and he had to rein it in. 'Well, we can't doubt their horsemanship, can we?' He tried to calm his mount, patting its neck, then spoke to Crealock, 'We will make an exception for Durnford's hard-riding Christians as long as he vouches for them personally. . . .' Then, more at the horse's volition than his own, His Lordship was moving off, spurring towards the Officer's Mess followed by Crealock who, in spite of being countermanded, showed no visible reaction to what his commander had decided.

Durnford watched them depart in quiet rage. Chelmsford had, somehow, left it that should one of the Sikalis ever, by chance, misuse his weapon it would be on Durnford's head. Was this to be the culmination of three decades of his Imperial service – to be thrust into an avoidable war, incompetently led? On field of battle, where knowledge of men and war and the enemy, where the power of clear-headed decision was the ultimate merit, Brevet Col. Anthony William Durnford had no difficulties, no self-doubts. But in these human skirmishes – for self-advantage, for personal power, to maintain one's own dignity and just position, he too often lost his way. Yet, he told himself, he didn't want *personal* victories – he was first, last and always a soldier, a soldier of Her Majesty whose call of duty surpassed personal advantage, personal ambition, safety of person, indeed of life. All other passions must be valued by these inculcated standards which gave real meaning to a soldier's existence.

A voice cut into his confused reverie. 'Colonel Durnford?'

He looked up to see, seated languidly on a long-maned white stallion, that damn fop over whom Fanny had gushed at Sir Henry Frere's garden fête. And with some fool manservant hanging on in the background, mounted on a silky black animal, of course. 'William Vereker, sir'.

'Yes, I remember.... You visit us at a difficult moment, Mr Vereker...'

Vereker smiled, engagingly, 'Not a visit, sir.... You complained, sir, of the lack of gentlemen in Natal who were willing to serve as officers ... I trust I'm not too late? I wish to volunteer in that capacity.'

Durnford was anxious to talk with CSM Kambula who still waited at the head of the Sikali troops. He had to quell his impatience. 'Gentlemen? ... Well, yes ... we need ... we are particularly interested in officers who can speak Zulu....'

Vereker looked at him directly, and spoke in Zulu, fluently, easily, with correct sounds, these words: 'Tell me what you want saying, one-armed warrior, and I will try to say it....'

Durnford, who understood Zulu but never felt fluent with it, looked at Vereker with more interest, 'I see ... yes ... also gentlemen who can ride? ... and shoot?...'

Vereker didn't reply for a moment. He glanced past Durnford; Durnford turned and noted a half carcass of a cow being hung up at a field-kitchen, 250 yards away, at which Vereker stared. Almost languidly, he slid his rifle, with its elaborately carved stock, from its saddle holder, snapped a bullet into the breech, backed the white horse a distance. Suddenly the animal catapulted forward at full gallop. Vereker rose high in his stirrups, cloak and hair streaming behind him, threw up the rifle in one hand and twisted in the stirrups to fire back at a steep angle: the half carcass hanging in the field-kitchen juddered under the impact of the heavy bullet. Durnford was impressed enough by that, but Vereker had not completed his demonstration. The horse plunged on, twisted like a polo pony in the narrowest possible circle of pivot, during which time, somehow or other, because he seemed completely occupied with the reins, Vereker was able to reload. Now, galloping back with his rifle on the wrong side, he twisted completely around, releasing a second shot with the same effect as the first. The cooks in the kitchen stared curiously at the suddenly swinging meat carcass.

Durnford looked towards CSM Kambula, who nodded approvingly. He was relieved – certain that he found the officer exactly suited for the job with the Sikali. And it pleased him to know that it wouldn't be one of the Subalterns of the Twenty-fourth he had heard Crealock suggesting.

9

The Officer's Mess for this encampment was housed under campaign-stained canvass tenting – but the more gracious accoutrements of their status and class were visible thereunder. A complement of white-jacketed African servants tended immediate needs. These were supervised by Sergeant Murphy, a tubby, beady-eyed Irishman with full red-veined cheeks whose attention to the staff officers bordered on the obsequious and to the subalterns on the maternal. Murphy denominated his rewards in free drinks, either bought for him, or as he put it, taken by the bottle on temporary loan. Vereker came through the guarded entrance in his new role accompanied by Lieutenant Raw. Chelmsford, Crealock and Lieutenant-Colonel Pulleine were having tea from a sterling silver service, at the same time working over tactical maps; the other lesser officers of this particular encampment were tippling and gossiping, the exception being Lieutenant Harford, totally absorbed at a space he had cleared for himself on a wooden dining table classifying his collection of African beetles into glass bottles gathered for the purpose. Complaints about Harford wasting good gin to preserve his specimens were frequent.

Heads raised as Raw called out, 'Stranger in the mess, my Lord!... Gentlemen...!', then quietly to Vereker, 'Announce yourself, sir.'

The mess waited for the name of the new man, but

Vereker looked about slowly, noted Chelmsford smiling in his direction, and said with an amiable nod, 'Good day, Frederic.'

The reaction of the officers was what Vereker anticipated. But Chelmsford, to his credit, merely rose and with smiling warmth crossed to Vereker with extended hand. 'Good day, William. Pleased you've decided to join us.' They shook hands. His Lordship looked about at the waiting room. 'Best announce yourself, William.'

Now, at his own timing, the young man was quite pleased to do so. He faced them easily and bowed slightly. 'William Vereker, by your leave.' Silence.

'Sergeant Murphy!' called out Raw, 'Stop stealing drink and bring some for our visitor!'

There was laughter – and acceptance. The rudeness and probing questions to the newcomer started. Yet, a proper distance had been established. Now he could participate in their high jinks and ritual of welcome, ultimately fight and possibly die alongside of them – but as the person he considered himself to be, not as some arbitrary replica of what a Queen's officer was supposed to be. The decision of fighting – on this side – came to him in quite a passionless way. He never had seen the Zulus as his enemy – but if he were to stay on this continent then it was impossible to avoid fighting in the war. The matter needed settling. The means were in the hands of exalted people like Chelmsford, Frere and Cetshwayo.

The raillery went on. Melvill introduced him to 'stranger's cup', wherein the newcomer was required to drink a huge measure of claret in a single quaff from an outlandishly large regimental pewter tankard – the penalty for the certain failure being the purchase by the newcomer of bottles for all on his account. Then Chelmsford felt constrained to make a speech of welcome, which developed into a formal statement of the purposes of the invasion. He was an orator of considerable persuasion: 'The task we have been given is to exact reparation for

79

violations of simple justice and to enforce better government on behalf of the unlucky Zulu people. Our first blow must be a heavy one. This cannot be a war of manoeuvre. . . .' He closed with the words, ' . . . our Imperial troops, *your* soldiers, gentlemen, are the anvil on which Her Majesty's intentions will be shaped . . .!'

Now, there was not doubt in His Lordship's mind that these royal intentions (though the Queen had not been consulted) were no more than the defence of Natal and the securing of the safety and well-being of its inhabitants. The invasion promulgated by Frere and to be executed by himself was simply the tactical implementation of that quite proper and wholly justified defence. The concept of the Imperial troops as an anvil was basic British dogma of the absolute effectiveness of steadily aimed, continuous Martini-Henry rifle-fire from highly disciplined Imperial foot soldiers. By simple arithmetic, this war should present no problems. Although 8000 Imperial troops had to take on 50,000 equally well, if differently, trained Zulu warriors – since the Martini-Henry rifle had reasonable effect at 1000 yards, and became deadly, even in the hands of an average marksman at 350 – the problem seemed to reduce to the probability of each rifleman stopping 6½ Zulus running in from 1000 yards before one got through for hand-to-hand, *assegai v*. bayonet. Indeed, if the Zulus co-operated in this simple tactical scheme, Chelmsford's strategy could be very simple: he would have only to form all his troops into one massive column across the Buffalo, advance seventy-five miles and take on the Zulu army at Ulundi, decimate it by sheer fire-power, and proclaim another victory and conquest in the name of Her Imperial Majesty, Queen Victoria.

Vereker listened to Chelmsford's confident prediction of victory with concern. Did the man not understand how the Zulus fought, the strategies they employed? With an army as fluid and mobile as theirs, there was no need to commit themselves to waiting in position for the defence of the royal *Kraal*. Even if razed by an uncontested enemy, it could be rebuilt in a matter of days. And with their attackers thus concentrated in a single column, which would take two weeks to traverse a distance which the Zulus, infinitely less encumbered, could cover in two days, there was nothing whatsoever to prevent Cetshwayo choosing any other southward route, around the British, and counter-invade! Chelmsford would be in possession of several miles of empty thatched huts, while the Great King destroyed the royal colony, its inhabitants and structures, unopposed. Vereker wondered grimly whether Chelmsford's theory – the single column, 8000 guns against 50,000 spears – would ever become a strategic reality.

As Chelmsford said in his speech, he needed early military confrontation to effect an immediate blow of overwhelming force. Selecting four invasion points along the border, he would send through not one but four columns into Zululand in a wide, four-pronged thrust which would converge only at their joint destination. Thus, the Zulus coming forward in any direction would have no option but to meet at least one of these columns (or retire in flight – and defeat – which of course they would never do). The main army of Cetshwayo would not wait for the joint attack but would have to move towards its south border to engage at least one of the columns. Here the arithmetic of dividing by four produced some less comforting numbers. Only 2000 Imperial troops per column meant 28, not 6½, Zulus to be brought down per rifle; the odds thus grew longer.

Furthermore, the estimate of 2000 Imperial troops per column may have been optimistic because Chelmsford needed substantial number of Redcoats to protect supply lines, outposts, home positions, etc. The columns, therefore, needed building up. Firstly, and above all, they needed riders to conduct scouting activities, mounted guard contingents, pickets, recce forces, escorts, supply guards, and so on unendingly. The War Office in its miserliness and possible lack of enthusiasm for Frere's war had failed to furnish Chelmsford with cavalry. Some of these needs were being supplied by local white volunteers formed into irregular commando groups, but not enough. So Durnford's recruitment campaign for native contingents, particularly for horsemen, became key to Chelmsford's plan to force early confrontation by using multiple columns for the invasion. Durnford had found, trained and armed 7000, plus irregular volunteers. When parcelled out this made 4000 effectives in each column. The Redcoat contingents in each column would now be undistracted by duties other than keeping up their murderous rifle-fire. Chelmsford was satsified that any one of these columns of 4000, adding some artillery support, could take the full impact of any attack even by the main Zulu army if necessary and emerge victorious – on its own.

Chelmsford felt an inner soaring – a plan, a mere thought process would, within hours, change into the reality of men marching, wagons and guns rolling, four separate armies taking position to begin an assault that would determine forever the future of this region of the world, indeed of the nations which contended for its control. True, some of the theory was less clear when examined by the criteria of that reality. Would, for instance, the native forces under Durnford be able to stand up to the tasks of war with an enemy known to them as the most fearsome in their world? Under pressure, with no real patriotism, would they fight – or run? And what about Durnford himself? Having done his job this well, would he then be reckoned, by those who judged later, as the architect of the entire victory, the true builder of the plan which he had, yes, implemented, advised well on, but – Chelmsford was sure – had not *created*. The man was known to be impulsive, idealistic, heroic and most dutiful. But over-confident of his new abilities, possibly arrogant in this respect. Didn't he put too much store in the ability of his untried native recruits? If they took the first brunt of a Zulu attack ... no, too uncertain a result to risk. In fact, Chelmsford had concluded, it was not necessary for Durnford's centre column to move from this side of the Buffalo at all. It could hold. With three columns coming into Zululand, the counter-invasion threat was not too likely, and Durnford's fewer guns could hold in an entrenched position. And, at the same time, keep the man out of mischief!

Durnford had not arrived at the Officer's Mess in time for Vereker's reception. He had sent Raw to introduce the new man. When he finally did arrive, he realized, with some dismay, that Chelmsford was making a major announcement and that he had missed most of it. Nor did His Lordship fail to note this tardy interruption with a quick and clearly annoyed look at the entrance. Durnford didn't dare move in further. Chelmsford went on speaking for his rapt audience, as he reached his conclusion:

'... our enemy, Cetshwayo, is predictable. He responds to events with habitual promptitude and indifference to any but the immediate results of his actions. But should he escape our three-pointed spear, and impose the threat of counter-invasion, I will leave Colonel Durnford in reserve at the centre with the awesome responsibility of the defence of Natal at that point. ...'

He went on, but Durnford heard no more of the speech. Chelmsford's declaration meant that he was being isolated from the main events, kept this side of the Buffalo, not permitted to consumate his efforts, nor play a fully active part in a war where his knowledge and experience made him uniquely valuable, where he could serve in the role for which most of his adulthood in the army here in Southern Africa had prepared him – and for which, he admitted, he had long been waiting.

The sound of hurrahs and whoops of delight jerked

83

Durnford's awareness to the others. He saw Melvill and Raw throw young Coghill in the air. There was handshakes and toasting of drinks all round. He forced his distracted memory to retrace the last few moments until he reconstructed the last words spoken – yes, Crealock has risen to formally deliver His Lordship's orders: the encampment was to head the column that would lead the invasion forces across the Upper Drift, Rorke's Drift as it was known. The move off was confirmed for tonight. The crossing into Zululand, this is what brought the joyous cheers, was tomorrow morning. 'But not', Durnford's mouth clasped grimly as he thought ' . . . but not me!' The shouting and joyous movement surrounded him. Then he became aware of a quieter presence alongside – it was Vereker. Vereker smiled at him and pointed to Sergeant Murphy who had swiftly picked up Harford's momentarily unattended jar of preserved beetles; as the two officers watched, Murphy quickly, furtively, tilted it to his mouth sieving out the black embalmed insects with his fingers and gulping down the gin which preserved them. Durnford smiled, realized that Vereker was helping him to get out of himself.

The young Honourable spoke sympathetically. 'I had anticipated serving more closely to you, sir.'

'As you realize,' replied Durnford, 'His Lordship has other . . . uses for me.'

Vereker nodded. 'If, as his Lordship states, the purpose of our action is to defend Natal, may I point out the best man available will now protect the border, where, as His Lordship realizes, it's most vulnerable – as he says, just in case.'

Durnford realized that he had been too hasty in his judgement of the young man.

10

Inside the band tent, Boy-Pullen, twelve years of age but already old of face, concentrated on the cards held in his smallish fists. Like many of the other boy buglers with him, Boy-Pullen was a soldier's orphan.

The buglers and drummers sat in a circle around the wooden ammunition box which served as a card table. Uniforms were unbuttoned for comfort; most of them dragged on cigar butts. They passed a rectangular-shaped gin bottle from one to the next, each taking time to note that none of the others took more, or for that matter less, than his share of the hard tipple. Through the slit-opened flaps of the tent, if any of the tough youngsters had bothered to look, they would have seen many of the camp's bell tents being brought down, and might have wondered why this was happening so early in the afternoon. But their attention was so riveted at the moment that not even the lad they'd assigned to act as watch observed either the fall of tents or the imminent entrance of the most dangerous intruder of all — himself, QM Bloomfield.

The Quartermaster swept in, eyes blazing, his pointed side-whiskers at angry thrust. The grubby packet of playing cards scattered wildly as the boys jumped to attention, knocking over the ammunition box. Bloomfield's swaggerstick stabbed out like a bayonet, pinioning Boy-Pullen's tunic just one undone button down from the one he was trying quickly to get fastened. Boy-Pullen stif-

fened under Bloomfield's grim inspection. The Quartermaster's words came, however, not in a roar, but as a
low, controlled-volume, deliberately paced sneer.

'I would like to acquaint you gentlemen – if you can
spare me the time. . . .' He paused lengthily . . . no one
moved or dared to look directly at the Quartermaster.
'. . . with some of me problems – which means *your* problems – which must be done, namely, by nightfall. To wit:
I must move from off me invoices, and on to the wagons,
more than one thousand and five hundred dead tons of
rations and weapons, not to mention equipment and sun-
dries, ammunition and so forth, et cetera, as they might
say. And you and me is going to keep that all moving and
in the right places and well accounted for until we meet
up with the murderin' black heathens we come here to
this land to fight – but what goes on here with all this to
be done? Me eyes see, but me head and me heart don't
believe!' He shook his head sadly, then with a stick swipe
he knocked the cards remaining on the overturned box
flying to the earth of the tent floor.

'A game of Brag!' He pulled Boy-Pullen's face around
by siezing the lad's ear. 'A bleeding game of Brag!' The
old-faced youngster grimaced in pain, cleared his throat,
smiled weakly. 'Sorry, Quartermaster Bloomfield.'

Bloomfield shook his head mournfully, exuding self-
righteousness.

'You'll be more sorry when the Zulu asks – nice and
polite, mind you – "Lad, what have you to offer me not
to slit your gut from this end to t'other?" What'll you
answer him, boy?' Bloomfield turned over the remaining
playing card Boy-Pullen still clasped in his hand, looked
at it and piped in a high-voiced quavering imitation of a
boy in terror, "The knave of hearts, Mister Zulu, sir, I'll
give you the knave of hearts!" . . . is that what you'll
say?'

The youngsters knew better than not to laugh at this
witticism, and Boy-Pullen knew better than not to hang

86

his head in shame, which he did forthwith. QM Bloomfield had made his point. 'Out! Everybody – this way!'

He strode out of the tent, taking one and a half steps for each one manageable by his boys brigade. Boy-Pullen fell in with the older man, adding skips to keep up.

Soon they were mobilized. Thousands of men and beasts of almost equal number were on the move – to the Drift. Artillery pieces, horse-drawn; rocket carriages and carts, mule-drawn; great wagons, oxen-drawn. All these sturdy animals strained forward into the night, the vehicles preceded by men carrying pitch torches producing orange smoky light. Wheels lurched and creaked, crashing over embedded rocks, sliding into deeply eroded ruts, followed by squads of overladen men having similar trouble with their booted legs. The column was accompanied by mounted officers supervising the lumbering progress through the mysterious blackness towards unknown destinations.

At the far end of the column came the Sutler's wagon, even at this time of night on the move, open for business. An NCO was hotly speaking, walking alongside, contesting the price of his gin – the Sutler having increased the price for goods sold en route. Boy-Pullen, moving against the flow of forward traffic appeared, tried but failed to get attention to his needs. Seeing the Sutler engaged in both controlling his two-horse team and arguing vociferously with his dissatisfied customer, the youngster stopped walking foward – until the rear of the cart was alongside him. Lithely he hoisted himself aboard, cautiously lifted the edge of the tarpaulin which covered the goods. He smiled – it was dark, noisy, and he wouldn't be noticed. He was in the act of extracting the gin for which Bloomfield had sent him, when three more soldier figures appeared, holding fingers to lips cautioning silence.

87

Boy-Pullen passed them their requirements also. Then, grinning, they vanished, he leapt off the wagon, the bugler boy stuffed a handful of cigars into his tunic, pocketed the shilling Bloomfield had given him to pay the Sutler, and crouching low, scurried forward again.

QM Bloomfield, lolling on one of the high-covered ammunition wagons, looked up when Boy-Pullen leapt on to the seat alongside. The bugler boy handed over the rectangular gin bottle – the drink the Zulus called the Queen's tears. The fiercely moustachioed QM extracted the cork with his teeth, drank deeply. He breathed out with fiery satisfaction, belched and said, 'Ugh ... poison!', and settled down staring foward into the black of the night. The boy had taken out a bugle mouthpiece, wet it, looked up at the older man. 'Will you hear "Last Post", sir?'

Bloomfield never spoke casually. He rubbed his moustache carefully, pursed his pudgy mouth, kept his look ahead. 'I listened extra careful to your "Stand To", this morning. . . .' he nodded slowly. Boy-Pullen glanced at him anxiously. 'It was perfect. . . .' The boy couldn't believe his ears. But the QM went one. 'Couldn't've done it better meself, not even when I was bugler to the Duke of Wellington. . . .' He reached across the wagon seat to touch the swollen nearside ear of his young charge, who immediately shied away, grimacing with some pain. '. . . Now tell me, who done that to you? – thought I warned you. . . .' 'It was the Cooks, sir', the boy said quickly. '. . . They saw me dip your shaving tin in the tea water . . . made their tea taste of Pears toilet soap they said. . . .'

Bloomfield studied the youngster's face. 'So it happened in line of duty, you might say?' The boy nodded eagerly. '. . . Point taken.' And he handed over the gin bottle, allowed the boy one good gulp, but stopped him on the second. Boy-Pullen, moved by his superior's generosity – and possibly his own desire to smoke –

decided to hand over one of the stolen cigars.

He produced a match to light both. 'Will we be fighting the Zulu soon?'

'Sooner than some might think. They know we're coming ... they know all right. . . .' He rolled his cigar in his mouth to wet the end more thoroughly.

'You afeared of the Zulus, Quartermaster?'

Bloomfield noted from the corner of his eye that the mouthpiece of the bugle in the boy's hand was being twisted nervously.

'One Zulu is only one man, and I fear no man. But the Zulus come in thousands ... like a black wave of living death ... in thousands. And they've got what we got – discipline, steel 'ard discipline. They know what their job is. But then, so do we.' He puffed in satisfaction with his choice of words to the boy. 'They know what's to be done and so do we. . . .'

The boy stared for a while into the darkness ahead. He sucked in a large mouthful of smoke from his cigar, blew it gently out through the bugle mouthpiece. Then compressing his lips into a bugler's *emboucher*, he very softly played 'Last Post'. It was a delicate rendition, the thin unsupported tone of mouthpiece only, penetrating softly into the night. Riders in nearby wagons of the column stopped talking to listen. He came to the end; the last note hung, faded, died. Bloomfield shook his head approvingly. 'That's good tonguing, lad – but maybe a mite too sad. The Zulus will be out there listening. . . .' Boy-Pullen turned to look. 'The next time . . .' said QM Bloomfield, 'I think you should try to put a bit more of your gut in it . . .!'

The darkness absorbed them.

11

The massed *Impis* ran-marched with their regimental
shields slung on their backs, outpacing their *udibi*, the
carriers who would catch them up later and provide the
food. The army stretched ten miles and advanced forty
miles at each stage. They covered in two days, out of
Ulundi, the distance for which Chelmsford, with his
heavy freight and modern military impedimenta, would
require a full two weeks. They had come the final forty
miles moving all through the night. Then, near to the
land of the enemy, the mass army split into two unequal
sections, the lesser one of them moving south-westward,
disposed so as to give observers from the approaching
enemy the impression that they would be seeing elements
of the Zulu main army gathering to their own south-east.
In truth the main army, at this splitting point, veered
north-west, taking a route difficult to traverse but, by the
same token, difficult to anticipate. The massed warriors
moved silently and with quite incredible swiftness, never
breaking formation, run-marching through the precipitous rocky contours of the upper reaches of the mountain
ranges which would lead ultimately to the peaks behind
the Nqutu plateau.

Along the adjacent flanking hills, paralleling the
rapidly moving main army by distances of several miles,
moved wraith-like units of spy guards who could silently
warn the principal army of any approaching enemy scout
units which might discover its position and course of

movement; when this happened the army of 25,000 warriors could in an instant vanish into the natural cover of the wild country about it.

But before the imminence of the enemy could present its challenge, the main army paused. Each of its *Impis* were required to undergo the Zulu sprinkling ceremonies. These ceremonies were conducted for the separate *Impis* by its own medicinemen; men of remarkable powers and countenance, men privy to secrets of the hidden spirit world which controlled, for good or evil, the events of the natural world. Now, before, going into battle, the warriors needed to reinforce their trained skills with the additional forces of magic invoked for them by their doctors. Each and all of many rituals were essential for the victory of each and all of the warrior participants.

The doctors smeared the warriors' faces with black powders; carrying a brand of fire, they waved its smoke to evoke the correct spirits, those which would protect Zulu fighters but confuse their opponents. The warriors cleaned themselves internally, using emetic war medicines which made them retch out the contents of their stomachs, and externally, in deep running water or under waterfalls. After this, from amongst the scouts on the far flanks, spies were sent in pairs, or in groups upwards to half a dozen, to probe out enemy movements. To the river umZingiat (called the Buffalo by the white men), which formed Zululand's most south-western border, at the place where the crossing was easiest, Bayele, with his friend Sekonyela, led a party of six scouts from the *inGobamakhosi* regiment of young men. Bayele's heart swelled. That his warriorhood would be fully established in this war he was certain. It was an important assignment, to scout here, for this crossing was considered a high probability choice for the Redcoats who called it Rorke's Drift. The scouts ran swiftly to their assigned observation points but always in cover. Enemy movements in the area had already been reported, but as

91

yet nothing to indicate mass exodus into Zululand.

This was the region of the border chieftain, Sihayo, who had offended the British by sending a kidnapping party in pursuit of an unfaithful wife who had fled across the river into Natal territory for refuge. She was caught and forcibly extradited back to Zululand to meet her judgment. Cetshwayo had refused to deliver Sihayo to British justice for this transgression of British sovereignity, and indeed the delivery of Sihayo and his marauders had been one of the conditions of Chelmsford's ultimatum to the Great King which had been, as were the others, ignored. In any event, Sihayo would be no friend of the Redcoats, and had good reasons to be loyal to Cetshwayo. Nonetheless, Sihayo was not regarded as a truly effective ally; therefore Bayele had been ordered to act independently of Sihayo's people. He, Sekonyela, and the four others positioned themselves on high ground near the crossing on the Zulu side, and waited.

The warmth of the rising sun of dawn was welcome for the summer night had been chilly. They had abandoned their sleeping mats and *karosses* in the interest of mobility when they went forward into the danger area. Bayele immediately sent a first runner back to report no immediate sighting. In their position of advantage, they settled to wait. Many other parties of hidden Zulu scouts, he knew, surveyed other stretches of the river as he did now. He could see for miles the twists of the river on either side. The waiting could be long. Bayele and Sekonyela, to pass time, sketched a *Mlaba-Laba* diagram (see Appendix, page 283) on the ground, found twelve brown stones and twelve white stones and started a game – but did not fail to keep continuous observation. Their cohorts shared the watch, and commented on the play. Some bet on Sekonyela, some on Bayele – they bet armrings and other ornaments. The two friends played thoughtfully, placing their stones strategically. Sekonyela exclaimed in triumph as he created a three-move web to a sure capture. Bayele wrinkled his nose, dismayed – then noted that instead of following up his advantage Sekonyela was staring off, straight ahead across the river. All were looking now, silent, wide-eyed. The first of the west column's wagons were emerging from the trees, and creaked forward to the river crossing point – the Drift. Many more vehicles and then men on foot and on horse appeared. Bayele felt his whole body charged with an excitement that nearly choked him. The enemy. The incredible enemy. With its awesome transport, with guns thick as a man's body and twice as long, drawn on wheels by straining horses, and men, unending lines of men, in red tunics and with glinting white head-dresses, coming to the west bank of the river. The first crossing was made by a troop of forward scouts on horseback.

Some of the scouts with Bayele clamoured for immediate departure – to tell the *indunas* that they had located the penetration point of the invader before they themselves were discovered by the men who would come on horseback faster than they could run away. But Bayele refused to panic – he sent two back, but maintained the rest in their lookout positions. Who knew what else there was to learn? Look, already rafts were on the flooded river, and the oxen-team-drawn great wagons were rolling down the far riverbank to begin their crossing. Some men with bright spears rode their horses down the bank to plunge in. The enemy. The fabled red-coated enemy – rulers of the world.

But Bayele welcomed them in his heart. That they were a strange and unfathomable enemy he had no doubt. There were many stories of their magic, their control of fire demons. But he had seen guns, and while he respected the power of such weapons to do damage, he felt they were not wholly reliable – the ancient musketry sold by gun-running traders provided the only index of judgement for a Zulu who still was to experience the engineering of a Martini-Henry – and the Zulus too had

93

magics of invulnerability which the King and his medicine men would put at their disposal. Yes, Bayele was glad to see this enemy, for there was among them one – at least one – whose blood would wash Bayele's stabbing spear. And only when he had thus washed his spear would he become a true and forever warrior for the King of the Children of Heaven. Welcome, oh welcome, enemy who comes to us across the river!

Gouts of Buffalo River water sluiced out of the supply wagon as its oxen team, leaving the river on the Zulu side, struggled to find purchase on the steep and muddy embankment. CSM Williams directed his water-logged troop of C Company to help the animals get the wagon upon shore. His mouth curled in exasperation.

'Push the wagon, not the oxen's arse, you bloody idiot...! What are you on?' he shouted at Private Williams.

'Yessir, S'arnt Williams, sir...!' replied Private Williams withdrawing his hands from the beast's behind and stepping back to salute as he usually did in moments of confusion. Promptly, his boots slipped from under him so that he flopped seat down onto the muddy bank, in which indecorous position he slid down the bank like a human sled, ending up in the flood-waters from which he had just emerged.

'*Private Williams...!*'

The fallen private succeeded in regaining his footing, an incredibly bedraggled heap of gangling soldiery.

'... What the hell do you mean by having the same name as me?' cried out CSM Williams in an anguish of despair.

'Sorry, S'arnt, dead sorry...'

More ox-teams lurched out of the water, punts and rafts arrived unloading Redcoats who ran up the embankment forming themselves into rectangular

94

squads, eyes alert on the horizon, rifles at ready. Lieutenant Raw barked a command and they fanned out further in sections, making for the lower slopes on either side.

Vereker and CSM Kambula had led the first crossing at the centre; they rode out of the water, side by side, clearing foward to allow their hundred or so followers of the Sikali Horse to come ashore behind them. They had to shield eyes from the straight-on eastern sun-glaze in order to examine the rising terrain before them. This frontal brightness acted as a protective curtain against the intruders, keeping the unknown less knowable. What was waiting for them behind that glaze? A moment later, a mount bearing a plumpish man in his mid thirties, dressed rather swankily in a belted khaki tropical outfit, though now wet to the hips from the river, and wearing a sun helmet with a red band at a rakish angle, reined alongside. The fellow was breathing hard, but delighted with events. He studied Vereker and Kambula studying the hills rising to either side.

'Looking to see if friend Cetshwayo's sent a party of greeting, Mr Vereker?'

The questioner had in fact been introduced to Vereker by Crealock – Norris-Newman, reporter from the London Standard. He was called 'Noggs'; generally, an amiable enthusiastic man with a reporter's capability for asking obvious, but difficult-to-answer questions.

Vereker kept his eyes shielded, scanning the elevations. 'Oh, they're there, no question – I'll simply try to stop them getting back to announce us'.

'You mean ... can you actually see them?'

But the Sikali were now all fallen in, and on signal from Kambula separated into three troops, galloping right, foward and left in a sweeping uprising arc, Vereker leading the last of these units. Noggs lifted binoculars to his eyes, watched Vereker's progress up the left side of the valley, then shifted the angle of the glasses higher to see what he could of Zulu spies. He saw nothing for the moment.

However, Bayele clearly saw the riders coming forward, the one group directly facing him led by a young white-helmeted rider galloping on an all-white horse. Clearly, it was approaching the time to evacuate this position — Bayele gestured his men to follow him on their stomachs. They slithered just over the far side of the crest, after which they could rise to a crouching run back along the top on the far side towards a route of departure, which Bayele had selected for such a contingency when they first arrived to wait.

Boy-Pullen, QM Bloomfield alongside, steered the horses of the ammunition wagon up the embankment into Zululand. The wheels lurched on some shore rocks, and a metal-banded ammunition box bounced off the back. QM Bloomfield heard rather than saw this, leapt off the wagon, ordered two bugler boys seated at the back to restore it to the wagon, cursing them for stowing it badly in the first place. He waited at the river's edge. Two drowned black bodies, of the Natal native corps, swirled toward Bloomfield in the flood-waters coursing past. One of the bodies caught on the rocks. Bloomfield leaned down, removed the corpse's ammunition pouch, opened it and studied its contents. Lieutenant Melvill came up beside him, leapt off his horse, squatted alongside the QM. He looked at the body, shaking his head in dismay. 'Tricky business, Mr Bloomfield. There should have been more rafts made. . . .'

Bloomfield was very disturbed. He showed Melvill the wet ammo pouch. It had only one bullet in it. 'Look at that . . . waste . . . each of them pouches contains five rounds Mr. Melvill, and each of them rounds has to be accounted for. . . .'

Melvill was looking down and muttering, '. . .quite dreadful . . . something should have been done. . . .'

'If they'd been put back in their boxes and screwed

down, sir, like His Lordship ordered. . . .'

'I'm talking about our drowned natives, Quarter-master!'

Bloomfield didn't like Melvill's tone. 'Natives is not on my invoices, Mr Melvill . . . ammunition is, and 'as to be accounted for . . . *and* the brass cartridge cases returned!'

Melvill sighed with irritation and regret. He looked up as the Battalion Commander for the NNC rode up. It was 'Maori' Browne, Commander Hamilton-Browne in fact, the tough Irish ex-builder whom Melvill had seen an hour before insist that his unwilling charges wade across a much too turbulent ford, somewhat upstream. Melvill looked up at him grimly. 'Yours sir . . . and several more went under I think. . . .'

Hamilton-Browne shrugged, started to rein about. Melvill stood up, spoke pointedly. 'Shouldn't we have a roll call, sir?'

The commander half-turned, smiling. 'Not practical, me lad . . . no one's even had time to make up the rolls yet.' Then the smile became a chuckle. 'Besides . . . not too sure how many we had before the crossing.'

He cantered away. Crude bastard, thought Melvill as he mounted. He too had urgent duties to attend.

Bayele badgered his men to move more quickly through the brush and rocks at the crest of the hill. There was a rock-strewn pass that cut down along the back of the hill just a few hundred yards ahead, and down which mounted men couldn't possibly pursue his scout party. But he was worried – he hadn't calculated on the speed of approach of those smartly uniformed black riders led by the young yellow-haired man. Then, to Bayele's annoyance, Sekonyela just ahead of him suddenly stopped and exclaimed – but in the next moment he understood. The riders who had proceeded straight up the

97

valley had in fact also cut off to the left further along, and were now climbing rapidly up the hill in front of them. They would reach the crest before Bayele's group reached the ravine which was to take them down safely. They were, Bayele realized, now trapped between two hard-riding columns, one behind coming on fast, and one in front to cut off his planned escape passage. Had they been seen? Was this a conscious tactic, or were they just quarry animals to these hunters being flushed out in case they were here – as indeed they were. In any event, the young warrior had to make a decision very quickly.

Below, elements of the column were still crossing. Chelmsford, deploying sections on arrival, was conferring with his staff officers all mounted alongside – his mobile HQ. Chelmsford wanted Colonel Harness to proceed in advance with his artillery, to place his seven-pounders as cover for the main advance when it was ready. Orders were sent. His Lordship glanced up at the surrounding hills, expressed pleasure that the vedettes of cavalry were spaced evenly along the heights. He was advised that the Sikali were scouring the hills to flush out and caputre, if possible, any Zulu scouts who might be lurking. Beyond Colonel Crealock's shoulders His Lordship noted the approach of a man in quasi-military gear. General Chelmsford thought that the rider was seated rather badly. He spoke quietly to his military secretary. 'What is the strange name this news reporter chappie is called?'

Crealock turned, 'Called "Noggs" sir ... actually name of Norris-Newman. Presented credentials from the *Standard*. If you wish me to....'

Chelmsford interrupted, 'I'll talk with him – our runners carry his dispatches, do they not?'

Crealock smiled, nodding. 'Of course, my Lord....'

But Noggs was already riding up to them. He was beaming with self-pleasure, 'I was amongst the first across, my Lord...!'

Chelmsford was pleasantly friendly. 'You were indeed. I saw you lead our cavalry, sir. Tell me, were they in good heart on arrival on to enemy territory?'

Noggs removed his sun helmet, gestured with it, 'They spurred on to the high ground as ordered, my Lord ... full of spirit and looking for the Zulu: Full of sport they were!'

Chelmsford looked at him squarely. 'Indeed – then I trust you will report exactly what you have observed.'

Noggs had a smile that was naturally sardonic. 'I know your views on the limited usefulness of the press to the military. Nonetheless, the Englishman back home wants to know what his regiments are doing. You agree that, don't you, Your Lordship?'

Chelmsford prepared to move off, 'Tell what you see, but write it well, sir ... and take care – to get it right.'

But Norris-Newman was well-versed in the art of keeping conversations going with reluctant interviewees. 'I have it right, would you agree, sir, that you lead an invasion into Zululand. I see that all about me, so it is beyond doubt. But Why? is the question that my readers will ask – Why? Or even perhaps – Aren't the Zulus our friends? Did we not crown their King Cetshwayo at his coronation, when it seemed to be to our interest?'

As Noggs asked his heavily loaded questions, Chelmsford's amiability vanished and his answers became more blunt. But the journalist had ready his justification for asking them.

'Those questions, my Lord, have already been asked in the House. The Secretary for the Colonies asked Disraeli ...'

'I am uninterested in their politicking, sir....'

'...the Secretary of State asked the Prime Minister and Dizzy answered...' Noggs chortled for a moment, '... that he knew not the answer. Now perhaps *you*, sir....'

But he had to stop because Chelmsford, signalling his

staff, simply rode off. The officers smiled wryly, then quickly frowned because quite intrepidly Norris-Newman spurred alongside. 'I have it, my Lord, that there is no answer. We attack for sport – or is it for reputations?'

Chelmsford checked his horse and stared at Noggs. When he spoke his tone was chill and impersonal. 'Do not confuse yourself. The Zulu army is fifty thousand strong, and require an enemy to attack. I choose not to wait on the rape of Her Majesty's Colony before I meet my responsibilities.'

Now Chelmsford waited for Noggs's reply. It was clear that he would be allowed that single opportunity only. Noggs nodded slowly, 'So ... I understand you to say that attack is in fact your defence ... and the Zulu King, Cetshwayo, he will meet your military requirements? He'll offer his Impis for destruction?'

Chelmsford smiled, 'Yes, you may say that – my only fear is that the Zulu will avoid engagement.'

He rode away, with Norris-Newman not at all certain whether he had something to dispatch or not. He saw the unfortunate Sutler take this moment to intercept Chelmsford with a pitiful cry, evidently expecting that justice in his favour be meted out. Sutlers considered themselves important adjuncts of service to the military in such climes. 'Your Highness, sir, Your Majesty – they robbed me of six cases of....'

Chelmsford usually saved the peaks of his fury for more important issues, but this was pure self-indulgence. 'Get those wagons out of my way, or they go into the river! Now!'

The Sutler stared open-mouthed, as Chelmsford raised his hand to signal his threat into action; but then the Sutler promptly whipped his horses, so that with a wrenching start-up they dragged the coupled carts lurching out of the officer's path. Chelmsford, feeling much better, rode on. The mobile HQ moved after him. Noggs

100

made a quick character note, which he would use for colour in a future dispatch.

In fact, when Vereker had led his troop of Sikali up the hillside, he had neither seen Bayele, nor even concrete evidence of the Zulu scouts' presence. But he had a strong feeling as to where such might choose to lurk should they be about. He had ordered the second Sikali troop to cut uphill further on in the tactic of enclosure which, although he didn't yet know it, had already trapped the men he had hoped might be flushed out. His own Sikalis were riding into nearby underbrush, their triangular bayonets fixed on their Martini-Henry rifles poking into the cover wherever it was too dense to see. Converging fifty yards beyond, only yards from reaching the crest, the forward Sikali troop was conducting similar manoeuvres. Suddenly, there was violent movement in the bushes twenty yards ahead of Vereker and the sought-for Zulu scouts revealed themselves, breaking cover to run full pelt down the far slope. Both troops of Sikali riders whooped and charged after them, over the crest, the horses sliding and back-footing down the gravelly hill-face of the far side, none the less rapidly catching up their quarry. The trapped Zulus turned in desperation as the first of the mounted Sikalis reached them. First blood went to the rearmost Zulu who, with his *assegai*, took the bayonet counter-thrust from the lead horseman on his shield, stabbed under the shield – into the horse's belly.

As the horse collapsed it threw the Sikali rider on to the hill face and the Zulu made his second thrust full into the fallen man's middle back. But in the very next moment, the dying Sikali was avenged by Kambula, whose bayonent thrust caught the Zulu in the throat as he turned to face his next attacker. The other three scouts fought desperately; two quickly fell to rifle shots; the last one, jumping and dodging madly, made it a distance downhill before he was ridden down by one Sikali and, so rolling downhill, bayoneted by a second Sikali leaning far over his saddle in a completely unlikely act of horsemanship.

Vereker had reined just below the crest when he realized that his own pursuit of the scouts was made redundant by the rest of the Sikalis. He watched the killing of the scouts with fascination but some dismay, then became aware of a movement at the top in the same thicket from where the group had emerged. More of the damned scouts had evidently remained hidden there! He shouted for support, spurred his horse back to the top. But by the time he scrambled to the crest he saw the backs of two Zulu figures running toward a ravine directly away from him. Vereker instantly understood that the first four who charged out had been decoys, sacrifices, for these two who were escaping along the route that would have minute earlier been blocked by the second Sikali troop. He got his pistol up, fired without aiming. One of the Zulus stumbled, fell, continued to drag himself forward, evidently having been victim of a lucky leg shot. The other Zulu hardly paused but, turning briefly shouted something to his fallen companion, then ran on.

Vereker spurred, firing, but this last Zulu broke left, leaping outward and down into a rocky ravine, plunging out of sight. Vereker's horse covered the distance in seconds, but when he reached the same point he had to rein. It was impossible to take the horse into this rocky gash in the hillside. There was an initial twelve-foot fall on to huge boulders, some of which filled the ravine as it wound down the hill between sheer sides, subdividing into branching ravines and gullies. Other riders now came up behind Vereker. It was agreed that pursuit on foot would be useless, that the number of branching escape routes for the fleeing man further down made nonsense of trying to organize a massed general search. They were dismayed. One man could carry away as much

102

information as could six. The wounded man was Sekonyela who was to have escaped with Bayele by the subterfuge that had drawn off the riders from them. When he fell to Vereker's unaimed shot he had held on to his *assegai*. He washed it in his own blood, which, under the circumstances, was a most noble use for it, and a brave warrior's death for Sekonyela. The order, 'Take prisoners, if possible', had become academic.

Deep in the ravine, moving downward between covering boulders, Bayele progressed with sure-footed speed. He was elated, because he knew that the information he was bringing to the *inDunas* would be of consummate importance. At this moment, he alone in the world knew where the first battle between his people and the Redcoats would take place. He was bringing information of many strange things which he only partly comprehended, but the wise *inDunas* would understand and interpret it all and act as was necessary. Bayele had wanted to stop to help Sekonyela when he fell to the white man's gun-shot. But Bayele remembered well the warning that since the scouts knew the position of the main Zulu army, they could not let themselves be captured, under any circumstances. This is what he had called to Sekonyela. What terrible last words to call out to one's dearest friend. He had no time to see Sekonyela's final deed, but he was certain that his friend was not now alive.

He paused briefly, but heard no sounds of pursuit. No matter, no man or group of men could ever catch him in such ravines. He had planned this as the route away in case of emergency, but hadn't realized how difficult they would make it for him to get to that route. Now Bayele alone was using it to return – the others had to die. But one man was enough. And the spirits who had been good to him would treat his comrades well also in the spirit world. For their deaths had made it possible for Bayele to return, to tell the Zulu leaders of their army that within two nightfalls the Redcoats should reach the mountain whose peak looked like the stomach of cattle – the Zulu word for which was *Isandhlwana*.

12

'*Isl ... Issel ... whl-a-hana ...,*' Brevet Lt. Col.
Henry Pulleine read slowly in what he considered to be
quite a reasonable rendition of one of those damn curious
spellings of Zulu words. And Crealock was being damned
superior about it too, trying to get him to say it correctly:
'*I-sand-hlwana.*'

'Doesn't matter, old chap...,' Pulleine pointed east,
'... eight miles past that tallest hill, straight track, camp
on the low slopes. I can read a map, you know, even if I
can't pronounce these damn names'.

'*I-sand-hlwana,*' repeated Crealock. He worried about
Pulleine. Splendid organizer and leader of men – good
initiative on direct jobs – but if circumstances required
tactical choice, say, decision in the face of alterna-
tives.... Crealock reset his steel rims on his nose, and
turned away from the thought. His Lordship had left
Durnford behind, so Pulleine was *his* problem. Keep
Durnford in line, yes, but don't cut off one's nose to spite
one's face.

Pulleine was already raising his hand in signal. His
adjutant responded from a high point, signalling 'Clear
ahead', and Pulleine waved 'Forward-on!' Column leaders along the line repeated the gesture.

Everywhere movement started. The two-mile-long
west column was moving on to meet the enemy on its
own ground. It was an arthritic saurian monster, ponder-
ous, made of endlessly awkward loosely joined segments,

105

creaking, groaning, slithering into life. On the hills flanking, Pulleine could see Vereker and his horsemen working hard in small groups, patrolling, searching, ceaselessly active. The platoons of Redcoats moved tactically from the beginning, rifles ready, at least one section of each platoon in a defensive position at each moment.

In spite of the patrols, the hills on all three sides posed a looming threat for those who had to travel beneath them. It soon was no longer possible to glance back to see British-ruled soil on the far side of the river. Only the unknown ahead. Every device on wheels posed problems virtually unsolvable, the sixteen to a team oxen-pulled great carts in particular, but any and all vehicles on this faintest of tracks, which differed hardly at all from the stony, gullied ground which led to the hills ahead, were sources of minute-to-minute difficulty.

Barely under way, Melvill rode up to QM Bloomfield, rather untypically raising his voice, angrily shouting: 'I want your wagons in open line, Mr Bloomfield, but not so damn open my company can't protect them! Forty feet, no more than forty feet between them!'

Bloomfield was beginning to dislike this arrogant youngster more and more. His answer was minatory, didactic, condescending. 'You see, sir, it's like this – the ox is a stupid beast, with slow reactions. Put the wagons too close, they're goin' to walk into each other ... not if we get two spans tangled up, then you can sit your men down for four hours whilst we....'

Melvill would have no more of it. 'Come, come, Mr Bloomfield, narrow your lines.' He rode off. Bloomfield, moustache quivering, started to shout at the drovers.

Transport was the overweight cross every British commander carried on his personal Calvary into these hostile outer world countries. Zulus on the march fed off the land and its villages. But modern army carried everything, in this case 500 tons of gear and rations for one column alone. Even the transport required transport – in the form of feed for the non-grazing beasts like mules, provisions for the drovers and herders. And animals such as the oxen required time to graze.

In fact, the drovers now being tongue-lashed by Bloomfield had been distracted by activity on the left-flanking hill crest. CSM Kambula had suddenly dashed up a ravine, followed by a troop of Sikali. There was an instant and palpable flutter of anxiety, and heightened tension until the riders reappeared further on, gave no signal of difficulty, then patrolled forward at normal pace. The column lurched on, and the sun rose higher.

By noon concern in the ranks about imminent attack had diminished – whether justifiably could not yet be judged – in favour of getting food into rumbling stomachs. The Imperial infantryman had a hard and very high-risk job; he was expected to live rough on campaigns without complaining, and also be ready to die. But come noon, some meat, fresh from the slaughter beeves, or salted out of the pork barrel, was due; bread from the bakery wagon in camp but hardtack biscuit out here on the march would do nicely, thank you; and hot tea. The half-hour of rest and the food at midday both contributed a bit to revive spirits depleted by the giant efforts of the last twenty-four hours. Even some cooling breezes were blowing down from the hills to relieve the intensity of midday heat that the unshielded sun generated. With the sun now higher and not glaring directly into eyes, the countryside revealed more colourful details, shades of green, contoured skylines, a dark blue instead of milky glary white dome of sky above. Food, scenery, a sense of confidence in the elegantly machined weapons on their shoulders, adventure ahead and the glory of victory – all seemed possible as the march inland resumed.

Easily seated in his saddle, a relaxed smile illumintating his youthful face, Lieutenant Coghill rode to the front of his marching platoon deeply inhaling the coolness of the breeze, patting his well-filled stomach in a mood of genuine contentment. All good things might come. He was transported, remembering a ship he once sailed in the Southampton Estuary.... His reverie was broken by a loud shout, a whooping call that could have been a warning. He looked up sharply and saw his friend Melvill galloping down the slope, shouting incomprehensibly, waving his arms. Coghill was alarmed, glanced about: the other marching units, in front of and behind his, seemed momentarily lost around twists in the trail. His hand swiftly withdrew his pistol from his holster, and he shouted an order, 'Number One Platoon. Halt! Loa ... oad!'

The Platoon slammed to a timed halt, instantly knelt, snapped open breeches, slammed in cartridges in a volley of metallic clicks. Then every alternate man stood sharply, waiting, rifles to shoulders. Coghill stood high in his stirrups and scanned the hilltops particularly those behind Melvill, who continued forward riding, gesturing, shouting.

There was nothing to be seen yet. Melvill came up, reined, breathing excitedly. He gestured expansively forward: Coghill's look followed the gesture. He saw the column section before them round a rock outcropping as its long lines of infantry and ox-and-wagon transport moved methodically towards the mountainous rises in the distance. To each side of it was sweeping country, a feeling of infinitude in greens, browns and blues, lovingly hued by the invigorating sunlight – empty of all threat.

Melvill was ecstatic. 'There, Coghill...! There! – Stretched out is my Lord Chelmsford's magnificent army! What a wonderful adventure we undertake ... what a marvellous spree!'

Coghill stared at his friend's glowing smile. Was this the same face which he usually saw crookedly arched in wicked attitudes of cynicism, its mouth pouring forth sardonic rebuke for mankind and all the world? Now this strange contradictory fellow whom he admired deeply was as innocently happy as a schoolboy at a truant's picnic. What's more, Coghill understood Melvill's elation completely. He shook his head, sighed, turned to his men still at ready with their rifles. 'Number One Platoon ... u .. un .. load!' Coghill's attention was caught by the next unit behind coming up. It was time to move on.

The artillery, shading in a vale of giant boulders which had rolled off the surrounding mountains in some geologic upset long ages ago, were finishing their eating. The horses were unhitched from the limbers; nosebags of feed were hung on their faces. The huge, black-skinned bombardier, naked to the waist, was running an oil-cloth over the shining barrels of the guns, which glinted with painful brightness in the noon sun. Colonel Harness, their commanding officer, rode in from a staff lunch with His Lordship. Maj. Stuart Smith sauntered forward to meet him, still chewing. The Colonel pulled his horse to.

'How soon can you move the batteries forward, Stuart? They're required for cover again.'

Smith sighed. 'That's what we're here for – but don't you think, Colonel, considering the time of the day and the distance we've to go. . . .'

Colonel Harness cut in, 'Five minutes, Stuart?'

Smith shrugged, 'The horses are just being fed now – perhaps thirty minutes?'

Colonel Harness shook his head more in sorrow than in impatience. 'Fed or hungry, Lord Chelmsford wants the batteries in forward position immediately.'

The Major compressed his lips, 'Yes, sir. But I do think someone should tell His Lordship. . . .'

Harness cut in, 'Stuart, the *Zulu* has been found . . .!' Smith looked up sharply and, without a word, moved into action.

Harness watched the horses resisting having their feedbags taken away, then balk at being put back, hungry, into the traces of the gun carriages. He was also trying to evaluate what he had seen and heard at Chelmsford's HQ just minutes earlier: His Lordship had opened some good wine to precede the food. Harness noticed two groups of riders galloping in at the same time; one, more distant, a pair of horsemen raising a dust trail, came from the south, while from the hillside to the north-west the rather magnificent Sergeant Kambula leaned close to his mount's neck sprinting towards them, members of his troop following, hooves pounding closer and closer.

Kambula reined in first, crying out, 'Zulu! We see Zulu!'

But under questioning, his information proved scanty. Crealock wanted Kambula to name the number of regiments, but it became evident that he was talking of possibly one hundred or so. Chelmsford thought that it must be an advance party, the spearhead of a major sortie. From Kambula's answers, however, it was soon deduced that these Zulus were probably not from the main *Impis*; they fitted what was known about the locals under Sihayo's chieftainship – the same Sihayo whose delivery to British justice was the subject of one term of Chelmsford's ultimatum to Cetshwayo. If so, they were not a major threat. But, Harness argued, could not the existence of hostile forces on any scale be a threat to British supply lines when they were more extended? Chelmsford seemed determined that any such hazard along the track to Ulundi be eliminated forthwith. They had seen Zulus allied to Cetshwayo ... main army or not. Colonel Harness recognized that His Lordship was elated, enlivened by an opportunity for taking immediate action.

It was decided to allow Pulleine to proceed with his section of the column already moving to Isandhlwana, but to hold sufficient forces to attack Sihayo's men first light, advancing before nightfall to an attack position, and bring up such reserves as might be required if the battle developed to larger proportions. And, Chelmsford added, he would likely employ Major Russell's rockets, which were a part of the artillery unit and therefore a matter of concern to harness. Russell's rockets, Harness pointed out, had been deployed back with Durnford's defence column at the Middle Drift. Orders were dispatched for Russell to come forward with his wonderful devices and the group of mechanical experts who worked them.

During the excitement generated by the heady news that the west column would see immediate action against a real enemy, the pair of riders from the south arrived, and were interviewed by Colonel Crealock. Crealock came from the riders towards the staff officers. It was evident that he brought dire news. 'My Lord....'

Chelmsford looked up, frowning at the sharpness of his secretary's tone.

'Colonel Durnford has crossed the river at the middle Drift.' Crealock thrust over the written message for his commander to read.

Chelmsford read and re-read the message, visibly flushing. 'Damn cheek.' He dashed the liquid from his wine glass to the ground; his voice shook with aggravation. 'Crossed over indeed! ... crossed over! In spite of.... Were my orders not clear? ... to defend only, hold and defend! Were those not my orders?'

Crealock nodded. 'Yes, my Lord.' Chelmsford re-read the message. Crealock spoke again. '... Perhaps Colonel Durnford has thought to conquer Zululand on his own....'

It was Crealock's rare attempt at sardonic whimsy, but Chelmsford didn't smile.

'The while leaving Natal defenceless at its middle!' Then, he added grimly, 'Order Colonel Durnford here, forthwith!'

Riders went out as required, and the staff officers,

111

exhibiting discreet satisfaction at Durnford's imminent disgrace, departed to their separate duties. Harness, on his way to move Stuart Smith and the guns forward, had a sense of let-down. Somehow this was not the way he thought the war with the Zulus would start. He had anticipated a Zulu initiative to be met of course by an impenetrable Redcoat defence. Now it was his side doing the attacking. But, in fact, would these Zulus merely wait for the British assault? Might they not instead take their own initiative?

Many others asked the same question when they were appraised of the action to take place on the morrow at daybreak. Zulus didn't wait for the enemy – the stealthy bastards picked their own times and places. News of the Zulu scout who had evaded Vereker and his Sikali Horsemen earlier was now generally out. Once that elusive scallywag returned to his black masters, surely the initiative would then belong to them. None the less, as shadows lengthened and the west-descending sun turned orange, the elements of tomorrow's attacking forces had been halted in fixed defensive positions, but ready to move into a strike stance when light returned.

Sentries prowled the darkening landscapes, rifles ready. Patrols moved between sentry posts, rifles loaded, bayonets fixed. The hills, where the Zulus were known to be, were visible in black outline. There were no fires permitted. Good soldiers can sleep whenever the chance arises, let the morrow bring what it may. But Boy-Pullen was twelve or thirteen and his boy's imagination was plagued by the QM Bloomfield's evocation of the evening before: '... they come by the thousands ... a black wave of death. ...' Everytime he closed his eyes, he could see them ... the thousands. ...

'Quartermaster?'

'What is it, lad?'

'Do you. ... I mean if the Zulu attacked us first ... you know, tonight like?'

112

Bloomfield came forward from the back of the wagon. It was too dark to continue checking supplies. 'The Zulu may not wear trousers and boots and the like, but that don't mean they got no brains. They'll watch us careful like ... and wait ... until they know our weaknesses.' He pulled out some burlap sacking.

'Oh. ...' Then, as the QM started to unroll his sleeping mat on top of the burlap, 'Quartermaster ... do *we* have weaknesses?'

Ten minutes later, all was silent and dark. Bang! A rifle-shot blasted the stillness, its nearby flash startling bright! Boy-Pullen ducked his head under his coat, Bloomfield sprang to the front of the wagon, pistol in hand. Redcoats were already kneeling with rifles swung to the direction of the shot, some buckling up their equipment to be ready for whatever was coming. Would more shots follow? The sentry posted at His Lordship's latern-lit tent peered about, but stared straight ahead when the great man himself poked his head out to look.

Then out of the night came a baleful roar combining anguish, rage and exasperation: it was the unmistakable voice of CSM Williams shouting. 'Pri ... vate Williams ... are ... you ... out of your bleedin' 'ead?!'

The army within hearing distance relaxed. The next voice was Coghill's:

'Is Private Williams a relation of yours, Sergeat-Major Williams?'

''e'll soon think 'e is, sir, because from this minute I'm gonna follow 'im round and every time I see 'im I'll put 'im on a bloody charge...! No! Don't reload! Private Williams!'

13

Chelmsford moved inside, adjusted the lantern on his desk to better see his documents while his servant refreshed his wine glass from a silver decanter. His Lordship quaffed half of this in a single swallow. The guard outside the tent appeared at the flap and said, 'Lieutenant Vereker is here, my Lord.' Chelmsford nodded, moved the documents aside. The guard held the tent flap open for Vereker's entrance, but Chelmsford immediately came to his feet, seized his young visitor's arm to draw him in, frustrating any attempt at a salute. 'I do apologize, William, if I'm depriving you of any sleep which you, above all, deserve, but I feel I haven't welcomed you yet – we've had no time at all to talk as old friends, family friends. He turned impatiently to the servant, made a quick pouring gesture, '... a glass for the Lieutenant....'

His order was obeyed with alacrity. A chair was drawn up and Vereker found himself seated, drinking and facing Chelmsford, wondering what meaning this curiously timed invitation to visit his commander might have.

Chelmsford held up his own glass, 'To reunions of old friends....'

Vereker accepted the toast with a nod, sipped, waited for Chelmsford's next words.

'Good job, flushing out those scouts this morning ... jolly good ... my congratulations.'

'Not as good as it might have been, sir'.

114

'Oh, the one who made off? Yes. Still, five of six, all in a day's war, as they say.' Chelmsford laughed. 'Unbuckle, William, drink up – splendid year....' He showed the wine label and also indicated that his own tunic was unbuttoned. Vereker complied, undoing his webbing, then sipping again from his glass in a manner to show he was savouring the vintage to which Chelmsford had called attention.

'First blood to you then, now that deserves another toast,' Chelmsford smiled knowingly, 'or perhaps ... a more *official* mention....'

'Ah, most of that was done by...' Vereker began to say, but Chelmsford was clearly not accepting any over-modest statements from his visitor.

'Good God, lad, I heard you bagged one at fifty yards with a pistol shot ... remember your first stag, William...? I do ... your father's autumn shoot ... '70 ... yes, '70 ... you were fifteen.... we discussed the matter ... I remember thinking boy William is no longer a boy. More than anything, I remember Ireland for that...' He paused again, a reflective smile appearing on his face. 'Memories of that pleasant greenland can be a godsend on this continent.... Do you find, too? – ever?'

Vereker inclined his head slightly almost but not quite, indicating an affirmative, tasted his drink. What did the man want? What was he getting at? This was too embarrassing.

His host waved his hand toward the tent flap and the servant vanished discreetly. Next Chelmsford clasped his hands behind his head, leaned back reflectively.

'The stag, nature's noblest, magnificent, beautiful.... Also, it will fight to death – and must be kept down. Let one relax one's vigil, and in time one can be dispossessed of one's own land.' He paused, looked at Vereker carefully, waited for a comment.

Vereker smiled, if somewhat wryly, 'I believe, Frederic, that you are creating an analogy for me – I am not certain why. I admit I was close to the Zulus. I've also enlisted to fight them. . . .' Was this it? Was his loyalty being questioned?

'Consider how often great nations have fallen to lesser breeds, Rome to the barbarians ... Attila ... Genghis Khan.'

'You think Cetshwayo belongs on that list?'

'Don't you? Or if not, could you take a chance? When history judges our action, what will it say?'

'I wouldn't care to guess, sir. Future Zulus, for instance, might prefer to list him with Napoleon or Caesar rather than Attila. . . . I've heard his ancestor Shaka called "the Black Napoleon" '.

'Why did you enlist, William?'

The young man thought, pursed his lips, 'Difficult. . . . Sense of survival, I'd say.'

'Precisely. Can you put that on a national basis then?'

What *did* Chelmsford want from him? Surely His Lordship hadn't developed a conscience about serving British territorial aspirations by military means. And even if so, what possible use was it to him to have his reasons for invasion underwritten by a junior of Vereker's low estate? The young man had to answer in some way, so he found himself saying, 'Colonel Durnford is a good example, sir. He feels that one must negotiate with them for as long as possible; none the less when a Zulu finally picks up his *assegai* and rushes at one. . . .'

Chelmsford leapt on the cue of Durnford's name. 'Yes, Durnford, exactly. When Durnford sat on the Boundary Dispute Commission ... what? eight, nine months ago, at most, he, more than any one of his fellow commissioners, was responsible for making the boundary awards in favour of the Zulus. Think of that in light of where things stand today.'

'But Frederic. . . .'

Chelmsford didn't want an answer. He was garrulous and, Vereker suspected, drunk from too much of the wine he gulped continuously.

'Crealock thinks Durnford has it in his head that it's not too late in life to gain a reputation from this war. But ... ', he paused to make certain that Vereker was fully attentive, 'consider Colonel Durnford's action whilst with the Boundary Commission, from an historic viewpoint! Should a man with a truly historical perspective, as we have a right to expect from a leader whose actions and decisions affect our future well-being, take an important decision that will weaken and embarrass the defence of his own side within a few months of that decision? Answer that!'

'Honestly, I don't feel I can, Frederic.'

Chelmsford's index finger now thrust forward, delivering judgment. 'No! But! even that is not our real concern. Our real concern is that he took this important – and damaging – position over the heads and expressed will of his superiors in these matters. I refer to the High Commissioner, my friend, Sir Henry Bartle Frere, and of equal importance, the majority of the people of Natal. Certainly today Durnford says, let's stop this man Cetshwayo, quite forgetting it was the report of the Boundary Commission, which he wrote, which encouraged the barbarian Chief to believe all his other demands should be given equal credence.' Chelmsford subsided, dabbled his mouth in his wine glass, chuckling to himself.

Vereker stared at the suddenly bemused man. . . . Yes, very drunk. He fathomed that somewhere in Chelmsford's obscure purpose, he was testing his, Vereker's loyalty as between the man who recruited him, Durnford, and himself, both his class equal and leader. Living as he had on the border, Vereker clearly remembered that the Boundary Commission's report was in favour of the Zulus. It had been a great shock to High Commissioner Frere, and most other colonials, and had indeed probably strengthened Cetshwayo's sense of hegemony; however, no one could say that the report had reached an unfair

117

conclusion. But, Chelmsford was not arguing against it as unfair. He was using it as a measuring-rod for Durnford's capacities to act in the best interests of the common cause of colonials in Southern Africa, when the power to do so was placed in his hands.

That was it! Chelmsford was worried about Durnford as a rival. He was criticizing him for taking on excessive authority. Every man's greatest rival is the one who has similar faults – this august General was suggesting that Durnford in his late forties was trying to snatch a late-life success to climax a so far inadequate career. What about His Lordship – in his late fifties?

What can I say that, first, can't be gainsaid; secondly, that Chelmsford would like to hear; and thirdly, that will not make me an absolute damn cad about Durnford? Thinking these thoughts, Vereker heard himself reply in stumbling, uncertain fashion, more to fill the gap of silence than for any good reason, 'I think it's generally agreed that ... that Colonel Durnford is headstrong and impulsive, however....'

Chelmsford's head snapped up. 'Precisely my point...! Would you follow him into battle, William?' He stared at Vereker, waiting for the correct answer.

'Er ... naturally, if such were my duty.... However...,' he paused while Chelmsford continued to grin, '... if it were my choice, which it is not, I would prefer perhaps a less impulsive fellow.'

'Precisely!' exclaimed Chelmsford delighted. 'Because you see, I do have to make the choice – I'm so glad you've confirmed my feeling. I'm in a lonely position, William, often have to take my own counsel, without faith in those available to me to give adequate consultation. Thank you, William.'

Damn, thought Vereker, have I crucified poor old Durnford without meaning to? The old boy seized on that word 'impulsive' so damn quickly. Lonely, that's it! No faith in his staff, he says. He needs a friend. Well, damn it, so do I, but it's not going to be him. . . .

Chelmsford, relaxed and amiable, continued to speak, the first few words of which Vereker had lost during his introspection; '. . . survival, precisely as you said. One hears your father's voice when you speak, William.' He finished off the wine glass yet again, brushed droplets from his trim moustache, gestured for Vereker to drink up also. Then he poured out two more from the decanter. Again he toasted, 'To survival . . . to survival!'

Vereker withheld drinking, and laughed, a touch self-deprecatingly, '. . . I must inform you, Frederic, that when one is a third son, with no hope whatsoever of title or money, surviving develops into an art. May I propose a toast. I just realized what a fool I've been. . . . I've failed to offer condolences for the passing of the first Baron, and my congratulations to you on your ascendancy to the title. . . .'

'Yes, yes – thank you. Let me amend then. 'To survival of third-borns *and* first-borns in our battle tomorrow'. . . .'

Dear God, thought Vereker, he's bleary-eyed drunk, and he's forming us into an exclusive club of the noble born and blessed in battle. Can I gently appraise him of the realities, dig him a bit without offending him?

'Little real danger, I'd hazard. These Zulus we found – they're only locals. The really able and young men will have all gone to join Cetshwayo, as mine did. . . .' Chelmsford didn't seem to react, so he added, 'I'd say, if we skirted them altogether, they'd be pleased to see our backs. . . .'

But Chelmsford's good mood was now unassailable – he drank again and chortled happily. 'Then we'll start with certain success. First blood and a rousing report in *The Times*. Keep Disraeli happy. And . . . ,' he raised his finger and winked sagely, instructing a young man in the sophisticated stratagems of high leadership, '. . . encouragement for our troops, confidence in their

119

superiority over the enemy. An opportunity sent to us by a kind providence, it would be a sin to forego it. . . . We attack at dawn! Attack!'

Vereker was now sagging with fatigue and the induced lethargy of the wine, but had no option than to sit there providing audience to a more than mellow and very talktative Chelmsford for quite a long time into the night.

14

Light bled slowly into the sky from beneath the horizon, heralding the day of attack. 'Stand to!' was sounded by a puff-cheek bugler boy, and at once the silent sleeping bivouac came to agitated life. The Natal Natives, harassed by their yelping NCOs ran into formation near the bottom of the slope they would shortly be assaulting; every fifth man of them with rifle and five rounds, the others carrying *assegais* and shields like the men they were going to engage; the sole insignia of their elevation to soldiership for Her Majesty in most cases amounted only to a bit of red rag tied on their naked biceps.

The Imperial troops of the second of the Twenty-fourth Foot were nimbly and expertly buckling packs, ammunition pouches, water bottles on to the white webbing which crisscrossed their scarlet tunics. QM Bloomfield, Bugler Boy-Pullen and other drum-and-bugler boys manned the ammunition wagons, passing out the seventy rounds set-issue per man, as the Redcoats filed past. The opening of each successive ammunition box, however, proved to be a trial. The African climate had oxidized the screws and metal bands, and the wood, too sturdy to merely split open, resisted hammer blows. Bloomfield refused to continue the distribution until his misplaced screw driver, heavy-duty, was located. It was his only one, a requisition for more having been refused or shelved.

The assault waited as other difficulties developed. The attack on the Zulus had to start with the disadvantage of an uphill charge: the focal point was no more than 500 yards up the slope where a rock-sided gash in the hill indicated an opening into a long, steep-sided gorge wherein lay the well-protected Sihayo *Kraal*. The sides of the gorge were almost perpendicular – too steep to attack from above. The slopes to the gorge opening were covered by tangled thickets of underbrush, rock outcroppings and clusters of thorn trees and acacia. Under the rocks were scorpions, in the grass were snakes and fire-ticks, and on the slopes some goats, which the herders quickly retired into the gorge when the first troops showed up below.

The most immediate hold-up was the placement of Major Russell's rockets, which task was not only occupying the Major and his highly specialist blue-coated crew, but also a number of curious Redcoats who had never seen the contraptions in operation. Russell had chosen as launch area a flat rock shelving part way up a slope adjacent to the one being attacked so that the trajectories for his wonderful rockets could be flatter and better aimed.

The soldiers who clustered curiously were intrigued by Russell, on hands and knees, getting his Major's tunic more and more greasy and crumpled as he wiped oil-black hands on the uniform. His helpers, erecting the rocket tube-troughs on bipod legs, were equally absorbed. The oblong one-foot and three-inch-long rockets, with spin stablizers, were being set in the troughs for the launching that would initiate the attack. His Lordship was convinced of the terrifying effect of these miracles of nineteenth century science on the barbaric minds of the enemy. Instant demoralization and submission was a conceivable reaction.

Major Russell, bald, short and broad, laboured with his black bombardier and eight Bluecoats carefully, tediously adjusting screw settings, taking readings of wind velocity, elevations and sea-level with an assortment of calibrated instruments. However, the bipod legs created difficultly in obtaining and maintaining the required angles and stabilized positions, and the screw settings were unendingly fiddly, and apparently subject to capricious and unaccountable change – as were the sighting instruments.

Finally, the members of the battery, exhaused but triumphant, straightened up. The row of rocket shells lay precisely in their firing troughs, the exhaust thrusts set to the second of an arc at the angle required by Major Russell; the hand-lit fuses waiting now only for the fiery touch which would launch the six-pound shells shrieking through the atmosphere towards their untutored, superstitious, spear-bearing, animal skin-wearing, black-bodied, human targets. The mules which served the rocket battery munched hay, the only uninterested observers of these novel scientific procedures.

The 'ready' signal was given by Russell waving an oily cloth down to the command post of the infantry waiting below. The launch signal was returned from the ground. Russell cried out, 'Touch the fuses for launch!' But the wheel of the flintlock was too worn to create a spark sufficient to ignite the touch paper with which to light the fuses. The spare flintlock was missing, so another had to be found. When this information reached the command post, His Lordship agreed to have the rocket launch used at a more tactical moment of the assault. Major Russell lost his audience of Redcoats, and the glory of opening the attack.

Hamilton-Browne turned from his Native Corps battalion with a look of disgust – he had no patience with them or their English officers. Behind the NNC formation, Melvill and Coghill had brought their C Company into position. On signal Melvill shouted, 'C Company . . .

fi ... ix ... bayonets!' Coghill, on his horse, watched the precision fix with satisfaction, and said out loud, 'Good soldiering ... excellent.' There was no doubt about the purpose of that row of glistening bayonets aimed at the backs of the Native battalion who were leading the charge. Hamilton-Browne had personally instructed the Redcoats that should unusually spirited resistance from the enemy cause faintness of heart amongst the NNC, causing their advance to waver, their only retreat would be into the prickled row of advancing fixed bayonets held by soldiers. He was most explicit in his orders to use them against *anything* coming in their direction, whether enemy or fleeing members of their own corps.

But, the charge developed with good force, when, about 200 yards up the slope, a spattering of rifle-fire broke out from the rises on both sides of the gorge entrance. The volume of smoke and the nature of the blast clearly identified the defending guns as muskets of ancient vintage. The charge halted momentarily, but there were no hits and it continued. Counter-fire of unknown effect poured back from Martini-Henrys, aimed at the musket smoke. More musketry, and the first NNC man went down, clutching his shoulder. All dived for cover. Those of the NNC in more exposed positions turned to escape back down-slope but saw the menacing bayonets waiting for them and abandoned the thought. To their relief, firing from both sides stopped. Silence, except for some insect chirruping. Then, a party fom the Native battalion, on an unheard command, skirmished forward and upward in a low crouch, more or less keeping cover, going from outcrop of rock or undergrowth, one to the next. They paused while some of their rifles were brought up to aim. Silence and waiting again.

Out of the vegetation at the mouth of the gorge, a grey-headed Zulu stood up, raised his spear and shield wide in outstretched arms to show no hostility. No one fired at him. Then he shouted, surprisingly in English, albeit heavily accented. He spaced his words for clarity, calling out each word in a loud clear shout.

'WHY-DO-YOU-COME-TO-OUR-KRAAL? WHO-ORDERS-YOU-TO-COME-HERE? WE-HAVE-NO WAR-WITH-YOU!'

Hands on hips, Hamilton-Browne shook his head in wonder, addressed Harford almost as a fellow human being. 'Mother of mercy, be damned, do you hear what I hear?'

Harford was standing erect, eyes glowing. 'May I answer, sir?' Hamilton-Browne shrugged indicating the depth of his unconcern about such niceties.

Harford cupped hands to mouth to shout back, 'By orders of the Great White Queen ... Queen of all Africa! Surrender now or bear the consequences!'

The grey-haired Zulu disappeared low. His answer was quick to follow. A volley of shots burst from the opening of the gorge and a sheaf of spears was hurled through the air in the direction of the most advanced skirmishers of the NNC. They took flight again. There was a shouted command, 'Forward, you bastards!', in the brogue of Hamilton-Browne. A second wave from the Native battalion ran uphill, shouting their war cries, holding their *assegais* aloft. The rifle owners among them fired, and dropped to their knees to reload as they had been taught. The rest of the line waited, waving their *assegais* threateningly, emitting dangerous shouts.

But there was a sudden new development from the defenders signalled by the abrupt appearance of some Zulu youths on the slope above but directly in line with the charge. They ran out from hiding, carrying sharpened poles which they immediately used to lever large boulders from what were, it was soon apparent, pre-set positions. The great round stones were instantly dislodged and rolled forward with increasing momentum, gathering a landslide of accompanying smaller stones, crashing and tumbling towards the attackers. The threat to life and limb was considerable as the volume of missiles crescendoed. The counter-attacking Zulus worked bravely at starting more and more stones downhill despite shell-fire splattering around them. Some of them indeed went down. But the boulders were also taking toll: the advance line of British native support broke, fled – but again not far. The Redcoat bayonets still waited for them. C Company's volley-shooting now came to bear fully on the rock-rollers in a hell-rain of swift deadly metal. Many young Zulu defenders died, and the others fled into the gorge.

'What now, Colonel?' asked Harford, scanning the empty terrain.

'Get ours together and we'll go in after them. . . .'

Orders were shouted and the European NCOs of the NNC used rifle-butts and curses without stint to reform the black-skinnned lines and point them towards the gorge again. C Company was brought into position to pour fire at the gorge opening to clear it for the next stage of the assault. Under orders from Coghill and Melvill the volume of fire grew, reverberating from hill to hill, startling all wild creatures except the men who created the sound. Harford was annoyed with Hamilton-Browne's coarse excesses. What the devil did he expect from the NNC considering the spurious terms of their involvement in this war? Doing damned well, rather, he thought.

15

Vereker and the Sikali were lined up just beyond the command post where Crealock sat writing out orders at a field table. The young man mused that Chelmsford's toast of the night previous on behalf of his safety in today's action had turned out to be a wasted gesture. Vereker and his unit were not to be engaged at all; in fact they were being sent forward to Isandhlwana to scout. He listened to the volley firing, watched the NNC being regrouped for another assault. But the real object of his curiosity was the proceedings inside Chelmsford's command tent, set twenty yards to one side of the field table where Crealock performed the visible work of command. Ranged beyond Chelmsford's quarters was a troop of Basuto riders which Vereker immediately identified as members of Durnford's Horse, who had come with their master as escort from the Middle Drift. Vereker assumed correctly that Durnford was at the moment inside the tent with his commander.

Chelmsford's public reaction to the message about Durnford's initiative across the Buffalo the day prior, left no doubt as to what the subject of this meeting would be. But Vereker's speculations were cut off as he was approached by a runner with written orders from Crealock covering his forward scouting action. He knew them, but re-read them. He signalled Kambula – and he and Kambula leading the Sikali, the scout party, rode off with their usual precision. The battle of Sihayo's *Kraal* went on behind them.

And the other battle, under the canvass of Chelmsford's tent, was coming to its own form of climax. Durnford stood at rigid attention, utterly frustrated in his desire to answer Chelmsford in matching tones of violence.

'Damn me, man, don't deny it! You intended to defeat the Zulu army on your own!'

Durnford replied in the careful manner of one who had made the same point several times already. 'My Lord, I received intelligence from sources of my own . . .'

Chelmsford cut in scathingly, 'Your *"own* sources" . . .!'

'Yes, my Lord. You have not objected when I have used these same sources to carry out recruitment, to determine disposition of potential support within enemy territory. . . .'

'Let's stay with the matter on hand, Colonel!' Chelmsford's tone was now cold, dangerous. 'Did it occur to you that this intelligence you received was deliberately planted to your informants – your so-called "sources" – just to draw you off, to open all of Natal to a possible counter-thrust at our vulnerable centre? And they succeeded – while you chased phantoms, the Zulu main army could have crossed the river where you abandoned the post *I* set you. . . .'

Durnford heard thoughts he hadn't meant to express pouring out. 'It is my opinion, sir,' and he heard the heat in his voice that he wished weren't there, 'that Cetshwayo is not prepared to assault across the boundary lines yet – Middle Drift or anywhere! He does not want this war! He is hoping in his perhaps over-simple way that his show of force will discourage us. An invasion on his part now is a commitment beyond which he wishes to take this war . . . he is not prepared for that. His *Impis* are under orders to rid their own country of aggressors, that is all;

not take that initiative on themselves. I have it on sources of utmost reliability...'

Durnford stopped, realizing that he was making no impression on Chelmsford. His own passion and sincerity had sprung from wells of deepest conviction and a certain knowledge of Cetshwayo's expressed feelings. It was true that his information about Zulu movements across the Middle Drift proved false. But on this larger issue – that Cetshwayo had no immediate aggressive plans, wanted only the integrity of his own territory – he was convinced. Surely His Lordship would have to take account of the depth of conviction of one who had continuously proved his grasp of all matters African to date. Durnford had accepted the principle of preventive invasion – but they were discussing short-term intention. Would Cetshwayo invade if he thought war was avoidable?

Chelmsford nodded curtly but added with an air of finality, very calmly and coldly, 'Colonel Durnford, if there is another occasion when my direct orders are flouted, it will be my regretful duty to remove you from all command.'

Durnford stood paralysed, beyond thought, surely beyond possibility of reply. He felt strangled, unable to breathe. He had just been informed of his dispensibility. Chelmsford waited until Durnford was able to muster a hoarse acknowledging '... my Lord....' with a faint acquiescing downward nod of his head. The Colonel's vision remained misted, his excessively long moustache seeming to droop even lower. He managed to straighten himself, shifting the weight of his useless left arm with his good right one.

Then Chelmsford went on, 'Now ... kindly return to your units at the Middle Drift. Move your central column through here, taking my route thus far. Proceed forthwith to Isandhlwana where you will support Colonel Pulleine. Aha, yes ... and young Vereker will join you as your ADC ... is all that clear?'

Durnford found himself even more dumbfounded by this order to move forward. He was stuttering his bewilderment, '... Then ... then ... the threat of counter-invasion no longer exists? The very matter for which...' He saw Chelmsford's eyes flaring. He stopped what he was saying. His voice and head lowered. He said simply, 'I agree, my Lord, my units will serve best as active reserves, as and where you wish to dispose them.'

Chelmsford rose, the matter closed. Durnford, moving stiffly left the tent to ride back to the Middle Drift, to organize the movement of the central column to its new position, this time inside Zululand – at Isandhlwana.

Alongside the field table outside, the reporter, Norris-Newman, was astride his horse examining the action on the slopes with his binoculars, a lately fashionable acquisition from London, contrasting with the less convenient, small-size military telescope that Crealock employed, standing up at the table. Noggs's attention seemed to be wholly on the fighting, but he turned the moment Durnford strode from the General's tent. He wheeled to follow him, calling out, 'Colonel, Colonel!'

But when the briefest glance identified who was doing the calling, Durnford pointedly ignored the newsman, mounted as his one-arm method required – swinging up from the wrong side of the saddle – and thundered off at a gallop, his Basuto escort following suit. Noggs had to rein back from the sweep of black, near-naked horsemen who treated his presence and physical safety with the pattern of unconcern demonstrated by their leader. As Durnford's Horse retreated south, Noggs managed a twisted smile. Very well, my good Colonel, I know the story from everybody's viewpoint but yours, and if that's the way it gets told, it was your choice.

Noggs turned as he heard a mass shout, indeed a roar of triumphant cheers, which echoed from the slopes behind him. He turned, galloped to Crealock who was excitedly sweeping the forward terrain with his brass telescope, as were others of the staff who had turned at the sound.

Noggs, fumbling to unstrap his binocular case again, called out to Crealock, 'Our men, Colonel?'

'They're through, they're through!' Crealock executed a quite uncharacteristic set of little jigging jumps of delight. Noggs now had his binoculars focused, and was able to see the forward companies of the Natal Natives pouring through the undefended opening to the gorge.

In an instant decision, Noggs spurred uphill. Crealock shouted at him to halt, but he was already too far off. Crealock, with a gesture, sent off two Lancers of the Seventeenth from His Lordship's personal guard to follow the intrepid, or foolish newsman as his horse charged up the slope into the danger zone. The Lancers swung their long-bladed weapons under arm at charge and galloped off in pursuit.

At the gorge entrance Hamilton-Browne was waving his pistol frantically as he shouted lurid commands, trying to give some sense of direction and design to the inpouring of his NNC troops. A European NCO, alongside his commander's horse, was giving emphasis to the foul-mouthed commands by repeating them in an even louder shout and jabbing out with his rifle-butt to get the attackers moving in skirmishing order in case they fell on to a counter-force of the defending Zulus. The rifle owners amongst the native troops, however, increased the din by firing shots into the air, prematurely celebrating the seeming rout as they entered into the territory of the enemy.

'No ... no! ... you gibbering idiots,' screamed the irate commander. 'Fire at your targets.... Sergeant!'

'Yessir,' responded the NCO, and with brutal alacrity drove the butt of his rifle at the head of the next offender, knocking him unconscious. Noggs, forcing his horse through the mêlée at the gorge entrance, came up behind

131

Hamilton-Browne just in time to see the Sergeant do his nasty work.

'Sir!' he shouted to the Commander, ' . . . should not the actions of our men be directed at the enemy?'

The Irish officer looked at his interlocuter with utter disdain, noted the arrival of the two Lancers who had been sent along as Noggs escort and then, looking beyond the three, exclaimed, 'Mother of God!' He spurred past them, shouting back to his NCO, 'Sergeant, find some stretchermen – officer fallen!'

Noggs pivoted his head round, saw a riderless horse and, from the askew sabre scabbard extending from it, what he presumed to be the face-down corpse of an officer. He and the Lancers spurred after Hamilton-Browne, who, reaching the fallen figure, leapt from his saddle to kneel anxiously alongside.

'You hit, Mr Harford?' His hand extended to turn the figure over, but held as the corpse instead lifted its head, turning to look around with a most pleased smile.

'N .. n .. n .. I am not, sir, but look what I found...! Sitting up he held out a magnificent leg-kicking black beetle. '*Bitula negra* ... ,' and then with quiet awe, ' . . . the first live one I've ever seen, sir.'

The young man stood, retrieved a bottle from a saddle-bag and plummeted his insect catch into a few inches of clear liquid visible at its bottom. The group watched dumbstruck. Hamilton-Browne crossed himself, closed his eyes, and exclaimed, 'Mother of Mercy ... not into good gin again!'

Although the resolution of the engagement was still several hours away, the decisive tactical triumph had occurred when the defence at the mouth to the gorge was breached. The tally of successes was quite impressive: The NNC had been tested under fire, performing better than most native contingents usually do when impressed into fighting for a cause only vaguely related to their own. The accurate fire-power of the Imperial troops had been an effective response to the defence tactic of boulder-rolling which, in the past, had proved a strong deterrent to less formidably weaponed attackers.

Later the defenders, having been forced to retire into their gorge, clambered on to the nearly perpendicular rock sides of the gorge, taking refuge in caves and crevices which they obviously knew well. From there they had little power of retaliation; on the other hand, dislodging them without too great cost in time and lives was giving Hamilton-Browne pause. Dismounted, he stood in the centre of the gorge contemplating a reasonable strategy with Harford alongside. The companies of the Twenty-fourth were marching in, and Noggs and his two accompanying Lancers, still attendant on the progress of events, joined the two officers.

Suddenly, an undetected party of Sihayo's defenders, probably slow in escaping to the cliffs and finding themselves trapped between the NNC forming up to attack the heights and the incoming Redcoats, decided to launch a surprise assault from behind a stony outcropping where they were in hiding. With a savage cry of 'U-Su-Tu!' one gnarly, scarred warrior leapt out, his *assegai* arm thrusting underhanded directly towards Hamilton-Browne's unguarded middle. However, fortunately, Noggs's Lancer reacted with life-saving swiftness. His lance flicked out – a shorter weapon would have been to no avail – parried the spear thrust and, in the next moment, flicked down over the surprised attacker's shield, piercing him mortally through the neck. Before the weight of the victim could drag the lance out of its user's grasp, an expert sideways flick disengaged it and let the body slip to the ground. The four companions of the dead man, who were following his charge stopped, gaped, instantly turned and fled up slope, hoping to get to the gorge walls, to the caves. But the two mounted

Lancers were instantly in pursuit, riding them down with consummate skill, impaling them with a dispatch and ease that sent Hamilton-Browne into a transport of praise.

He turned to Noggs, delighted. 'See that! Couldn't we use a few hundred of those lads? See that ... deceived him with the down and took him with the up! Perfection!' This last comment was upon the dispatch of the last of the Zulus who, trapped at the cliff face, turned to make a stand with *assegai* and shield, but was felled in a trice. 'Show me the Zulu who'll stand up to that!' exulted the Commander. 'Could do with a few more than just for parading around with Chelmsford. Tell the War Office that, will you! Give me some more damn Lancers!'

Noggs wondered how long the bad-tempered, loud-mouthed ex-contractor would last with His Lordship if that kind of remark were indeed reported. The newsman reached down with the long barrel of his Winchester Repeating rifle. He used the end of it to move the war shield which had fallen over the face of the Lancer's first victim, the one who had almost dispatched Hamilton-Browne. The dead, grey-black face that stared up was hollowed and wrinkled with a goodly count of years. Noggs shook his head sadly, addressed Hamilton-Browne, 'You've been fighting grandfathers and boys – I'll tell you about your Lancers when they take on some of Cetshwayo's real warriors...!' He stopped talking and looked up in astonishment as a crescendoing, reverberating howl grew overhead.

The rockets at last were making their spectacular appearance. Emitting ear-piercing wails, throwing out showers of sparks and fire from exhaust nozzles and snake trails of noxious smoke, came a flight of rockets, each dispersing on its own erratic course, culminating in three great explosions on no particular targets, although creating significant pyrotechnical effect. A bank of three more followed, the flight patterns as diverse as the numbers, as were the explosive landings. Almost immediately there was a mass emergence of the holed-up Zulus, ostentatiously casting aside weapons, holding hands aloft in surrender, submitting to being herded towards the mouth of the gorge by the triumphant Natal Natives. Hamilton-Browne cantered his horse alongside the captives with Noggs and Harford abreast.

'Look at them ... will you look...,' Noggs was grinning at the vile Irishman's chagrin. He looked back to note that the Lancers shared his amusement. '... they must be the filthiest, stupidest, most useless things a mother ever dropped ... *but*, they're my prisoners, and I love them all.'

They were marched down the slope. The staff officers came out to review the prisoners. The rocketeers and their mules came in at the same time, Major Russell beaming. Harness rode over to them. 'Splendid, chaps. Absolutely spectacular!'

Russell dismounted the mule he'd borrowed to bring himself downhill.

'Terribly sorry, we were a bit late ... weren't we?'

Harness wouldn't have any apologies. 'Nonsense. Perfectly timed for maximum effect. Scared the living daylights out of them.'

Hamilton-Browne listened with disgust to the artillery congratulate itself. He grunted after Harness's last comment. 'Scared the bejazes out of me, too,' he winked at Noggs, 'until I realized they didn't have a chance of hitting a damn thing! Most bloody useless things I've ever seen.'

Chelmsford had come forward from his tent, and all turned to him. Evidently he had overheard Hamilton-Browne's comments. His Lordship was smiling, but his disapproval of the rowdy Irishman's forthrightness was evident.

'Caused your prisoners to surrender, nonetheless, didn't they, dear fellow?'

135

Hamilton-Browne shrugged, pointed to the pathetic line-up, 'I speak with the greatest of respect, my Lord, but who the hell needs them?'

And although His Lordship's short 'ha, ha' seemed to treat the remark as just another drollery from the crude Commandant Hamilton-Browne, there was no mirth in the sound whatsoever.

16

The divining doctor, the same one who had smelled out that Bayele would bring back information of vital importance, was consulted again by the council of the *indunas*. He was required to repeat evaluations for the next foray of scouts who were to follow up on the movements of the invaders as depicted in Bayele's report. Even Bayele himself had to be tested again to ensure that the good spirits who had helped his success at the Upper Drift crossing hadn't since abandoned the young warrior, nor that his talents had been somehow weakened by an unknown *umthakathi*, that is, an evil wizard, perhaps one employed by the Redcoats, or by a traitorous chief who wished the Great King's downfall. Three scouts were to be picked from eight possibles. This particular *isangoma*, in his divining, used a calabash pierced with many holes. His body was painted with a whitish dye, and his face streaked with other plant dyes. His eyes flashed, and strange noises in the language of the spirit world issued from his corded throat. He poured water into the pierced calabash to divine from the direction and nature of the streams of liquid that issued from it what the future held for the young scouts who had been brought for the testing.

Bayele could sense the deep and mystic wisdom in the creased black features of the powerful doctor, who had come from the royal *Kraal*, it was said. Doctors were each unique in their dress, each one constrained only by the limits of his (or sometimes her) own imagination. This *isangoma* wore many powerful carved charms strung around his neck. They were made from the bones and parts of powerful beasts, leopards, lions, reptiles, and some of them were hung on to the narrowly woven plaits of hair which swung like a hundred writhing snakes around his face as he spun in a circle with the showering calabash arching out streams of water towards the candidates. As he whirled he produced sharp throaty noises and uttered powerful secret words. He sprinkled equally potent medicines from pouches and baskets which hung and swung at his waist. But Bayele had no self-doubt. The strength of the good spirits who had helped him thus far in the service of his King and people still surged within him – he felt them. And the *isangoma* confirmed this by suddenly crying out a declaration that Bayele, of all the young men, was the most auspiciously graced for the tasks ahead. Selected with him were two others in whom Bayele had great personal confidence: Batloka, a compactly built powerful young man, shorter than most warrior Zulus, but known for his dexterity and fleetness, and Sigmanda, clever and witty and wise in planning and judging, and for reacting well in a crisis. Bayele marvelled at the accuracy of the *isangoma's* selection. He, who knew all the men because they were in his *inGobamakhosi* regiment, personal friends – he couldn't have picked better himself.

The selection ceremony was being held in a grove at slight remove from where the decoy army had split off from the main *Impis*. It would be the job of these scouts, they were now told by the *inDunas*, to reveal themselves at an appropriate time and let themselves be followed to within sight of the decoy army, so that the enemy would think that they had discovered the whereabouts of the main Zulu army by their own cleverness. To complete the deception, the scouts would then allow themselves to be captured so that under interrogation (and only after resistance to make their 'co-operation' seem genuine) would they confirm the misinformation, as if submitting under the brutal form of questioning they knew would take place. It was a fraught mission, but one of highest honour.

The selection-of-the-scouts ceremony had had several uninvited witnesses. One was Siswe, the herdboy, who, with a few other youngsters, watched the goings-on concealed by brush at the edge of the clearing where it took place. Siswe, who was so proud of his brother's honours, now felt grief in his heart, and felt hot tears course down his cheeks. He knew that this time brother Bayele had been selected to offer himself for torture, and for probable death.

The three selected scouts were led by Uhama at a run for more than two miles westward. As they came over a ridge Uhama cautioned stealth. They looked into a shallow valley through which a stream of glittering water wandered. There was a thicket of trees following its course, and a low, one-man tent was pitched at the edge of these trees. A horse was tethered there and was being fed handfuls of some substance by a fattish, bulging white man wearing stained Khaki clothing and mud-caked riding boots. While the scouts watched the fat white man began to strike his little encampment, then to saddle up the animal.

Uhama quickly explained the man's presence and relationship to the purpose on hand: 'He is the English trader. Fannin is his name. He amuses our Great King and it is said he brings him valuable information about his fellow whites. But like the snake who speaks twice, he also tells the British what he learns when he returns from Zululand. We have already 'allowed' him to catch sight of the decoy Impi section which split off from the main army. With this information he is now anxious to reach the British to trade with it for his own benefit and honours amongst his own kind.'

139

Fannin, having disposed of the camping equipment about the body of his animal, added the additional insult of his own gross weight and started the sagging horse away at a walking pace.

Uhama and the young scouts were smiling. 'Follow him', said Uhama, 'and by the day's end he will bring you to the white soldiers. Let him see you. Then he will tell the soldiers of your presence. It is difficult to predict how quickly they will take you, but when they do, tell them nothing, but when you are crushed and cannot breathe because of the bones they will break in your chest, and when you fear your eyes being taken from you forever – then confirm to them that our main *Impis* are to the east of them and will attack them from the east. Be assured that their own scouts who will follow you or your directions will see just enough to confirm what you tell them. . . .'

As Uhama questioned them on the deception they were to carry out, Fannin started away. He disappeared over a hill towards Isandhlwana. Bayele, then Batloka and Sigmanda started after him at a strong-paced run, which they could maintain indefinitely.

Fannin had his oversized pistol in his hand as he dismounted, because he had been belaboured by the feeling that he was being followed. True, he travelled under the protection of Cetshwayo, but then he wasn't sure how pervasively that knowledge had seeped throughout the territory he had to transgress. He also suspected that the information he travelled with had been provided a bit too easily by the Zulus, but if he gave it to the British soldiers, it would be their task to separate the wheat from the chaff. Right now his horse required water and rest, and if any hostile snooper were on his tail, they'd have to get by the business end of his six-shooter. Holding it at arm's length he held himself still, tautly listening. Nothing close, although the thickets of waist-high grass and brush could conceal a host of threats. He studied the

140

clumps of vegetation for odd movements – nothing. Satisfied, he disengaged the water-bag from the saddle, hung it from the projecting fork of a broken branch on a handy sapling tree. He returned to the horse, loosening the metal bits at its mouth corners.

At that moment his eyes, pinpoint bright in fat pouches of pink skin, caught a movement, off to the right. A ripple of brown skin showed briefly. Fannin fired automatically, Batloka whirled upward for a moment, into sight as if by the force of a hit – and then pitched earthward, apparently lifeless, disappearing into the high grass. Silence. Nervously, sweating a torrent, Fannin took several paces forward, raising himself on tiptoes to see what damage he had done. The grass concealed the body – if body it was. He stared, not daring to make a decision.

On the opposite of the clearing, Bayele grinned at Sigamanda from their crouched concealed positions, then rose easily behind Fannin's back, hurled his *assegai* and instantly ducked low. With a loud thud the spear pierced the water-bag hanging on the sapling. Fannin heard the *thunk* of the *assegai* imbedding itself in the wood, and whirled around to see the bag spouting its water on to the earth, while the spear still vibrated in the thin tree trunk. He looked in the direction from which the spear had come. There was nothing to see there either. He was surrounded. Fannin had had enough. He heaved himself back into the saddle and got the unwatered, unfed beast going at a gallop. He wasn't halted, but for a time didn't dare look back. The young scouts, including the 'dead' Batloka, let him get a fair distance ahead and then, crouching, continued their chase. Requiring water, rest and food, Fannin would cause no more delays to their mission.

When Pulleine's column arrived at the lower slopes of

141

Isandhlwana, Vereker and the Sikali were already in formation to greet them. They reported no enemy signs, as yet. Pulleine was pleased, but hardly had this been said, when a shot rang out from the top of the plain. They whirled round to see Fannin, spurring in, his six-shooter aloft, firing to attract their attention. Vereker and the Sikalis dashed up slope to intercept him – he pointed urgently in an area of undergrowth towards which the Sikali Horseman immediately swerved, whooping. In no time they flushed out the three Zulu scouts. As Uhama had predicted as possible, they were captured sooner than they might have wished – once more it was the unexpected presence of this young white officer and his unusual black riding scouts, but the outcome of the mission, Bayele told himself, would not be affected.

Vereker ordered the Sikali troopers to bring the Zulu scouts to Colonel Pulleine. They responded with alacrity. The young officer watched the captives being herded from horseback, stumbling, sprawling when ungentle prods from rifle-butts to keep them moving were applied over-zealously. Then he rode his horse to Fannin, who had slid from his saddle and was now leaning heavily against his horse, gasping for breath and clutching his chest as if in pain. Fannin looked up, hoarsely choking out his words between gasps. 'Fannin ... name of Fannin, sir, Captain.'

'It's only Lieutenant, Mr Fannin,' he held back a smile, 'name of Vereker.' He nodded towards the captured Zulus. '... that all of them?'

Fannin wiped his dry lips with the back of his hand, 'Dozens of them ... followed me, followed me ... I killed seven, maybe eight, well ... them is all as hung on ... I guess.' He swallowed with a show of difficulty, moving his hands to his throat. 'Don't have a bit of brandy, sir, Captain, I mean Lieutenant ...? Don't feel too good ... sick as a dog ...'

Vereker reached into his saddle-bag and extraced a

142

bottle. He watched the group of Sikali riders scouring now at quite a distance up the slope while Fannin took several generous gulps. He noted several all-clear signals being passed along to Kambula. Then behind him came agitated shouting from the group with Colonel Pulleine surrounding the Zulu captives. Vereker glanced back briefly catching sight of two of the Zulus being slammed to the ground by rifle-butts in the hands of the European NCOs. He turned back to speak to Fannin. 'I think they've the lot now sir. I wouldn't worry.'

Fannin had taken several heavy swigs from the bottle and now passed it back. Vereker affected not to notice its near depletion. He studied the portly trader carefully. 'Why did they attack you?'

Fannin looked up, slightly startled but then replied quite smoothly, 'I discovered their army, your honour ... saw a whole valley full of them ... and beyond...'

Vereker looked to where Fannin was pointing, more or less North up the slope, skirting inside the humpbacked peak to the mountains of the western Nqutus. Vereker frowned. 'But that's not the direction you rode in from....'

Fannin smiled craftily. 'No sir, we came from the east. Saw plenty of Zulus there. But not the main army. They thought they could fool me but they didn't no sir.' Again he pointed upwards to the peaks of the mountains. 'That's where they'll be coming from, sir, you'll see. Bet they circled behind those mountains. You'll see.'

Vereker gestured with his head, 'Come along, sir....'

While Fannin hefted himself back onto his saddle, Vereker rode down-slope to Pulleine where the Zulu captives were being interrogated. Two of the Zulus were stretched out on the ground, curled up foetally protecting the middles of their bodies with clenched arms. The third was being held with his arms twisted at his back while one of the NCOs was barking out questions in the Zulu language, none of which seemed to be getting any response. Pulleine sighed in despair, clearly not enjoying the form of questioning but accepting its necessity, then nodded with his head to indicate that the questioning be relaxed while he spoke with Vereker. Fannin was already advancing from the background.

'Odd looking chap,' said Pulleine quietly, clearly referring to the fat figure riding forward. 'Say who he is?'

'Some sort of trader, I'd say,' said Vereker. 'I believe I've heard of him – Fannin. Sells guns to the Zulus, that sort of thing. It's difficult to know whether to believe him or not.'

The European NCO intruded, 'The same with this crafty lot, sir,' pointing to the captive Zulus. 'Can't get a straight answer out of one of them.'

Vereker turned in his saddle to look more closely at the one young Zulu who was still upright. He became aware of the intensity with which his look was returned. Vereker shifted his gaze to Pulleine. 'Did they say anything – I suppose not.'

The Lieutenant Colonel shrugged. 'They claim they are deserters ... followed him,' he nodded towards Fannin who had now almost arrived. 'Solely, I was informed, that they might give themselves up to us ... on the theory that we would give them protection from Cetshwayo's wrath. When we defeated the old villain we would allow them to go home to their *Kraals*, that sort of rubbish. Would you accept that story, old boy?'

Vereker turned to look more closely at the erect captive. Bayele stood his ground, unblinking, staring upwards at the blond young British officer, aware of how carefully he was being scrutinized. His heart accelerated – if this white man recognized him as the scout at the river crossing who had escaped just two days before, then the role he was now playing of a recent deserter would not be believed. But he was reasonably certain, also, that this recognition was not too likely. After all, the man had only seen a fleeing back – except for Bayele's momentary

144

turn-back when Sekonyela had fallen. None of this concern showed on his face ... and shortly it was evident that there was nothing in the red-coated officer's manner to indicate that he knew his captive.

Bayele had conceived an instant hate and contempt for this man who had coincidentally been present on the first two encounters with the enemy. He felt within himself a surge of power, feeling for one furious moment that he could tear himself from the grasp of the men who were holding him, drag the blond officer from his horse and thus take with him one companion at least to warrior's heaven – his personal enemy, the blond man on the horse. But this was an indulgence he could not allow himself. Uhama, who had given him orders in the name of the King, must be served. Their will must be executed. But he would remember this yellow-haired, pink-faced young officer and, perhaps if Unkulunkulu so ordained, there would be a third encounter, for final reckoning.

Vereker saw no indication of these thoughts in the young captive's face, but he did see an unfathomable world of feeling and of experience to which he had no real access. He wondered for a brief moment if under different circumstances, ever, he could learn to talk to a young man like this as he had learned to talk with Thola. He heard Pulleine speaking, 'Do you think we ought to believe them, old boy?'

Vereker shook his head, 'I'd say ignore any information volunteered too easily.' Pulleine nodded, turned to the hard-faced NCO. He said, 'You heard the officer, Sergeant!'

'Right sir!' the NCO barked out sharply and then, grinning, turned to the prisoners.

The interrogation started with a rifle-butt thrust with force into Bayele's solar plexus. Bayele crumbled to the ground, unconscious.

17

The encampment had formed itself on the lower east slope of Isandhlwana in the course of the afternoon, so that the sun which, when seen from the other side, had come from behind its peak to make the dawn of morning, was now moving to descend behind it again, but on the West side, to bring the night.

An observer standing a thousand yards directly to the south of the encampment would note the following features: the peak of Isandhlwana was to the north-west, that is, to observer's front and left. The column had arrived from due west, passing the lower slope of the mountain on arrival, then turning itself sharply left up the slope to find its bivouac on the eastern base. The wagons and Company encampments stretched due north in a direct line perpendicular to the observer's point of view. The Zulu enemy, if it came, would presumably be coming from Ulundi, more or less directly from the east — that is, to the right of the observer. Arcing behind the encampment were the mountains of the Nqutu range, spreading off distantly to the right, that is, to the north-east. Five hundred feet lower than the top peak of the Nqutu range was the Nqutu plateau, extending for at least four miles, a flat shelf dominating the camp and all its northern approaches. Closer to our theoretical observer was another lesser rise directly in front of Isandhlwana called Stoney Hill: and in fact it was between Stoney Hill and Isandhlwana, forming the sides of a saddle-shaped pass, that the column first arrived at this site. If, instead of bearing left to encamp on the east slope of Isandhlwana, the troops had continued forward another 1200 or 1500 yards, that is, on past the observer to his right, they would have come to a long deep ditch which also ran more or less directly northward. This ditch – South Africans call them *dongas* and this particular one 'Big Donga' – through which a muddy trickle of water ran, could provide a natural eastern defensive barrier if manned as a trench with a few Companies of rifles. However, the Isandhlwana camp-site was viewed by Chelmsford as merely a better than average stopping-off point for his penetration into Zululand, defensible from forward attack, protected at its back and north by mountains, he didn't expect the principal encounter to occur here, although he didn't mind if it did.

The date was 21 January 1879; there were no Zulus in sight except for the three caught, taken that morning and safely secured as prisoners. The afternoon was coming to a pleasant sunny ending and spirits were high. The cooking areas which occupied the centre of the camp were being established, and the wood for the fires used in preparation of the evening meal was gathered.

Chelmsford arrived with his contingents, and was duly informed of the capture of the three scouts. He considered the matter briefly, presumed also that their information would be unreliable; but, in any event, if he had further questions to ask of them he would rather make a judgement based on his own observations. Thus, while the camp was settling into place, Chelmsford rode with his personal escorting force to examine the high ground off to the right. They went as far as the time allowed them by a rapidly descending sun, but no Zulus were to be seen, either on the plateau above the camp nor amidst the peaks of the range above that.

In the meantime the tents went up and bright patches of colour – the fires steaming with the food for a well-earned evening meal – appeared. At the north-east corner of the camp, where Stuart Smith's guns had been placed, the artillery crews were engaged, as ever, in burnishing the metal barrels to ever higher degrees of glittering brightness. They caught and reflected the hot orange rays of the descending sun in halating flashes which would be seen for miles.

The Boer volunteers, who were attached to the mounted troups gathered at the lower south end of the camp, surveyed the arrangements, frowning, clearly dissatisfied. They spoke with each other in Afrikaans and, walking their horses, went for a visit to the camp centre where the camp Commandant, Lt. Col. Pulleine, had his tent pitched. They found the commandant standing outside the tent flaps, watching the camp activity, turning his gaze occasionally to the heights which at the moment seemed to be quite benign and unthreatening in the softening light of late day. Pulleine's servant emerged from the tent, refilled the long-stemmed wine glass held by his master. The drink was savoured appreciatively, then Pulleine's eyes turned up to note the arrival of the two agitated Boer volunteers, indicating that they had his permission to speak. He listened to them expostulate on the overwhelming importance of bringing the wagons into a *laager*, the Afrikaans term for an end-to-end closed circle, which could then be used as an entrenched defensive position in case of a surprise attack. Of course this was not news to Pulleine, but the Boers went on to recount many grim incidents when this requirement had been ignored by previous parties foraying into Zululand.

Pulleine argued gently the difference between doing this for a small party of men with few wagons as opposed to an army equipped as they were with hundreds of heavy duty transport vehicles. The practicalties, he tried to point out, were on an entirely different basis. The Boers, on the other hand, understood no practicality other than that of survival. They emphasized the possibility also that the peaceful vista which now engaged the commandant's vision could prove to be a deception, probably a fatal deception. They knew that Lord Chelmsford had personally scouted the Nqutu plateau, but questioned whether it would have been in the time, closely enough or far enough observed. The capability of a huge number of Zulus to move silently and with a swiftness quite inconceivable was not denied by Pulleine, but it was clear that beneath the surface of his eminent politeness lay some scepticism. Zulus were neither supermen, nor invisible ones. The admonitions of the Boers grew repititious – they spoke from an experience earned by the blood of many of their kind – and tedious.

From the corner of his eye Pulleine detected Chelmsford returning from his scouting endeavours to the north-east and, muttering his excuses, walked forward to greet his General with the deference due. The elder Boer exchanged a cheerless glance with his nephew, shaking his head with despair at ever getting through to these pleasant but arrogant men in their splendidly colourful uniforms. They saw no commands resulting from the two Englishmen's conference to indicate that their warning would be heeded.

The two Boers moved away, leading their horses and carrying their bedrolls. As they came to the perimeter of the south-east end of the camp, moving towards the boulders that splattered the lower slopes of the Stoney Hill out-cropping, they saw the Sikali Horsemen carefully attending and checking and cleaning their Martini-Henry weapons. Sergeant Simeon Kambula observed the course of their movement and cocked his head, saying in a slightly quizzical tone, 'You are leaving us, Master Boer?'

The elder Boer replied, pointing to the boulders several hundred yards farther on at the mountain base. 'We sleep over there ... amongst the rocks. . . .'

The night ran its course, and was uneventful. The

camp slept undisturbed and, except for the movement of the sentries, peacefully.

Bayele, Batloka and Sigmanda, the three captive Zulu scouts, did not share the camp's peaceful night. But then one must expect certain difficulties in achieving restful sleep in a standing position, with wrists and arms bound tightly to the wheels of an ox cart. Bayele had tried to relieve the maddeningly tedious discomfort and the throb of the bruises he had received in the previous day's beating by recalling his moment of triumph in combat with Nomzaza on behalf of his regiment at the royal *Kraal*. The Great King himself had shown his approval. Earlier on that same day he had participated in the *giya*, the exaggerated dance-mime performed by the regiment before the King, wherein was enacted the fantasy of how the shields they were begging would be used in engagement against the enemy. But the *giya* of some of the warriors were not fictions. They were accounts of true feats in battle, or in the hunt. After this day Bayele could perform such a *giya*: he imagined himself in the presence of his fellow warriors of the regiment: they calling out their approval, beating their shields, encouraging him to tell how he had deluded the red-coated soldiers, had escaped under gunfire, and now finally how he had contributed to the defeat of this army of many-armed men and wagons pulled by beasts, and huge guns on wheels, each as big as a hundred ordinary guns all bound together – wheeled guns they were, so large that they required their own animals to pull them, and twelve men to attend each one. Plunged into this fantasized *giya*, he could partially ignore his discomfort and pain.

When he had withstood their beating until there could be no doubt in their mind but that he was trying to save his own skin, he had told them where to find the false *Impi*, to the east. He understood immediately from the nature of the commands that were issued that his words would be checked, that their own scouts would be sent out to find substantiating evidence for his tale – which would of course be found. During the long night he had turned his mind completely to the composition of the *giya* that would dramatize his adventures of the past three days. He worked out the movements, the words, and the melodic forms in which the *giya* would be couched. He didn't ask himself the gloomy question – whether he would one day be able to actually use the *giya*, though he believed he would. The main *Impis* would come and crush these Redcoat warriors, and free him and bring him back into the warm welcoming life of tribal participation which had embraced him for the whole of his life. Sometimes he dozed still on his feet and his imaginings faded over into dreams, but the dreams too were on the subject of combat and fighting and the glory of many victories. Then he would sag against his bonds and the pain would awaken him.

During the course of the night he had heard Batloka moan weakly, but when he spoke with him to encourage him there was no reply. Later, Batloka had stopped making any sounds what-so-ever; Bayele listened for breathing noises but he could not detect those either. Sigmanda had been tied to a wagon further away, so Bayele made no attempt to communicate with him. No, it was better to keep his mind on the composing of his new *giya*: he reviewed the dance steps and reheard the melodies with which the words he composed to tell of his deeds would be given emphasis. After a time his Zulu audiences would themselves learn his songs, so that they could join in and chant his fame, his praise, and his courage as a great warrior of the King. And if the songs of his *giya* were of sufficient calibre and his feats of sufficient stature, generations of Zulus who followed him would still know and repeat his songs.

Bayele was awakened from a final lengthier doze by the

151

brassy sounds of the 'Stand-to' which also awoke the rest of the camp. There was enough light from the new dawn for him to verify his deduction made in the black of the night – Batloka hung lifelessly tied to the wheel of the wagon directly opposite. Perhaps his warrior's soul had already risen to the heaven of the Zulus where Unklunkulu waited to receive those who died in the service of God's earthly representative, the Great King Cetshwayo. He grieved for Batloka, as he had grieved for Sekonyela and the others who had already fallen in these battles of a war not yet wholly started. And he grieved for himself and for the pain of his bonds and for the terrible thirst that assailed him and for the cracked rawness of his lips and mouth, and for the over-bright sun-rays which now pierced from the east directly through the gap in the wagons to burn into his puffed and bruised and sleep-deprived eyes. He wanted to scream out and go mad.

But, he thought, he must keep his mind fixed on the idea that he had been honoured by the King and had been allowed to be the first to carry the spear of war into the heart of the enemy. He must take pleasure in the knowledge that in the battles where his scouting comrades had already fallen, the victories were his. Could these whites here in the place begin to conceive of how important these victories were? No, they waited here, unknowing, to be assaulted by the great armies of the Great King, and it was Bayele, the long-to-be-remembered, who showed them the way. Remember this, Bayele told himself, and you will feel no pain....

The camp, as he could see it beyond the wagons, was now alive. Men on foot ran into formations, and groups of horsemen assembled and the preparatory movement of many of the wagons and their animals had begun. If Bayele's well-acted deceptions were going to prove effective the Redcoat army would next move off to the east, thus making the encircling movement by the Zulu main army already waiting above them behind the plateau that much easier.

The Great King had told his armies not to engage this particular enemy, armed as it was with many rifles, while it was in an entrenched position. It was much better to fight it on the move, stretched out with its defences disorganized and its fire-power not grouped. The young warrior realized that he would shortly know the result of his efforts, although the break-up of the camp could very well bring forward the question of his disposal. He did not dwell for long on what would happen to him personally. But he wanted to see the outcome of the battle, certain that it would end with the destruction of these men who had already caused the painful death of men he knew as good and close friends. And he would like to have some of the final justice meted out by his own hand, by the thrusts of his own *assegai*.

He tensed as the four guards who had left him bound the night before made their first morning appearance at the gap between the wagons, then moved towards him. They were talking in words he couldn't comprehend, nor could he otherwise decipher their immediate intentions. To his surprise and considerable relief one of them poured out some water from a bottle which hung from his white belt, and held up the cup so that Bayele could drink it. The coolness of the water stung the injuries on his mouth but this was of no consequence. Its deliciousness as it coursed down his throat, its entry into his dehydrated body, made it seem the single most precious drink of his life. The men turned from him now and cut down the body of Batloka. Two of them carried it away. Then the remaining two left him briefly, but they returned soon with Sigmanda. They had cut the ropes that had bound Sigmanda's feet although his arms were still tightly tethered behind his back. He was clearly in bad shape. He was shoved forward and tottered, then collapsed to the ground.

153

The guards were about to pick up his fallen friend, but just then more figures appeared at the gap between the wagons. The guards came to immediate attention. Bayele saw amongst the new arrivals the yellow-haired young officer. But there were also other white *indunas*, older men evidently of great importance to judge from the richness of their uniforms and the haughtiness of their bearing. Bayele even surmised that the eldest of them all, with the pointed white-tipped beard on his face might indeed be first *induna* of the British army. He was attended by another grim-faced *induna* who deferred only to the elder one, and with them also was the fat trader who was supposed to be friends with the Great King and whom they had chased here to this encampment before it formed yesterday. Bayele wished he could understand all the things they were saying. Thereupon, the young yellow-haired officer surprised him greatly by speaking to him in the Zulu tongue, with a strange pronounciation but with considerable fluency.

Vereker said to Bayele, 'You claim to be fugitive deserters ... very well, tell me *why* did you and your friends desert your *Impi?*'

Bayele wondered what trap lay in this questioning. He realized that this man was asking a different kind of question. His first interrogaters had demanded direct answers, such as to where the *impis* were marching, from where they had come, their numbers, and so on. This young man was asking him questions that began with the word 'why'. But Bayele had a prepared answer.

'I am of *inGobamakhosi*. Cetshwayo allowed the veterans of the *unThuluwana* to select brides from our *Kraal*. They took my sweetheart Mantana to whom I was betrothed. They did the same with my friends and robbed them of their sweethearts. That is why we ran away and wanted to come to the land of the white men. So that we would not be subject to the cruel laws of the old days, from the days of Shaka.'

The young white officer looked at him carefully. 'Tell me, how long ago did you desert?' he asked.

Bayele had this answer ready too. 'Twenty days ago. We ran away before our regiments went to *umKhosi* (the ingathering) at the royal *Kraal*. We have been looking for your army for many days so that we could surrender and be taken back to your land. Or perhaps to fight with you and to help you with information.' He immediately saw the scepticism in his questioner's eyes. That was the question which had the trap in it. What had he said that was wrong?

The young man told him, 'If you were fugitive and hiding from your own kind for so many days the skin over your stomach would not be smooth from being so well-fed, nor your thighs and calves rubbed with oil. You would be dusty and dry of skin. Look, the skin on your stomach and arms is not wasted from hunger. How did you eat in that time? You are lying! Every word you speak is a lie. You say the main army is to the east – that is a lie, too, is it not?'

Bayele shook his head vigorously and was surprised with the tones of sincerity that he was able to produce in his answer. 'I do not tell lies. For several days we found an old woman in a mud *Kraal* that had been deserted by the warriors who joined the *umKhosi Impis*. She hid us in her *Kraal*, she even gave us oil to rub our skins so that we would not look like deserters, and fed us. And I can only tell you what I saw; I saw the main armies to the east. They were waiting in hiding there, and although they could have moved, it did not seem to me that would happen from the way they were waiting.'

Vereker smiled cynically. 'Yes, and our own scouts verify that there were a considerable number of your fellow warriors there. But we know the tricks of the Zulu army and we know that they could have been put there for our benefit. I don't like to see you punished and hurt the way you have been. But unless you speak the truth it will have to go on. Do you understand that?'

Bayele only repeated desperately, 'I tell you the truth, I tell you what I saw.' He lowered his eyes. He saw Sigmanda looking up from the ground where he had collapsed. None of the White men seemed to see him there. He was of no consequence to them. He was a piece of dirt, he was a stone; he was not a fallen human being, who was, also, a dear and beloved friend of Bayele. The white men were talking amongst themselves again in their strange tongue, and their expressions told little of their meaning or even of what they felt. The older man, the leader of them all, Bayele had now established, was listening to the young officer, who evidently was reporting their exchange.

Chelmsford listened, sighed, fundamentally disinterested. 'Tell me, William, do you credit any part of the information he has divulged to you?'

Vereker shrugged, 'He says only what he has been told to say . . . he was very well coached. I would presume he speaks the opposite of the truth in most cases.'

Chelmsford threw up his hand, 'This fellow' – he pointed to Fannin – 'this fellow says they are to the north . . . this one says they wait in the east. I believe neither one of them, but on the balance of my own information I reject the north and north-east, not because of what either said, but because I have it on different intelligence, because I understand geographic facts, and because I believe I know something of our opponent's principles of strategy in deploying armies for combat. . . .'

Fannin chose this moment to intrude. 'Wherever they are, Your Honour, I tell you there are sixty thousand of them dark devils coming at us *now* . . . at this moment.'

Chelmsford cut in wearily, 'They multiply, Mr Fannin . . . they multiply.' He paused and surveyed the ungainly fat and agitated man. 'Tell me, sir, do you speak the Zulu tongue? I presume you do.'

'Like a native, sir, Your Honour.'

Chelmsford wouldn't let him go on. 'Then ride with Colonel Crealock here,' he nodded to his military secretary standing alongside. 'I go east, and I am short of interpreters. You will serve in that capacity.'

Fannin gasped in alarm, 'But Your Honour, Your Lordship, I'm not a soldier and you're going east, I mean ... that is *further* into Zululand ... I must go back to Natal....'

'Otherwise, sir, you will be arrested!' Fannin swallowed his reply, weakly nodded. Chelmsford turned from him.

Crealock stepped aside, gesturing Fannin to precede him. 'This way, Mr Fannin...!' Chelmsford followed at an easier pace accompanied by young Vereker. The Lord General started to re-explain the strategic basis of his plans to the mere Lieutenant. Absolutely amazing, thought Vereker, although he had no choice but to listen since Chelmsford said he wanted Vereker to understand: he had decided to move half of the invading forces under his direct command forthwith to the south and east, not so much on the basis of what the captive scouts had told them, nor upon its subsequent confirmation by observation from their own forward scouting parties, but because of his certain feelings of what the Zulus were capable of doing and were likely to do within those capabilities. In any event, the camp could defend itself.

Chelmsford's willingness to speak so freely about his own inner processes, however, did not in the least release Vereker from his own constraints. It did not behove him to say that he felt that His Lordship was underestimating the capabilities of his opponents. For instance, Chelmsford dismissed the idea that the main army would be brought via the difficult route of the Nqutu range, or, in the unlikely case that it had been, that it could have reached a strike position in such a short time. Chelmsford himself had scouted out in that direction the day before and had seen nothing, no signs to indicate that there were Zulus anywhere in the region. Vereker felt that it was not correct for him to say what undoubtedly Chelmsford had heard many times before, that it was almost as possible for 20,000 men with their mobility, their training and their superb organization to co-ordinate movement with unequalled efficiency; some said a Zulu army moved as one single man of prowess. Or that the entirety of the Zulu army could conceal itself on a plain, 20,000 thousand men becoming invisible amongst boulders and grass and ditches and underbrush, again as if they were one. Or that they could climb peaks and mountains through the dark of night with the unity of purpose of a single driven individual.

Of course he could affirm it once more, and Chelmsford might even listen once more, partly believing, but finally rejecting the notion that Zulus were capable of anything truly extraordinary. To Chelmsford, armies moving meant goods to be transported, machines carried, men and animals to be endlessly fed and watered and catered to in all the endless details of their various human or beastly needs. It was beyond his powers of conception to see a military force, that need be reckoned, which rejected all such impediments, and was as one with its natural environment. Here, the mountains and endless plains, the rivers flooding, the stubborn boulders and strange unpredictable beasts, the Zulu armies and the Zulu people *were* the environment. Above all, Chelmsford had the perfect confidence that his forces divided in two could each take on the entire main army of the Zulu. The dogma of the unassailability of the defensive force of British rifle-power pervaded his being, was the sum total, in many ways, of his knowledge. Let the damn Zulus show up here, there, anywhere. The sooner the better.

'I move to find and engage the enemy.' He gestured towards the column already on the move, extending to the south-east, its rear units already a quarter of a mile away from the camp. Only Crealock, with Chelmsford's personal escort, including his Lancers, were still waiting for his Lordship to join the departure. They were accoutred for action, with swords, pistols, binoculars, and other such scientific aids with which to outfight and then coerce and subdue the barbarous enemy.

Chelmsford paused a few yards before reaching his escort group, dropped the volume of his voice, pulled at Vereker's sleeve, drawing him closer. 'Colonel Pulleine has my orders to defend this position. Colonel Durnford will be bringing support forward ... he should be here in no more than a few hours. I hope you don't mind, but I have notified both him and Colonel Pulleine that you will serve as Durnford's A D C. ...' He smiled at William and lowered his voice to an even more confidential tone. '... Now, dear William, I recognize that you are much junior to both of these gentlemen. But none the less ... I trust that you ... that you will give them your very best advice. ... I am certain you understand what I am saying to you, William.'

With this, Chelmsford abruptly swung about, approached his horse and then, dismissing the hand of the aide who was standing there to give him a boot up, seized the saddle and placed a boot in the stirrup. His Lordship, if one considers his age, noted Vereker, mounted deftly on his own. There was a signal and His Lordship with the mounted escort moved forward in a close trotting formation to catch up with the column which was snaking away along the plain to the south-east.

18

Vereker watched them depart. He had been acutely embarrassed by Chelmsford's unwanted confidences about his senior officers. He found himself hoping that if anything untoward did happen here at the encampment below the humpback peak that its upper command was less confused than he felt at this moment. And the encampment, now depleted by half, or more, of men, artillery and wagons seemed many times more vulnerable. He saw other Redcoats nearby staring forlornly after the disappearing column. He was not alone in his feelings of being deserted . The activity of the camp had come to a virtual halt. The skirling sounds of Chelmsford's Scots pipers at the increasing distance became less and less distinguishable from the keening of a fresh wind that seemed to have come down from the mountains to take up the vacuum of space left by the departing troops. When Chelmsford's column vanished beyond undulations in the south-east plain, many glances instinctively turned to survey the hills behind them. The sunlight on the peaks was now bright, but still the rugged terrain appeared to be filled with many dark areas of secretive shadow, deep ravines, and ominous hidden places – where an enemy could lurk unseen.

Although Bayele's angle of vision was constrained by the narrowness of the gap between the wagons where he was tied, he had been able to deduce that there was a large scale movement of men and vehicles away from camp and from the sounds that those departing were travelling south-east. The guards had walked away to watch the departing column also, and he was alone with Sigmanda. He became exultant as he realized what it was that was taking place.

'Sigmanda, Sigmanda!' He spoke quietly, quickly, urgently, 'can you hear? . . . they are moving to the south-east! Our mission is successful! . . . and they divide themselves into two, for no useful reason.' Sigmanda, from the ground, looked up weakly, tried to respond. But his physical state was clearly poor. And so it was that although Bayele had no one to share his feelings of triumph, he was able to visualize the vast horde of men, his thousands upon thousands of warrior brothers squatting in the ravined valley beyond the plateau, and beyond the peaks about it, to the north-east. A horde of 25,000 men of war who, at the appropriate moment, would form themselves into a mighty bull's head, which would lunge at these foolish white soldiers, now thinned out and weakened, spread vulnerably on the wide slopes, to trap and toss them on horns encompassing four miles, then crush their remains on the loins of the Zulu war beast. So, all arrogant enemies of the Great King died.

Colonel Pulleine stood with Lieutenants Coghill and Melvill rather morbidly examining the obscure region of mountains and crevices to the north. Two separate troops of horsemen dispatched by him were moving out towards the hills. One troop, moving more or less due north, was easily identified as the Sikali troop, distinctively uniformed and led by a white officer and a black CSM. Riding to the north-east were the second troop, comprised of some white irregulars led by trooper Lieutenant James, and support riders, Basutos, led by Lieutenant

Raw. The three officers watched them, then Pulleine's eyes fixed on the artillery unit of four guns set out at the north-east corner of the camp. He looked, suddenly startled, as an idea, not a frequent experience for him, flashed its unexpected light.

'I say', said Pulleine to the two young Lieutenants, 'Do you notice how Major Smith has his guns disposed . . .?'

'Seem lovely to me.' Coghill frowned, puzzledly studying the arrangement. But Melvill understood instantly. 'By Jove, you're absolutely right. Two to the east, two to the south-east. Absolute waste.'

'Lieutenant Coghill. Would you mind riding to Stuart Smith and ask him to bring his artillery about. . . .' He pointed to the north-east. '*All* of it!'

Coghill smiled, at last understanding. 'Oh, of course, sir, Zulus aren't likely to launch at us from the direction His Lordship is marching, are they?' He saluted and galloped off to do as he was commanded.

Pulleine and Melvill watched him for a few moments. Even Melvill was affected by the loneliness of the expanse that confronted them. He studied the rise to the plateau, wagged his head sadly. 'I say, we are a bit over-exposed should they come down . . . I mean . . . how could they have got up there? What do you think?'

Colonel Pulleine shook his head dubiously. 'I have it on the highest authority available to us, dear Melvill, that is most unlikely. . . . As you say . . . how? So, if our only concern is of little concern', he laughed, 'I shouldn't worry!'

But then, abruptly, the outriding Sikali Horsemen headed by Vereker spurred forward to a sharp warning cry which could be heard even at this distance. They galloped full tilt up the slope, raising a cloud of dust, and within a few moments disappeared amongst the rock out-croppings. Pulleine worriedly bit at his upper lip; Melvill's usual composure was disturbed even further by this inexplicable movement.

162

'I do believe', he said, 'our "Honourable" may have spotted something.'

Pulleine nodded, compressed his lips further, came to a decision, turned sharply. A wave of his hand brought an adjutant who saluted, turned running, calling out, 'Bugler! Bugler!'

Pulleine returned his worried gaze to the mountains to the north, scanning the plateau that ran north-east. 'By Jove, don't tell me they've managed to get up there after all. . . .'

Melvill smiled, a bit of his old self. 'One consolation, sir – if they have, won't His Lordship be jolly annoyed?'

Now the bugler sounded 'Stand to'. The Redcoat companies scrambled up from their late breakfasts, buckling their equipment, grabbing rifles, hastening to fall in, in front of the wagons. As they began to take up their assigned places it rapidly became evident that there would be huge unseemly gaps between the sections; the double ranks had to stretch close to a mile to fully protect the rectangular layout of the wagons, which defined the shape of the camp. It was overpoweringly clear that the elements which had been extracted by Chelmsford left extensive gaps. At first, there was calling from the officers and NCOs for the men to space out, to try to fill out and join up with the next company as if merely taking this act of further spacing would account for the uncomfortable spread of an army that felt most secure when fighting in close formation.

Pulleine watched this frustrating procedure for a few moments and then turned his eyes to the north-east corner of the encampment where he had the momentary satisfaction of seeing Coghill ride up to Major Smith's artillery batteries. He saw the gun crews, tiny at the distance, run to each of the unlimbered guns that had been pointing south-east, bringing them about to be trained upon the danger area represented by the plateau. One problem of their positions, Pulleine realized, was that the steep shelving to the plateau meant its surface could not be seen from this low angle. An attacking army would be pouring over its edge before it became visible. Pulleine sighed deeply – nothing one could do about that. Have to wait until the scouts returned. He now looked south, then rode to Melvill's side.

'Mr Melvill, kindly send a lookout. . . .' He pointed to Stoney Hill at the south-west bottom of the camp. 'Post him atop there and have him call out the instant he spies Colonel Durnford's column coming to reinforce us . . . they'll help us fill in our gaps. Just have patience.'

Melvill looked at him quizzically. 'Does he bring *Imperial* troops with him, sir?'

'He brings his . . . er . . . Basutos, Mr Melvill, as you know damn well. Excellent riders and . . . sturdy soldiers in a desperate situation . . . I believe. . . .' Melvill's saturnine right eyebrow arched more cynically than ever.

19

Chelmsford, attended by his troop of Lancers, Colonel Crealock, other senior officers of the staff and the newsman known as Noggs, led his column searching the ground to the south-east. Isandhlwana was now a hazy peak several miles away in the background. His Lordship noted Noggs reining his horse to come alongside, but he frustrated the newsman's question by getting in his own, first.

'What o'clock is it, Mr Noggs?'

Noggs checked a large, steel-cased timepiece that hung at his waistcoat. 'Ten o'clock, My Lord.'

Chelmsford patted his stomach and turned to his military secretary. 'Colonel Crealock, if our good friend's clock is accurate I would say that Colonel Durnford will ... at least should be ... this very minute approaching Colonel Pulleine. And this brings me to the thought that it might be an appropriate time for us to breakfast here. I want to scout that height,' he pointed to a rise in the terrain in the direction of their movement, 'and I will be back with an appetite in, let us say, just under one hour....'

Whereupon this expression of his wishes was converted into a series of commands. The column stopped, and His Lordship spurred forward with his escort of Lancers of the Seventeenth.

The pain caused by the bonds around Bayele's arms and legs alternated between feelings of unbearable throbbing, agonized burning sensations or a sense of dread numbness, as if he were losing the capability of ever using them again. What more could they want from him? Had they forgotten him? He looked down and his despair was deepened when he saw that Sigmanda, who had seemed more dead than alive, was writhing on the ground in a sudden rhythmic spasm of movement, and then suddenly subsided with a kind of horrifying inertness. He watched for a few moments thinking that the very worst had happened; then he noticed that shallow breathing resumed, although the rasping sussurant sound was not very reassuring. He called Sigmanda's name several times, but there was no response. Then he looked around as he heard footsteps. His guards were returning. Good, something would happen, something, whatever it was, would be better than this unbearable waiting in unending pain. What would they do now? He didn't want to die, but on the other hand he couldn't rule out the possibility. His usefulness to the Redcoat soldiers must be over now. Why should they keep him alive any longer? He wouldn't if their positions were reversed.

They came closer. His eyes turned and stared without any revelation of the turbulence of emotion he felt. If his death was what they came for, they wouldn't see a Zulu warrior show anything but his contempt for them. But now, for some unrevealed reason there was an outburst of cheering and calls from the encampment behind, and his guards turned. In the next instant Bayele could see what was causing the excitement. In the distance, charging up the slopes from the main trail, he saw 300 Basuto horsemen led by a white officer who seemed to have only one arm with which to hold the reins. The hooves thundered on the ground, the whoops of the riders crescendoing. Behind came other elements of a column, evidently reinforcements for the portion of the army that had been left here, but in spite of the volume of sound from the horses, the total of new arrivals no way equalled in number nor in force those which had departed. More important, Bayele's guards decided to run back from the gap in the wagons to join the other soldiers at the camp centre who waved and cheered their welcome to the approaching reinforcements.

The distraction was suddenly as welcome to Bayele as it was to the British soldiers. This was his last chance – he must make the most of it. If only Sigmanda could be made to respond, even to a small degree; a plan had formed in Bayele's mind which just might relieve his desperate plight. Savagely, teeth gritted, he called Sigmanda's name, again and again, in a harsh whisper, although the noise from the camp, where soldiers were running out to greet the arrivals, adequately masked his calls. Then, wonder of wonders, Sigmanda lifted his head and his eyes seemed to be clear, showing understanding. Bayele spoke urgently, rapidly, 'Sigmanda, you have borne your pain bravely, like a great warrior – can you still move to help me, brother?'

Sigmanda stared at him, clearly not comprehending how he, lying there with his arms behind his back, and in this weakened condition, could be of any help. Bayele struggled desperately. For the thousandth time he twisted against the bonds that held his biceps and wrists, gritting his teeth at the searing pain. It was as useless as his many prior attempts. Panting heavily he turned his attention to the ropes binding his legs. Earlier, he had felt a slight slackening of the tension of these, but the raw pain of the rough bonds against the flesh of his ankles worn bare from his struggles had stopped him from testing them further. Now, grimacing, he squeezed his eyelids together, blocking out the burning anguish as he furiously twisted and tugged his legs. Skin peeled away and perhaps it was the slickness of raw flesh that allowed one foot to be dragged through the corded rope, yielding, tearing, then jerking free. The remaining loops of the rope dropped slackly around the other ankle. The possibilities of what he could do had suddenly increased beyond measure as compared with the former immobility ... his arms were still helplessly bound, but his legs were free!

He glanced down the alleyway between the wagons to the gap at the western end. One of the guards still stood there, back turned to Bayele, but the other one had run forward to join the milling crowd who were slapping backs, pumping hands, or stroking the muzzles of the horses that carried in the leaders of Durnford's column. For Bayele it was now – now, his foot free, his plan matured – now or never. He must instill Sigmanda with some of his own strength and determination.

'Sigmanda, listen to me. I will call the white soldier back – your legs are not bound; try to bring him down when he passes you. Bring him down so that he falls to me. Do you understand?'

Sigmanda stared at him in a way that said neither yes nor no, but there wasn't more time to make certain. Bayele started to shout and struggle madly, as if he had gone berserk in his agony! At the top of his voice he screamed out, *'U-Su-Tu! U-Su-Tu! Ana Ingli.'* Again and again he shouted out these words, the direct translation of which were, 'Kill! Kill! Kill the English!' The guard turned, annoyed, paced towards the raging captive. But he stopped himself after a few steps, and admonished Bayele as he would a naughty boy, ''Ere! 'Ere you, shut up that yelling!' He wanted to return to watching the newly arrived soldiers.

Of course, Bayele did not understand the words although it was evident from his gesturing and tone of voice what the guard was saying and what he wanted. This merely encouraged Bayele to continue his wild shouting. The sentry lost patience, snarled with irritation, moved forward, clearly intending to take whatever

168

physical action was necessary to stop this obstreperous savage.

'I said stop it, and you *stop* it, boy!'

Then, as he made his last stride forward, lifting his hand to cuff Bayele, Sigmanda, bound on the ground, thrust his legs between those of the advancing man, tripping him. The guard pitched full length to the ground, his head coming near to Bayele's freed feet. He sprawled there only for an instant and immediately began to raise himself from the ground, but the instant was enough. Bayele had lifted his powerful right foreleg waist high in the classic Zulu stamping position and brought it down with a mortal crunch on to the sentry's lower neck as he was coming up, driving him face down into the ground. The one incredibly forceful blow was enough, but Bayele took no risks. He repeated the stamping action with blinding speed and ferocity. The man was corpse.

Then Sigmanda responded to Bayele's furious whispered instructions. He somehow was able to roll on the ground towards the dead guard to seize his rifle with its fixed bayonet. It was a difficult manoeuvre for the injured Zulu, with his hands bound behind his back, but finally he seized it, and turned it upright behind himself and, using it for a support, he rose to his knees. He wavered there, panting desperately, ill and depleted by his wounds, his torture, making this infinite effort Bayele demanded from him in urgently repeated whispered commands. He managed from this half-risen position to manoeuvre the bayonet of the rifle between Bayele and the wagon wheel to which he was bound. All this was done with his own back turned, as Bayele coached him in each detail of his movement. Bayele watched the gasping, swooning, mortally ill man fight to keep himself conscious, to execute his commands. At last ... at last the moment had come. The bonds at Bayele's wrists were resting against the blade of the bayonet. If Sigmanda could hold it...! There was an interminable length of

169

time as Bayele sawed the wrist ropes against the blade, ill himself with pain, panting, watching Sigmanda, watching desperately to see if the other guard was going to turn from the activity at the camp centre to return to his duty. The ropes began to part, strands frayed ... then they were cut through and fell away! He was able to reach down and remove those which still dangled at his left ankle, and step from the wagon, completely unbound!

Sigmanda had collapsed. Working as rapidly as he could, Bayele cut Sigmanda's bonds – dearest Sigmanda who had come to his rescue with such courage and determination, but who had now fallen inertly to the ground again. Bayele, ever watching the turned guard, urged his comrade to move, pleaded with him to respond. But Sigmanda gave no indication that he was alive, or even conscious. In a fury of frustration Bayele stood up, seized the bayonet-fixed rifle between two hands, then confirmed the death of the first sentry by driving the blade into the man's belly and ripping upward. At the same moment he saw the other sentry start back towards the wagon, although his attention was still on the camp centre. Bayele lifted Sigmanda's head once again; there was no response and then there was no time. He knelt down quickly alongside his friend and he said, 'Go to your Fathers ... go to the Wise Ones. Many of us will join you today. Good-bye Sigmanda.' He thrust with his bayonet into Sigmanda's heart. As the sentry turned, he dived beneath the forward wagon, crawled to the far end, rose, and in a low crouching run moved towards the hills.

The returning sentry had not seen Bayele's move away, and only slowly, as the scene between the wagons became clear, did realization of what had happened take shape. Alarm! The captive was gone! And there was no indication whatsoever of when exactly or in which direction Bayele had escaped. Of course, there was ample and horrible evidence of what Bayele had done in order to escape.

Durnford came to the command tent with Pulleine. There were many matters requiring consultation. However, he paused at the entrance, turning to Lieutenant Melvill, who had been accompanying them. He looked at the junior officer, quizzically. 'The men are still at "Stand to"...?'

Pulleine looked alarmed, mistaking the statement as criticism. He said quickly 'Order "Stand down" immediately, Mr Melvill!'

Now Melvill looked dubiously at his senior officers, glancing meaningfully towards the north hills. Durnford followed the glance and then said, '... perhaps the men could eat breakfast with, say, their equipment unbuckled? ... Colonel?'

Pulleine nodded quickly, 'Oh, yes ... an excellent idea. Good.' He then re-instructed Melvill, 'Breakfast then, in battle order ... with their rifles at hand....' He looked at Durnford, who nodded approvingly.

Boy-Pullen sounded 'Stand down'. Melvill and Coghill each galloped along the lines passing the command that breakfast be eaten in battle order. Inside the command tent, Pulleine hosted Colonel Durnford to kidneys and bacon. Durnford ate gustily, manoeuvred his eating utensils most dextrously with his good arm. Pulleine had taken up his own plate of food to stand at the tent flap, gazing out at the camp as he ate. There was a certain constraint between the two gentlemen officers, for there was the delicate matter of command to be discussed. Pulleine, after all, had been given orders in this repect, but Durnford arrived on the scene with seniority – and no specific orders. For some moments they ate in relative silence and then Pulleine spoke quite loudly as he surveyed the scene, 'And so they breakfast at the ready!' He

171

laughed briefly, then turned to Durnford, looked at him a bit carefully. 'I saw young Vereker report to you. Has he brought you up to date?'

Durnford shrugged. 'Only that he suspects it is possible that the main Zulu army is perched directly over our head. . . .' His head nodded northward.

Pulleine laughed slightly. 'That's not quite what I meant, but it is rather nonsense . . . I would say.'

'How do you know that?'

Pulleine tweaked his small blonde moustache. 'Well, for one, His Lordship is of the certain opinion that it is much too difficult an approach to be chosen by the Zulu command, at least in the time they've had. It would mean that they had twenty or thirty thousand men running over mountain tops for the past two or three nights.'

'I have probably said it before, Henry, but Zulus excel at that sort of running under those conditions and the momentum they would gain in a down-slope charge would attract a Zulu commander greatly.' He gestured across the encircling north arc of the imagined down slope advance. 'The head, the loins, and the two horns. . .! The details vary – the form, never. . . .' He chewed his food reflectively while Pulleine sombrely looked north and north-east again. 'I met young Chard on my way here. He was on his way back to improve the crossing at the Drift. Now *he* saw Zulus on the plateau. More than just a few. Enough to indicate the possibility of a goodly force. . . .' He finished off his last mouthful of food and joined Pulleine at the tent flap, shared his probing of the dark places in the moutains above them for sight of some clue to their particular question of the moment. 'It might not be a bad idea to pre-empt that possibility. Yes, the more I dwell on it . . . the more I am inclined to think that it might serve several excellent purposes.'

Pulleine instantly turned to him, alarmed. 'You mean go out there? Our orders were very clearly to defend.'

Durnford kept his voice moderated. 'Your orders, my dear Henry, not mine. Mine were to support.' And then, before Pulleine could protest, he added. 'Each of us commands his own unit today.'

Pulleine spoke with precise firmness. 'You *are* senior to me, Colonel.'

Durnford, of course, was aware of the problem but merely sighed at confronting the complexities it offered.

'Yes ... that is so. Nonetheless, when His Lordship says, "support," he does not mean "take command". And I am very much afraid that until we are given some other words on our orders, we must interpret His Lordship's intentions.'

Pulleine scratched his chin nervously, 'Yes, I see what you mean — pity we can't actually know them.'

Durnford paced slightly. 'I think we should be clear, it's really a question of the best tactics in the face of a possibly dire threat — not perhaps a real one, but it is the potential of such a threat we must take into account....'

'But His Lordship very clearly ordered....'

Durnford did not accept the interruption. '... as I see it we are obliged to deter the possibility of such attack, if we can.' He pointed to the Nqutu peaks visible through the tent flap. 'Suppose I take my three hundred riders up there — even if we can presume that His Lordship will confront the main army...,' he pointed south-east, 'might there not be a considerable force, perhaps a full *Impi*, perhaps several, deployed up there? He pointed north-east. 'Such an *Impi* could be used to cut south to form the right horn of the bull for attack on Chelmsford's flank. Either that, *or* to attack us. If I take three hundred horsemen to that direction, north-east, and they see us, I think they will think twice about which way to move. And I will be in an ideal position to take defensive action to slow them down in whichever direction they choose to force move. If they press in this direction, well — after all, we are mounted. As fast as a running Zulu is, we on our mounts will be faster. We can, in the last resort, even race to close the defences of your camp. As you know, Henry, the Zulus don't like fighting mounted men. We can use our superior mobility to slow them down whether they come forward to us, or circle south to close on His Lordship. It's a plan which makes the best use of my mounted units. Yes. Now, that's my opinion, and I would like to hear yours.' Pulleine blinked, his brow furrowed. It was clear that Durnford had given him to intricate a strategic scheme to consider quickly. 'I do wish ... , 'he said after a moment, '... you wouldn't leave....'

Durnford shook his head, moved to the tent flap. Pulleine spoke quickly causing him to pause and turn. 'What are a few hundred of you against possible tens of thousands....'

'We are mounted, Henry,' Durnford said patiently. 'If it's necessary we can withdraw all the way back here to help close your defence. Nothing will have changed.' Durnford allowed a rare smile to play at the corner of his lips. 'Unless you want to give me two of your Imperial companies to take out with me. In that case, we might be able to make a stand.'

Pulleine took him quite seriously and answered hastily, 'Oh, no! I couldn't I can't spare them. And that would be directly flouting His Lordship.'

Durnford was amused by Pulleine's distress at the mere mention of taking original action; however, he didn't bother to say that it was not a serious proposal.

'I'll leave Lieutenant Vereker with you – I think it's best to keep the Sikali as a free-moving reserve. They can scout the full perimeter and then move to support wherever and if you require. I'll take Major Russell with me, but just beyond the north-east perimeter, and have him position his rockets to support me and defend the camp ... give the Zulu cause for thought when they see a few of those.'

174

After quite a long time, and a fair bit of moustache-tweaking, Pulleine nodded his head ... but only very slightly, producing the minimum semblance of acquiescence. However, such was all Durnford required.

'Thank you, Henry,' he said, 'I'm glad you agree.'

'I do wish,' Pulleine said aggrievedly, 'you could wait until Lieutenant Raw returns. I've told him to mount the crest beyond the plateau, and he may come back with vital information.'

'I'm going further east, Henry,' replied Durnford, still patiently, 'and I also may come back with vital information. I am trying to convince you, I *will* be coming back.'

It seemed that Pulleine wanted to prolong the interchange, because he now added rapidly, 'I've given orders to the companies of the Twenty-fourth under Lieutenants Cavaye and Mostyn, move north to slow that downhill charge if it comes.... Do you think that....?'

Durnford was hardly listening; he was anxious to move off. 'Yes, Henry, I think that was a good idea.' He turned and strode out of the tent.

20

Bayele had reached the edge of the plateau, where he paused panting, exhausted of all strength. He sprawled flat on his stomach until some of his breath recovered. He was able to observe the spread of the camp without fear of being observed. Below him he saw a movement of troops departing, the line of wagons coming towards him. The Redcoats under Cavaye and Mostyn marched forward in formation at least 1500 yards north of the camp to find a suitable fire line. What foolishness, reflected Bayele. First more than half of the encampment had departed south-east, leaving it that much more vulnerable for the great attack, and now they were fragmenting it even more, even with these small numbers. But now there followed an even more surprising action.

Riding in a diagonal below him to the east, but bearing slightly northward at a high pace was the one-armed commander with the Basuto horsemen who had arrived so short a time ago, Bayele presumed to reinforce the camp. They would soon reach the plateau also, but far to his left. A small contingent of white soldiers broke away from this latest exodus, moving north to his left, below the plateau, then halted. These had some mules, and strange little tubular objects which might be another type of wheeled gun, but which did not look like guns. Bayele could not yet conceptualize 'rockets'.

The one-armed *inDuna* and his men rode further and further east. The encampment below looked weaker and more vulnerable than ever, spread out as it was on the vast sloping plain from the base of Isandhlwana. Bayele had at first intended to continue his struggle to the top of the Nqutu range, in the direction where he knew the main *Impis* waited. But he was in a terribly weakened state, and it occured to him that he could wait here hidden in this handy little crevice where he found himself, wait for his fellow warriors to arrive, as eventually they must. He might join them in their attack, and then the fantasy of the revenge which had kept him going through the night might still become actuality. He settled down to wait, burying his head in his arms to rest, trying to ignore the throbbing pains of his injuries.

A half an hour earlier Lieutenant Raw, leading his group of mounted scouts, had passed within several feet of where Bayele now rested. They had crossed the plateau and on to the next rise where they moved eastward and northward, their horses sliding and struggling on the precarious terrain. As they approached a second crest there was a degree of flattening out. They moved around an oversized obstructing boulder, saw a stretch of grass and other undergrowth and, 500 yards ahead, almost at the top, a herd of Zulu cattle grazing! They paused in astonishment – how had the animals come here, to these heights?

They saw the native herd-boys become aware of their presence, and after one startled glance start to herd their animals up to the crest in an attempt to get them over that edge and out of sight. Trooper James and his men came around the other side of the boulder, immediately kicked their horses and, whooping, gave chase. Trooper James shouted across to Raw's group, 'Steak on the hoof! Let's take it!'

James was a bulbous-nosed, red-cheeked, over-robust man who somehow seemed too large for the horse he rode

177

and now was delighted to find relief from the boredom of looking for something that had refused to appear. With laughing yells his men spurred around the herd to cut it off. The Zulu herders, boys and youths, began to abandon the cattle, some of them fleeing over the lip. The two nearest to James stopped and futilely threw their undersized *assegais*. James reined back as the spears fell short and the youngsters instantly started to turn to make their escape.

James flung up his rifle to shoot, barely above the hip. One shot rang out, and one of the boys fell to the ground. The other one, who was Siswe, froze for an instant of horrified reaction, then plunged into the bushes. James, ignoring the fallen boy who was convulsed on the ground, galloped forward to the lip, keen to repeat his success if he could find another target. But when he reached the top he stopped his horse, then slowly, staring in disbelief, eased himself from the saddle, stepped to the mountain edge, transfixed by what he saw in the valley below. Staring, jaw slack, he called in a hollow voice.

'Mr Raw, Sir ... Mr Raw! Come and look at this ... my God, sir.'

But Lieutenant Raw didn't hear James. Huge and ungainly himself, but of an entirely different sympathy than his trooper, he pulled up his horse alongside the dying Zulu boy on the ground. The boy saw him, whimpered in dread. Raw slid off his saddle to help the youngster, but even as he started to kneel the young herder subsided. The dimunitive shield which had been clutched protectively in front of the expiring boy fell to the ground. Raw compressed his lips – then strode upwards a few yards to where James stood, still staring down at the vista below and beyond the crest.

Raw was angry, 'Trooper, you know what you've done? You've managed to bring down a boy of twelve ... no more....!'

But James merely continued to stare across the valley, and Raw's words had already started to falter as he too took in the sight.

Human powers of estimating large numbers are not sufficiently refined to distinguish between 20,000 human figures or 30,000. But Lieutenant Raw and Trooper James, within the rush of many other emotions which paralysed normal thought processes, found themselves trying to put number to what they were seeing – for the valley they overlooked was filled with Zulus, warrior Zulus, squatting at rest as was their fashion. All of Cetshwayo's main *Impis*, close-packed, sat silently on their haunches, covering the whole of the valley floor, and perching on every inch of its rising sides. 20,000 certainly – perhaps 30,000 – warriors of the Great King. As Raw and James stood together gaping, other riders of the two troops of scouts, Basutos included, rode up to the lip and as each arrived, were caught by the same sight, and transfixed by the same paralysis.

But this appearance of mounted men also caught the eyes of some of the Zulus far below. Some pointed, and a few rose to their feet.

'I do believe,' said Lieutenant Raw in an awed whisper to the man arrived alongside, 'that my Lord Chelmsford does search in the wrong place for the Zulu army....'

Tens, then hundreds, then in the next moment, thousands of Zulus stood up, still silent, still staring up at their observers.

'Ride! Ride quickly to the camp!' Raw was now talking much more urgently, 'Warn them – then on to Chelmsford! Tell His Lordship that we have found what he looks for!' A rider spurred down-grade to the plateau. Raw mounted the horse he had been standing alongside, signalled, and the troop wheeled to follow Raw while he looked for a skirmishing position where he could make what must be at most a token attempt to create some delaying activity against the infinite army now moving

179

towards the side of the valley. The moment of attack had been determined by chance. But now it was irrevocable.

21

It is recorded in history that the Zulus who waited there in that valley were to have remained thus throughout the afternoon and the following night, and were to have made their strike upon the camp at the earliest dawn hours of the following morning. But the instant they saw those tiny figures appear high on the rim of the ravine edge above them, not a single one of the warriors needed instruction that the battle scheduled for the morrow was now begun.

The army rose, and moved. The huge formations flowed into a shape. The right horn on the west of the valley began to rise towards its crest to comprise the force which, at the correct time, would encircle, flank and crush down upon the defenders who would have already committed themselves eastward to meet the forward rushing head of the Zulu bull charge. The head itself, at the appropriate time, would split right and left to join the crushing pincers of the encircling horns.

The more immediate problem of the troopers was the warriors who started to swarm up the steep near face of the ravine directly at them. They mounted with stunning alacrity and poured over the crest, running at a pace that nearly equalled that of the mounted men retreating. But the troopers who had discovered the Zulus were not going to yield immediately. Their firing seemed to have little deterrent effect. Their withdrawal was neither as paced nor as orderly as Raw tried to keep it, their aim from the saddle uncertain, and the continuous threat was of their own encirclement. From the Zulu side there was some firing also, but even less accurate and from much less effective weapons. There were fewer casualties amongst the troopers but they could afford much fewer. And the steep slope of their retreat was most hazardous to the secure footing of their horses. The penalty for being thrown was almost instant death from a multitude of furiously stabbing spears. And it happened several times.

Vereker and Kambula, who were scouting the lower slopes more to the west, pulled up and searched the ridges beyond and to the north-east to determine that exact source of the sporadic firing they heard. Vereker raised a pair of binoculars to aid his search CSM Kambula watched the young officer manipulate the focus of his remarkable optical instrument. The CSM then turned and gestured to the Sikali Horse to prepare for the next command. Then Vereker lowered his glasses and spoke sombrely to his Sergeant.

'Send to Lord Chelmsford, Sergeant-Major. Tell him that his battle is here – at Isandhlwana.'

Colonel Durnford, leading his Basutos, eyes forward on the north-east horizon, felt that the focus of his eyes had for a moment been disturbed. For one moment the shape of that horizon appeared to move slightly, and then in the next instant it was totally transformed as a two-mile-long line of shields appeared along its edge. The line moved forward and was followed by a second row of similar length, and then a third behind and on, it seemed endlessly: all in an uncountable moment there swarmed a multiplicity of figures on to the plateau in a wide, sweeping, inclusive and inescapable arc. Riding in front of one small convex segment of it were Raw's troops, firing small puffs of smoke to stem a black avalanche. Durnford knew that these front lines were only the head of the bull, and that two more formations of equal length would sweep forward at both ends to represent the horns.

Major Russell was exercising his usual meticulousness to achieve mathematically perfect positioning of his rockets. On Durnford's instruction, he had moved a half mile beyond the north-east perimeter, while Durnford continued more directly east with the main body of his mounted forces. If Russell had thought about it he would have realized that he was very much out on his own, in spite of the fact that he had been left with a small Company of Natal Natives, headed by Lieutenant Nourse, who had set themselves up defensively in a position forward of the rocket launching site. The mules of his rocket contingent were grazing as their masters went through their complicated scientific and engineering procedures for a rocket launch.

Russell was confident that given a bit more time for preparation he could prove the effectiveness of his new demonic weapons. He was sensitive to the fact that modern rocketry still had to prove itself effective beyond its psychological potential. He intended this time to compute trajectories that would end in a significant body-count of the enemy. The instrumentation, sightings and calibrations were producing a set of figures which he scribbled down quickly while the rocket-launching team waited for his final precise orders. He needed a bit of time, that was all, just a bit of time.

The first sense he had that he might not be given the time he required came from the sound of rifles and the cracking volleys echoing from across the plateau in front of him. But standing as he was below the edge of the plateau it was not possible to see anything that happened very far beyond the rim. Russell and his men paused in

183

their work just long enough to crane their necks to get some sign of what was causing the rifle fire.

The mystery was cleared up for them with dismaying speed. Raw's troop appeared on the edge of the plateau, pausing for a final round of firing, and then started to gallop down the slope behind them. Then the lines of Zulus rising from the background appeared, swarming forward. Russell's eyes scanned right and left. The Zulu front line was miles in length, shaping itself, and a significant section of it was coming directly towards the rocketeers.

Russell's mind raced.... Could he get off an immediate fusillade just to give them halt? But even the roughest calculation revealed the difficulties, 'My God, oh, my God,' he said. 'The elevation – they're too high for us.' He looked about desperately and noticed a knoll that rose thirty or forty feet above their own ground level some 200 yards behind them to the west. He pointed, shouting, 'Over there! ... on the rise! ... for God's sake! Quickly!'

There was a frantic mêlée to get the rockets hitched up to the mules. The animals were set in the traces almost immediately and then whipped into a gallop, and it became a panic race to re-position the rockets. The Zulus advanced.

But first they would be required to face the fire of Nourse's Natal Natives, who were being kept lined up only by the brutal threat of their European NCOs. Their uncertainty was increased when glancing back they saw the rocket carriages being re-positioned. They realized rapidly that their effectiveness against the Zulus would be tested before the rockets could do much to wreak the havoc that they were reputedly capable of doing. And only one in five of Nourse's Natives even possessed a rifle. Trying to respond to Nourse's shouted command to sight and aim, half of the rifle owners managed to fire one uneven volley.

184

Lieutenant Nourse reacted with instant rage, 'Hold fire! Wait for the command! ... wait till they're in range! Mark your targets at four hundred yards!'

As he shouted each command it was translated into several dialects. The Natal Native contingent waited trembling, the soldiers suppressing their instinct to press the triggers too soon. The advancing Zulu line came to a sudden halt – precisely out of range. There was a moment of silence and then, timed by a thrust of an *assegai* to the sky in the clenched fist of an Induna, and his shouted command, the 'kill' chant, '*U-Su-Tu, U-Su-Tu*' started. The spears began to pound on their shields, crescendoing louder and louder. This tactic of threat through various sounds was no less terrorizing for knowing such was the Zulu intention. The rising volume from the beating of the shields shattered nerves, jellied the resolve of the fiercest of foes. The '*U-Su-Tu*' chant had cowered a hundred armies over thousands of square miles to give military dominance to the mighty Zulu: it had no less an effect upon the pathetically inadequate NNC line waiting to defend the rockets.

Russell, sweating, working desperately to make delicate alignments under untenable conditions, his teeth clenching, tears coursing down his fat cheeks, was uttering a strangled prayer, 'Hold them, please God, give me three minutes, please hold them ... three minutes....'

Then the sound rose to a level beyond which it could not go: it mutated into a baleful howl. The spears which had been beating the shields were raised to a thrust position, and the charge flooded forward. Russell's prayer had not been heard.

Further into Zululand (along the track which, if followed another fifty miles would lead to the royal *Kraal* at Ulundi) approximately eight miles south-east of the mountain Isandhlwana (where war had started) there sounded the incongruous tinkle of good glass, the solid clinking of fine silver being set out on the superbly crisp, white surface of a finest linen tablecloth. Lord Chelmsford, Colonel Crealock, Lieutenant Harford, Commander Hamilton-Browne, and other officers of that day in good grace, stood within the screened area where the servants were preparing the table for the midday meal, chatting, drinking claret from long-stemmed goblets. Gleaming hot dishes were being carried through the sunlight from a small field-kitchen set up behind a second screen.

Noggs the newsman was amongst the guests, observing that Chelmsford was talking amiably with Hamilton-Browne. Noggs made a mental note that on those few occasions when some underling had stood up to His Lordship, perhaps from a brief moment of unusual courage, or out of sheer uncontrollable chagrin, Chelmsford subsequently tried to win back the underling's favour, seeking good will somehow lost. Further evidence lay in the courteous good grace being extended to the crude Irish commander. There were other instances Noggs could recall. That young chap Vereker, for instance, why was Chelmsford so often soliciting his approval? Often as not, in response to behaviour that seemed downright negligent, if not offensive. Noggs didn't want to put too fine a point on it, but considering Chelmsford's long history of exercising his inherited right to power, it did seem a bit strange; as if somehow it indicated a substratum of uncertainty in the great man. The newsman wondered how he could work this observation into one of his dispatches. He swallowed his wine and wandered forward to a servant who stood near Chelmsford's group, ostensibly seeking a refill.

Chelmsford, just as Noggs came alongside, was addressing Crealock, 'I have found another superb site for my next stopping place....'

Hamilton-Browne cut in, saying, 'Defensible, I hope, my Lord?'

186

Again Noggs saw anger suppressed. The implication of the remark was clear, and yet Chelmsford chose to treat it as a Hamilton-Browne absurdity rather than as a direct insult. At this point, an adjutant stepped forward and gestured, indicating that the food was all laid on the table and ready for consumption.

Chelmsford assented with a nod, and gestured that his guests move before him to the table. But Hamilton-Browne stood still. Chelmsford looked at him quizzically. 'Not joining us, Commander?'

Hamilton-Browne looked back sourly. 'Colonel Crealock gave me your orders to get back to the camp, sir. Do they no longer stand?'

'But after you've dined, dear chap.'

Hamilton-Browne ignored the second gesture to proceed to the table. 'My natives haven't eaten since last night. And there won't be supplies for them until I get them back to Isandhlwana.'

Chelmsford shrugged. 'Well, then let them start off now.' He laughed, 'Surely they won't hurry with you not there to curse them on. You can catch them up, after you've eaten'.

Hamilton-Browne's lips compressed angrily; if anything the Gaelic burr in his voice became more pronounced. 'Thank you, my Lord, but I don't think it would be proper of me to sit at your table whilst their bellies are flat against their backbones!'

The commander tossed off the remainder of the wine in his beaker, saluted, smartly pivoted about-face, and walked away from the screened area. Noggs watched Chelmsford tremble violently for a moment before he controlled himself, then managed a guffaw at the commander's outrageous manners. Noggs decided to pursue Hamilton-Browne and see if he could entice some quotable words from him while he was in this excellent opprobrious mood.

Harford stepped forward apologetically, and Chelms-

187

ford glared at him. The boy's jaws went into spasm, 'M ... m ... my .. L ... Lord – My commander departs. I m ... m ... must go with your l .. l ... eave.'

'You have my leave, Lieutenant. But mark, learn nothing from that Irishman ... except how *not* to behave!'

Several of the officers attendant upon the conversation assayed to laugh, and were most pleased when Chelmsford joined them. Hamilton-Browne's departure had been made into a grand jest. When Harford stepped beyond the screened area he noted that one of the Sikali riders had come in from the encampment and was gesturing excitedly, trying to communicate to a group from Chelmsford's escort who seemed to be barring the rider's way. Then one of the escort moved swiftly past Harford to enter His Lordship's dining area behind the protective screen of thin palings. The fact that this might be urgent news registered with Harford, but on the other hand he saw Hamilton-Browne and his NCOs going through their usual rough tactics for whipping the native groups into some semblance of order. Harford's duty was there. In any event, they were going back towards the mountain peak and whatever the news was from that source, probably being conveyed at this moment to His Lordship, it would soon be known to the young man by direct contact.

At this point he saw Hamilton-Browne pointedly walk away from some badgering questions with which Noggs the newsman was annoying him, only to be confronted by the fat, white trader Fannin. When Harford got closer it was clear from what Fannin was saying that he had been released by Chelmsford to return to the Natal border and he was trying to move with their group as a protective escort back to Isandhlwana *en route* to Rorke's Drift. Harford wondered if it had occurred to the fat cowardly gentleman who was so pleased to move back west that he might be meeting an even more dire situation in that direction. On the other hand, at the present rate of organization it would clearly be some time before they covered the eight miles back to the distant but clearly visible peak.

22

The trooper who had entered Chelmsford's guarded eating area had passed his message on to Crealock, who then moved forward thoughtfully to pass it on to his chief. Chelmsford was lifting a spoonful of steamy, thick potage to his lips with his right hand as the extended index finger of his left pressed the lower edge of his moustache upward, to prevent it from being stained by the frothy but delicious-looking liquid. He tilted the spoon, quaffing and savouring its contents, smacked his lips with appreciation. Aware of Crealock's hovering presence he looked up, indicated that he was prepared to listen as he dined. Crealock bent forward and spoke in a confidential whisper as His Lordship sipped his second spoonful.

'A strange message from Pulleine at the mountain ... apparently, he has a battle on his hands ... its dimensions are difficult to determine ... no details.'

Chelmsford considered the matter for a moment, and then leaned across the table to the youthful naval attaché, Milne, who had been on duty with them from the start and was distinguished for the meticulousness of his uniform, and the length and resolving power of the heavy brass naval telescope which he carried in a long leather case attached to the saddle of the horse he rode. Until now, his role had been almost wholly that of an observer.

'Mr Milne...' Milne looked up eagerly, pleased to be addressed directly by the General, '... kindly take your telescope to a high point. Note what you can of Isandhlwana.... We await your report.' Chelmsford returned his attention to the soup course. Rising with considerable eagerness he snapped his boots and departed the party.

Mr Milne carried the telescope on horseback to a small prominence several hundred yards beyond the eating area. But, powerful as it was, it was not going to detect anything more over the eight-mile distance from Isandhlwana than a few puffs of smoke from the larger guns.

There was no chance whatsoever of seeing anything the size of a human being, even assembled in so vast an array as the left horn of the Zulu army which moved swiftly through the broken, fleeing ranks of Nourse's Natal Natives. Dispatching the few who stood against them caused hardly a ripple in the Zulu line's forward progress, and even less of a ripple as it engulfed the rocket crews, their animals and their weapons, and their brave, squat, engineer commander wielding his over-length sword for just a few effective moments before he too fell to the simultaneous stabs of riposting *assegais*. Could Major Russell's last thoughts have been that his medieval sword did more damage than his marvellous scientific wonders? Then he disappeared under the giant black wave which rolled on to try the main camp.

An extension of the same line which inundated Russell's rockets, curved two miles south-east to form the horn tip which moved forward in unfaltering formation. It would soon meet head-on with Durnford and his troop of mounted defenders who waited for it, hoping to deform or even possibly stop its advance. The west right horn, despite travelling over more severely bouldered and steeply downgrade terrain, would shortly encounter the companies of Imperial soldiers who had marched out under Lieutenants Cavaye and Mostyn to defend the north approach to the camp. East and West, the horns closed.

Cutting across the plain at the north of the camp where

the Mostyn and Cavaye companies were preparing to defend, was a long *donga* at right angles to the approach of the as yet invisible Zulus. The companies were crouched in that *donga*, an advantageous waiting position; the Zulus wouldn't be visible until they reached the south edge of the plateau.

Corporal Field had ordered Private Store to carry a set of flagged pegs which would serve as range markers. The Corporal was briskly pacing out the yards due north from the defence lines while Private Store followed behind, setting the markers at every twenty yards, i.e. at the ten double-pace intervals indicated by his Corporal.

'... ninety seven ... ninety eight ... ninety nine ... .' Corporal Field stopped, apparently having lost count of which 'hundred' he had reached. '... what comes next, Private Store?'

There was no answer, Field turned, shouting 'Store !!' There was no Store and the last marker had not been set. It took him only a moment to discover that Store had moved off to a bush clump that concealed him from the company lines behind, but not from his Corporal. He stood there, his hands at this crotch, arching a stream of yellow urine on to the ground.

Field shook his head in despair, waiting on the spot. 'You useless bastard ... hurry that up.' Store of course didn't hurry, but let nature take its course.

However, Private Store's moment of blithe relief was only momentary for in the next instant he looked up: his jaw dropped weakly, and his water stopped.

Frantically buttoning up, he shouted to Corporal Field, 'Look ... Corp, quick look!'

But Field made no attempt to turn around to look up at the *Impi* that had now reached the edge of the plateau and was beginning to flood over its edge. It was still 1500 yards away but that distance was vanishing with great rapidity. Field called out to the transfixed private, 'If you've finished, Store, get to work!'

'I ain't finished – I got cut orff! Corp! You ain't lookin' at what I see!'

Now, finally, Field did turn his head in the direction, slowly, deliberately and apparently with no passion whatsoever. He then looked at Store and said, 'I saw them when we marked eighty yards.' He pointed to the near ground, 'I'll set one here, follow me fast, put one at three hundred fifty. And meet me at four hundred.'

The Corporal paced steadily forward, increasing the frequency but not the length of his pace. Private Store swallowed, looked back longingly for a moment at the relative safety of the *donga* where the comrades of his company were waiting with their rifles shoved over the lip, and then, such was the madness of his occupation, Store marched after his Corporal not *away from* but *in the direction of* the oncoming hordes of Zulus. He ran forward to the 350-mark that Corporal Field had indicated, plunged the marker into the ground, and then ran forward, puffing and panting from the uphill effort, in time to set the final marker just at the point where Field reached his 400th pace in front of the defending companies.

A mere further 400 yards ahead of them the Zulus, who had broken rank only to transgress a particularly uneven section of downhill slope, had come to a momentary halt to reform their lines. Store's last marker had hit a stone, failing to stick into the ground.

'Get it in', barked Field, 'That's the most important one. Right! Now back, on the double.'

Together they whirled and raced back like sprinters going for a meet record. They had hardly covered 100 yards before Field dove to the ground at the same time shouting, 'Down, Store! down!'

Store obeyed with due alacrity for he too had heard the command that came from the lines at the *donga*, 'Set your sights at four hundred yards! Aim!' Hardly had Store and Field flattened themselves out on to the ground when a

193

double volley sent whistling bullets over their heads. And the Zulu lines which, just at that point reached 400 yards, for a moment wavered as the first flight of metal ripped through shields tough enough to withstand ferocious spear thrusts to penetrate the flesh and vitals of the oncoming warriors.

This thunderous start of synchronous volley-firing, less than a mile on the north, had an instant effect upon the main forces within the camp. Pulleine, sitting in his tent writing letters raised his head at the echoing crash of the volley, paused writing in mid-sentence, then added the few necessary words to complete the thought, rose and walked to the tent opening.

Under the arching canvas of an ammunition wagon Boy-Pullen and the other buglers and drummer boys had started their card game again. The holders of weak hands for this particular deal wanted to terminate the play on the instant of the sound, but Boy-Pullen, who had a strong hand, demanded that they play on. The game terminated in any event because Quartermaster Bloomfield, who had been checking his stores by comparing against invoices, reacted with an old warrior's instincts, and decided that the time had come to look into the problem of readying the next supply which might be required from the ammunition boxes. When the card players' lookout saw the QM starting forward, the cards were promptly hidden and the boys stood awaiting their next orders. Dead centre of the camp, Melvill and Coghill were strolling along the lines of their C Company, both pausing mid-stride as they calculated the meaning of the firing.

But the meaning needed no calculations – a volley of this sort could only be response to a serious enemy charge no more than 400 or 500 yards in front of it. The single possible deduction was that a major offensive had started.

194

Melvill pursed his lips thoughtfully, 'Building up a bit, don't you think?' Coghill nodded in agreement. But then, Coghill nearly always nodded in agreement.

It was at this moment that the two young officers saw the rider who had been sent in by Lieutenant Raw galloping towards them, shouting 'Zulu ...! Zulu!', and then he passed them as he headed straight for Pulleine's tent. When they saw that Pulleine had emerged and was moving forward to meet the rider they followed quickly to find out the details of what was being said.

After the first volleys, Private Store and Corporal Field came to their feet during a reload command. They managed to get a hundred yards nearer to their lines when the commands for sighting and aiming were given, and once more hurled themselves to the ground well in advance of the final command of 'Fire!' The volley crashed out with even more deadly effect at the Zulus, now at the 300-yard mark. The toll was severe; the front of the Zulu line halted, going to the ground and taking cover while the survivors waited for detachments from the lines behind to come forward to fill out the spaces created by the dead.

The officers had no intention of wasting rounds on anything but erect targets. The next command from the company lines was, 'Hold your fire!' Store, delighted by the respite, started rising to resume his run back to the lines, but he had come only halfway to his feet when he noticed that his Corporal was not taking the opportunity to move.

'Better move, Corp, or you'll be a Zulu carpet....'

No! it was worse than he'd thought; the man was sprawled out motionless, and the blood of the wound in his head was seeping copiously. Store gaped at him in dismay, glanced back at the lines where his protection lay, but then, issuing a foul curse, flattened himself against the ground alongside his fallen Corporal. He stared at the lifeless bullet-pierced head. 'I tell you, Corp, one of our own stupid bastards wasn't looking at your markers, that's for sure.'

The Zulus were forming up again in front. From behind, Store heard the next set of commands to prepare for volley firing. He hugged the ground with his body, at the same time searching through Corporal Field's tunic pockets until he found what he was looking for – money. He turned his head to yell at the company lines behind, 'Shoot straight, not at the ground you bastards!'

The next two volleys again whined overhead. Store yelled, 'That's better!' He had run out of time and he had to go but he spent a lingering moment looking at Corporal Field's money in his hand and then at the inert body. He sighed, 'What comes next? – the answer, Corp, is two bottles of Mother's Ruin ... on you.' The line of Zulus hadn't started forward again, and there was a command to hold fire. Store, clutching Field's money, sprinted to the lines, and this time managed to get to them.

Durnford was more than two miles east of the encampment when the tip of the left horn of the Zulu attack appeared to his north-east. At first he felt a throb of satisfaction – his anticipation of a substantial presence of the Zulus was being confirmed. But as the shape and numbers of the swiftly appearing army began to become evident, the moment of elation was rapidly replaced by the sickening realization that he had not even begun to imagine the strength of numbers in which the Zulu force would appear. What he now saw was beyond doubt Cetshwayo's main army. By looking leftwards from his extended position he could see the full four-mile-undulation of the Zulu front line. It was clear to him as it had never been before that a cosmic viewer from a great height would see it precisely as it was meant to be, the

196

lunging head of a gigantic bull. And he, Durnford, with his pitifully small contingent of several hundred Basuto horseman, had to dally with one small section of the beast's left horn while the main thrust carrying the full weight of the head, the loins and the other horn which he could see to the north and west was bearing down to destroy the camp with its close on to 2000 inhabitants.

It was enormously dismaying, no question of that, but all was not necessarily lost. It was important that the defence coalesce at its centre. He admitted to himself that in his hurry to move forward to meet the enemy he had not spent as much time as he might have with Pulleine to be certain that the disposition of the defence within the camp was all that it should be. His obligation now, however, was self-evident. Using the somewhat greater mobility and speed of a mounted troop he must, at all odds, delay the advance of the left horn which would, if it were unimpeded, flank and encircle the camp as its lower right end. He must give Pulleine as much time as possible to consolidate. Only then, with the rifle-power of the Imperial companies amassed, and aimed in every required direction at the attackers, its flanks and back at minimum exposure and with its supply lines of ammunition free and unimpeded, was there a reasonable chance that the killing rate would be enough to stem these racing hordes — even at the improbable odds of twelve (or fifteen) to one.

Durnford realized that he was in all likelihood recapitulating Chelmsford's own diagnosis, that correctly deployed, either column had within itself the power to mount an adequate defence. On such a rationale, His Lordship had taken the chance of splitting the Rorke's Drift column into two. But it was an arrogant decision, thought Durnford. It made so many presumptions about what the Zulu would do or could do. He, Durnford, admitted to himself that he had not known from where the main army attack would come. But knowing was so

197

different from presuming, or of making the huge presumptive error of splitting an army. And now the price of that presumption was about to be discovered; that it would be high was already past questioning, but that it be kept within acceptable limits was a matter now for courage, for coolness under incalculable pressures and, added Durnford dryly to himself, perhaps for prayer also.

Durnford's Basutos had been recruited for scouting, but now they were being required to take on the full load of cavalry combat. Their riding was excellent and dashing if not quite up to the remarkable precision achievements of the Sikalis. Durnford had trained them particularly in the mode of tactical skirmishing during defensive retreat, which they would employ this day. Essentially they were divided into two troops of 150 horsemen each. Mounted, they could keep a fairly extended formation, engaging a goodly section of the advancing Zulu horn considering their own small numbers. The forward line of 150 horsemen, for the most part armed with carbines, would bring their horses around in a straight line, confronting the Zulus about 200 yards from its running front line, fire off their volley, split at its centre and then spurring left and right in reverse arcs, firing at will, race behind the waiting line of the second troop of 150 horsemen another 100 yards to the rear of the first. As the first cleared, the rifles of the second line would be already raised and loaded and ready to fire their volley at its most effective distance. Then the horsemen would repeat the split and race away, free-firing to the right and left, to clear for the first line-up who, by this time, would have already thrust new cartridges into their weapons, thus, repeatedly could each line succeed the other in inflicting a considerable toll on the advancing enemy, at the same time keeping a taunting self-protective distance from the hand-to-hand engagement that the Zulu sought.

Of course, the attackers had some guns of their own, which even if not as effective as the defenders', did fire

198

off potentially deadly metal which hit riders or brought down horses. From time to time also the plunging horses on the insecure ground would stumble and lose a rider. In either case, losing one's mount proved inevitably fatal if the man involved could not somehow recapture his horse in a trice, or, on occasion, be given a lift by a near companion. In cases where none of these was possible, death by stabbing was sure, and often horrible.

Durnford had another worry additional to what was happening at the encampment. Major Russell and his rockets, with only a small contingent of the NNC, had been left at least a mile and a half behind. He had pointed Russell to a position somewhat north of his own move eastward and had last seen them marching towards it. From what he could determine the Zulus must have already engulfed the position where Russell and his rockets were supposed to have remained to daunt whatever attack would be coming from that direction. He thought, indeed, that he seen low-trajectory rocket-fire, briefly, then nothing. He considered detaching a section of troops to see whether they could aid the rocketeers, as well as Nourse and his Natives. But perhaps all had chances to flee back to the camp; and such a foray was clearly not practical, in any sense.

As the whirling, racing defence against the Zulus continued, with each fall-back and reformation of the line, the defenders came closer to the long *donga* from which Durnford had planned to make a more concerted stand. While this mobile, continuously rearward defence was effective, it was only partially achieving its real aim of slowing the left horn's approach to the camp centre. The walls of the *donga* would provide a much firmer base for rifle-fire, and permit the marksmanship of his troops to be much more accurate. As he raced behind his front line, reining about with his one good arm, and then at intervals dropping the reins and controlling his well-trained horse only with his knees, raising his own rifle to aim it one-handed to add its occasional fire-power to that of his men, he realized keenly the difficulties of achieving real accuracy from the saddle. He was certain that his troops would be able to gain a good deal of time for the camp defenders to contract its defences once his men were entrenched in the *donga*. The *donga* was far enough away from the east front of the camp to prevent any partial spillover of Zulus from making a significant attack upon it, and close enough to establish the all-important line of supply for refurbishing the ammunition pouches of his men when they required, as they certainly would, fresh supplies.

Then there was a momentary lull in the Zulu advance, possibly as they considered their own tactical problems in respect of the unaccustomed defence which Durnford was mounting. Durnford found his binoculars, swept the camp behind him, trying to estimate the problems they might be having, and then tried to find out where Russell, Nourse and the rockets might be. The pinnacled outcropping hid that secret, but from the position of the Zulus he could not come to any optimistic conclusion. He signalled a subaltern, who rode quickly to him.

'Ride to Lord Chelmsford,' he said, pointing to the south-east along a path that seemed less likely to be cut off imminently. 'You will find him six, possibly eight, miles along ... and report that the battle he longs for has started, and that he must move back in support, quickly!'

Durnford was aware that by the time Chelmsford could react to a message, the course of the battle would probably be fully determined. Still, if the defence could maintain itself, and if the Zulus were slightly less firm of will in the face of the huge losses that the massed rifles would inflict, there was some possibility that even a lumbering reinforcement from Chelmsford would be useful. The subaltern had saluted and Durnford watched him ride south-east, at a gallop. He returned to search for Russell.

23

Russell and his rockets were no more. But it should be more thoroughly recorded that his efforts to launch the rockets had not failed completely. First, the infantry units of Lieutenant Nourse's Natal Natives crumpled. Was it not too much to expect a fully committed fight against such overwhelming odds from men who, through all their lives, had heard stories and saw evidence of the fearsome, all-conquering might of Zulu warriors? Moreover, they themselves in one way or another were connected by their descent to the Zulu nationality. Russell was not surprised to see most of them waver and turn. He was more impressed with a substantial minority who stood, and fell. He was less offended than pitying for the number who sped back towards the camp, in the futile hope that there might be some safety there.

It was only at this last-ditch moment that Russell managed to touch fire to the fuse of one, then another, of the rockets. With flamboyant sparking and burning they took off on a low trajectory. They flew, leaving a long train of fiery effects – smoke, sparks, flame – snaking at low level not too far above the heads of the attackers, wailing and spluttering their pyrotechnics, a daunting sight. The Zulus stopped running forward. This brief halt represented rocketry's one moment of promise. A Zulu, named UmBeje, cried out his opinion that the British had captured the King of the Fire Demons, to produce for them this new and horrendously destructive weapon. In the pause Russell managed to light a third fuse but it spluttered and went out. The first two rockets lurched erratically, one exploding against a rock face while the other fell behind a stone outcropping.

The *inDuna* of the attacking regiment looked derisively at UmBeje. 'What say you – the *King* of the Fire Demons? It is a stupid, senseless demon who spits fire and sparks uselessly, into the wind, at nothing.' The *inDuna* pantomimed broadly and sarcastically and the warriors around him laughed. The Zulus, many of whom had suffered their moment of doubt, joined in the laughter, raised their spears and charged against the rockets and their crews.

Russell's last act was to reach alongside his tool-kit to retrieve the sword which he had earlier unbuckled because it was impeding his efforts to mount the rockets. In the next moments, the Zulu tide, stabbing without reservation, treating the mules of the rocket team, the artillery men and the officers alike, dispatched them all into history.

24

Chelmsford's midday meal had progressed slowly through its several excellently prepared courses, to climax with the serving of a sweet pancake based on fresh eggs captured from Sihayo's *Kraal* and now soaked in an excellent brandy which was lighted just prior to serving. It was a superb touch out here in the wilds of Zululand and appreciated by His Lordship's guests.

An hour earlier the festive meal had been interrupted by several reports; only one of these was not from Isandhlwana behind them, but from forward positions. The mists on the mountains *ahead* of the Chelmsford's column, to the east, had been cleared by the rising sun. Some Zulu outposts became visible and there were signs that camp-fires, a great number of camp-fires in fact, had been burning there the night before. The deduction was that the main Zulu army was waiting ahead but had deployed back so as not to encounter Chelmsford's advancing troops. (The true main army which had waited, at least 25,000 strong, in the rocky ravine above the Nqutu plateau did not indulge itself in the lighting of camp-fires. It had produced no visible light, nor had it created any noise.)

A part of the NCC had been sent forward to make prisoners of whatever elements of Zulus there were waiting before them; but the Zulus had retreated and made no stand. This was quite consistent, Chelmsford explained to the diners, with his policy of containing the

Zulu army, preventing its march towards invasion of Natal, forcing it back towards Ulundi from whence it came, or until there was no more fall-back position, at which point the great battle would take place at a time coerced if not dictated by the British. In fact, this confirmation of Zulus ahead had been so encouraging to Lord Chelmsford that he dispatched orders to Pulleine to de-camp from Isandhlwana, and to move forward to re-join with him as soon as possible.

Then the *flambé* pancakes were brought out, drawing a chorus of approval and congratulations for the cook and for His Lordship's originality at concocting a menu. The good port was served. Shortly after, many of the officers dispersed to duties that had been set to them, while those of higher rank stayed on for a command decision meeting which Chelmsford had indicated he would like to hold. Noggs had enjoyed the good eating, and had garnered several amusing observations which would serve as colour for his dispatches; but he was slightly depressed by the feeling that unless something of great military significance started happening in this forsaken region, there were better and more comfortable places to dine. He noted that, rather unusually, Crealock was not occupied either with his commander or with other of his incessant duties. It was a rare opportunity for Noggs – he stepped forward quickly.

'Crealock, old fellah?' For once Chelmsford's military secretary didn't positively shun Noggs, as was his habit. 'I'm doing a few notes for my dispatch ... would like to clear up a few military points. Don't want to bother His Lordship, you understand?'

Crealock, unquestionably softened by the copious supply of alcohol, indeed seemed to show some minor affability, as he waited for Noggs to continue.

'Damned pleased His Lordship is bringing the Isand-hlwana encampment forward. Always had it drummed into my thick skull that a good commander never wil-

205

lingly splits his force – especially in an enemy's country, and before knowing their true deployment. Is my information wrong?'

Crealock smiled slightly, but allowed Noggs to see no meaning in the smile. 'Ah yes ... if we were facing a European enemy, perhaps, armed with rifles, artillery, etcetera, I think your point would be correct, Noggs. Beyond that, I'm not qualified to make further comment. I would also remind you that I do not create nor even participate in the strategies upon which you wish to comment.' The usually staid man now even assayed a smiling, wry note of self-deprecation. With an exaggerated whisper he said, 'Do try to remember, I am *only* His Lordship's military secretary.'

Noggs felt annoyance flooding in him at Crealock's carefully cultivated style of continuous evasion, even now when lubricated with drink. The newsman leaned forward, grinning savagely, 'Don't take overly comfort from that, Crealock, old fellah ... if His Lordship sinks, then *you* sink with him...! I say, is there any more of that disgusting claret we had midmeal? I've a stomach full of beastly gin and its dilution is an urgent necessity....'

Crealock looked at him with cold disdain, 'Diluting alcohol with alcohol is reinforcement, sir, not dilution!'

Nogg's grin broadened, 'Reinforcement! As, yes – now that sounds like good advice for you to proffer to Chelmsford.... Instead of bringing Pulleine forward, don't you think it would be better if His Lordship, as you call him, turned back now, the sooner to join his army together? That is, especially, if he wishes to be present at his own principal battle?'

At which point, all affability fled Crealock. 'You probe in the wrong corner, sir, I will have no more!' He started to move off, but Noggs followed immediately, his voice rising to a harangue:

'Reinforcement, Crealock, dear fellah, is *still* my advice ... it would take only two or three hours at the double for this lot to return to Isandhlwana.' He tapped his nose knowingly. 'This seldom, let me say *never*, fails me in my search for news. I tell you that's where the news is: *I-Sand-hl-wana!*'

Crealock whirled in his tracks and faced Noggs with the full blast of his no-longer suppressed anger. 'Then let that ugly nose of yours inform the readers of the *Standard* that it quarrels with Lord Chelmsford's nose – then see whether they'll agree with you or agree with him! I don't give a damn!' This time when Crealock strode away, Noggs did not follow. But he did stand and stare towards the mountain behind them, full-knowing that movement, 'at the double', for this lot was not even a probability. If men fought at Isandhlwana now, they would fight and die alone.

Vereker and Kambula waited with the Sikali Horse at the centre of the camp in response to Durnford's earlier orders that they act as a free-moving reserve to support any element of the defence that began to show signs of collapse. Vereker felt that this somehow contradicted Chelmsford's direct orders to him to act as ADC for Colonel Durnford, with its connotation of serving him at first hand, not simply by doing what he commanded. The Imperial Companies of the First of the Twenty-fourth who waited in their defensive squares had, of course, not yet been engaged. The opening salvos had come from directly north, where companies under Lieutenants Mostyn and Cavaye, sent there by Pulleine, had to meet the downhill onslaught.

But, at the moment, as well as could be told through binoculars at this distance, they were maintaining their positions. The firing from the north was going well and steadily, and Vereker presumed the toll against the Zulus to be very severe. Looking just south-east, to Durnford's extended position, he had been able to calculate that man's intentions. He noted the delaying fall-back tactics of the mounted Basutos, and presumed that they would make a concerted stand once they reached the Big Donga and the natural protection that if offered. But even as he watched he detected that a note of disorganization had crept into the heretofore rhythmic fall-back tactics that Durnford was using to combat the advance of the left horn. Vereker was able to deduce that this was caused by some failure of ammunition supply because of the decreased volume of firing that came from the mounted Basutos. He reacted immediately. He shouted to Kambula who was checking the lines of the Sikali, taking in every detail, looking at the contents of each man's ammunition pouch, and the state of other vital equipment. Vereker signalled that he be followed, and spurred ahead.

Kambula, as it often seemed by telepathy, invisibly commanded the troops' co-ordinated start. With its usual even but furious precision, lines maintaining perfect formation in spite of being at full gallop and over calamitously uneven ground, the Sikali rode out to support Durnford in his extended south-east position. Pulleine, wating alongside the Imperial contingent, noted, as Vereker had, that the danger of the moment seemed to be from the south-east, and that all else was holding quite nicely. He shouted to Coghill, 'There! Ride to Stuart Smith! Tell him to bring his guns about and cover Durnford and Vereker for a fall-back.'

Coghill responded, spurring to the north-east where the artillery unit was firing with considerable effectiveness at the Zulu units that were sweeping down in front of them, descending from the plateau but not yet wholly on the plain.

The trouble at Durnford's front had been, as Vereker guessed, one of ammunition shortage. The consequent reduced rate of firing had allowed the left tip of the horn to penetrate into a position where they threatened to cut behind the ultimate retreat route of the Basuto horsemen towards the Big Donga. It was at this advanced spur towards which Vereker and the Sikali charged, shooting with formidable accuracy, even at full gallop. The left tip of the horn withered under the force of the attack, and then scattered. The Sikali now directed their fire in support of the forward section. Durnford felt an enormous uplift at this sudden strengthening, and shouted his command for the retreat to the Big Donga while the going was good. When the Basutos reached the *donga*, by prearrangement they leapt from their horses and scrambled down with them into the nearly mile-and-a-half-long ditch. These well-trained black soldiers, now threw up their rifles over the edge of the ditch, prepared for their hold-fast. Vereker and Kambula rode down into the *Donga*. Durnford, on foot, striding behind his men, was already commanding their firing; aiming, reloading and repeat firing into effective volleys. He greeted his rescuers with a warmth that made all their efforts seem worthwhile.

'I am in a position to say it,' smiled Durnford. 'You, Sergeant, are a chip off the old block.'

Kambula appreciated the compliment. 'Even the brave and mighty Zulus stepped back from this Sikali. . . .' The truth of this statement, which was made not boastfully but as a fact, was unassailable.

Durnford smiled, nodding in agreement. They had functioned as he knew they would, he told them, and now he felt sufficiently secure in this position. He ordered them to take up their camp posts again, to serve in the same way, as a flying reserve. 'But send out some ammunition quickly. We are already dividing up what we have.'

Vereker expressed his puzzlement. He said that he had deduced the requirement and had transmitted orders for an ammunition supply to be brought forward instantly, but now glancing back to the camp centre he could not discern anyone bringing anything at all in this direction. He was furious. Damn fools – some ass passes an order along incorrectly and in the circumstances like this, the penalty could be the death of men.

'Don't worry, sir,' he said, as he and Kambula departed, 'you'll have what you need if I have to bring it myself.'

But before he fully left the site he saw a wave of Zulus hurtle over the top edge of the *donga* at its far end, and a fierce hand-to-hand – bayonet versus *assegai* – duel, ensue. Immediately a second wave of Zulus charged forward to follow into the breach of the *donga* defences. But then the first artillery shell burst in their patch, scattering bodies and creating a chaos of dispersal by men who had never experienced such a frightening explosion in their midst. Vereker felt better about retiring his Sikali Horse now that Durnford had the support of the artillery. He galloped the Sikali back to the centre of camp, leaving Durnford running up and down the length of the *donga* shouting encouragement and orders at his men. When Vereker last saw him, Durnford was moving to the far end of the *donga* where the hand-to-hand fighting was still going on. Vereker was amazed at the older man's unflagging energy in combat.

Lieutenant Colonel Pulleine had now ridden over to the artillery himself. He was more than pleased with the effect of the well-aimed shells upon the Zulus who confronted Durnford at the far south-eastern approach. He watched the huge sweating black bombardiers stockpiling the shells near the loading team, who inserted them with expert speed into the gun breach, snapped and closed it, and then stepped back four smart paces to cheer together as each shell landed to wreak havoc, dismemberment and death amongst the human contingents that were their targets.

Pulleine waved his sword in the air and shouted approval to Maj. Stuart Smith. Smith, from behind the guns, grinned and shouted back to him through the noise. 'If I had two more batteries, Colonel, and two more crews such at these, I would give your battle to you right now, sir – alone!'

Pulleine laughed exultantly, pointed his sword 1000 yards to the north and west where the companies under Cavaye and Mostyn defended the high outer periphery, firing their volleys with steady fierceness. He shouted back, 'And there, Major Smith, is the best infantry the whole of this world produces. Major Smith – I say our chances can only be excellent!'

Sceptical commentators, including some Englishmen, were wont to remark that this exuberance with which the Imperial forces relied on stationary, square-block fire-power was a product of mind and souls not sufficiently agile to deal with the tactical finesse of mobile warfare, or of shifting deployment of forces. Whether this kind of comment is true or not, at the moment, Pulleine's confidence was shared by all those men who stood together working the levers of their breach-loaders, with well-learned, automatic, and highly efficient precision.

Not that they weren't suffering casualties from the much less efficient counter-fire from the antique guns that had been sold to the enemy by traders like Fannin and his ilk, and further casualties from some hurled *assegais*, and sometimes from overpowering waves of charging Zulus so sustained that the last few who didn't fall to the volleys were able to climb over the bodies of their comrades to reach the defenders and engage them in hand-to-hand, until bayonets or more bullets wiped out these also. But counting their own substantial casualties, the much higher number of the enemy who were dropping to the deadly leaden hail as well as to the greater explosive force of the artillery pieces encouraged them vastly. There was a renewal of hope, a delightful feeling, after the first discouraging sight of the Zulu hordes as well as swallowing the sour-tasting fact that the enemy had arrived in a way and in a place which was wholly surprising. The Martini-Henrys were overheating, burning the flesh of the hands that held and fired them at peak rate. The cost and the effort were both great; so were the stakes – their lives and the credibility of the great nation and high crown they represented. It began to look now that some of the first – their lives – and all of the second – their honour – could be preserved.

For instance, Private Store, having made his way back to the lines carrying his corporal's money and some pain in his heart for having to desert this man who had so often abused him but who had also led and counselled him when he needed leadership and good counselling, had taken up his position among the defenders. He was aiming and killing with a great deal of satisfaction, each squeeze of his trigger working out a sense of revenge for the dead corporal who lay out there, still and bloody, between Store, his mates, and their ready-to-die enemy. The steadiness of Store's firing faltered when he reached into his ammunition pouch and found it empty. He reached for the additional supply he carried; it had also diminished – to his last two rounds. And then he began to wonder if the thinning of the last volleys, as measured by the decreased volume of sound they produced, might be caused by the fact that there were others in the line at this north end of the camp who were also running short and searching, or having to borrow from the next man. His hand snagged out, trapping the sleeve of a bugler boy who was passing behind him. The youth understood Store's requirement but shook his head negatively and handed over a mere two cartridges.

'Won't do, lad!' Store was loading with the pathetic additional supply even as he talked. 'Run back for a proper supply, bugler, and scamper fast, you lazy lout, or we'll lose this bleeding war!'

The bugler boy was offended by the tone. 'Been twice already . . . they ain't got them out. . . .'

'Make it three times then!' he gave the boy a shove, back to the centre of the camp. 'Can't hurt yer!'

The bugler boy sprinted away, his small legs carrying him at a racer's pace. Store now aimed and fired again. He saw the black face of an advancing Zulu 200 yards away smear into an instance mess of flesh, splintered bone and blood. He grinned. 'They smash you out, don't they, these soft bullets. . . .,' he remarked joyfully to the man next to him as he reloaded with his last one.

But the man he spoke to was also loading with his last one. He looked at it woefully then inserted it into the breach of his gun, 'Oy, but bullets get used up – and them bloody spears don't.'

Store aimed, refused to become downhearted. 'Me trigger finger's getting tired anyhow. And look at me left hand – bloody burnt meat. . . .'

Lieutenant Cavaye paced behind them calling out with droning rhythm, 'Watch the markers . . . watch the markers. Adjust your range. At two hundred yards. . . .'

Of course at that distance and in the din of battle it wasn't possible for any of the *inDunas* who led the attackers to have heard Cavaye's calling out, even if they could have understood what he was saying. But at least one among this group of elder, battle-experienced men grasped the significance of those regularly spaced white-flagged objects in the ground. The front attacking line suddenly vanished, as it seemed capable of doing at will, and next there appeared individual Zulus, either running in a low crouch or slithering forward on their stomachs, getting to the markers and then pulling them out. Many died carrying out that assignment, but many of them also succeeded. The kill per bullet ratio of the defenders became too low for the decreasing supply when there were not more markers against which to set sights. But firing couldn't stop.

25

A half mile further north at the base of the plateau, another *Impi* of Zulus sat, as was the Zulu style, with their backs to the battle. Now they were given their signal. They arose in unison, turned and ran downhill towards the north defenders. It was a vast new reserve. Cavaye, who was beginning to worry at the loss of his markers, now had a new concern; he saw the huge wave of plume-topped shields starting forward. And he was intensely aware of the fact that his riflemen were running out of ammunition.

As a matter of fact, the pause gave him time to dwell on several additional concerns. His company had been sent too far north of the camp. The supply line for ammunition should have been shorter; then this particular threat might be less. And when he glanced backwards he noticed that the left flank behind him, which compromised the north-west corner of the basic huge square with which the entire camp was defending itself, was manned wholly by Natal Native Corps. He had seen that the Zulu reserve line was advancing at an enormous pace while its westward end was forming into a long horn that was undoubtedly aimed at the vulnerable north-west corner. If the NNC blokes caved in, the undefended rear of his company, together with that of his companion, Lieutenant Mostyn, would be assaulted by a great, great number of blood-thirsty, infinitely determined black enemy. His confidence began to ebb – one attack front was proving too much as it was.

When the bugler boy sent for ammunition by Private Store arrived at the wagons where it was being doled out, little had changed from the time before. The other bugler boys were waiting there restively, while Quartermaster Bloomfield stood over one of the boxes, exerting the greatest possible pressure with his long-handled screwdriver to force the oxidized screwheads out of their sockets. Well, at least thought the young man, they have managed to get out a few more boxes. All these needed now was opening. The bugler boy from Cavaye's lines watched the Quartermaster sweating, but failing to unloose the reluctant screws. Then, all of a moment, the group round the ammunition wagons became aware of an ominous change. The noises of the battle everywhere had stopped. They all now looked, distracted from their total concentration on the ammunition boxes. Their eyes searched the huge perimeter of the defence. There was no firing because all the Zulus had somehow vanished. There was only this huge and terribly threatening silence.

Then, out of the silence, at the very lowest threshold of audibility, came a buzzing sound that immediately began to increase in volume and in direness. It was a terror tactic of the Zulus of which they had been warned, but that did not reduce its effect.

The buzzing crescendoed. The Imperial defenders could not avoid listening to it, nor reduce their apprehension, and even those voices that were raised to call out, or mock or challenge sounded weak and unconvincing. The retaliatory efforts ceased, and all the while the buzzing grew louder, and the waiting more tense.

Quartermaster Bloomfield turned to his job. The last screw yielded, and then he was able to pry off the crossed metal bands, also using the heavy screwdriver blade.

215

When the top came off, there was a cheer from the buglers who waited. He pushed the box to Boy-Pullen who took charge of the distribution, while Bloomfield went to the next heavily banded, screwed-down ammunition box. Then from the corner of his quick eye, he noted that first and second in the line of those Boy-Pullen was serving, waiting with open pouches, stood two native runners, one from the NNC defenders at the north-west corner, and the other wearing the insignia of the company of natives at the north-east who were supposed to protect the artillery. Bloomfield's reaction was instantaneous and sharp with disapproval.

'Boy-Pullen!'

Boy-Pullen stopped his action with the guilt and promptitude of a cat caught on the dining table. 'You will not, ever, issue ammunition from this wagon to any but authorised companies.'

Nothing of what Bloomfield or Boy-Pullen said was understood by the native runners who merely stood confused and immobile when Boy-Pullen failed to fill their sacks and tried to get them to move on. Politely but firmly Bloomfield took a step in their direction, to move them on out of line. 'I am sorry, my good man, but we can't have you lot disorganizing everything.' He pointed to another set of wagons some 100 yards further on. 'Now get to your *own* wagons. I am certain they'll help you.'

The buzzing of the Zulus had reached a sustained peak. In the distance the native troops were holding up their useless rifles, waving them towards the supply wagons. Bloomfield was suddenly annoyed, impatient. 'Off with you! Both of you, off!' Bewildered, the native ammunition runners sped in the direction that he pointed, even though this was where they had come from, having failed to get the supply of ammunition they sought. The white-skinned runners stood waiting while yet another banded and screwed down ammunition box was dragged forward as Boy-Pullen too quickly emptied the one that Bloomfield had just succeeded in opening.

'Please, sir,' urged Boy-Pullen, 'couldn't we set some of the lads to opening 'em as well as taking 'em out. . . .'

Bloomfield merely shook his head. 'I had sixteen extra strong, extra long screwdrivers requisitioned. I'll show you my duplicate form.'

'Yes, sir,' said Boy-Pullen urgently but trying not to upset the Quartermaster, 'but they just ain't here, sir. I know it ain't right, sir, but couldn't some of the lads try to open 'em with some rocks. We could try, sir, couldn't we?'

Bloomfield sighed deeply. It was a horrendous idea to him, banging open ammunition boxes with rocks, splintering them, wasting them forever, spilling cartridges on the ground. He studied the problem to a depth that he had never gone before. Then he nodded slowly, 'Very well, Boy-Pullen', he said, 'we'll try it, but just this once, see. . . .'

Boy-Pullen gave rapid orders and the other bugler boys hauled out some more of the sturdy, banded boxes. Bloomfield attacked the one before him with the same methodical effort he had used on the others, trying to budge the stubborn oxidized long screws into some movement. Circumstances had forced him to agree to use irregular methods but he knew that it wouldn't make much difference really. He could see clearly in his mind the ammunition box that had taken a long fall from the back of the ammunition supply wagon as it jolted up the embankment out of the Buffalo River on the crossing. It had landed full force on the jagged end of a huge boulder in the river. The heavy fall had produced barely a visible dent in the sturdy hardwood of which the box was fabricated. These lads would have to do an awful lot of pounding with very large rocks to get them open at a rate required. The battle had lulled but only briefly, while the Zulus buzzed, and buzzed, and buzzed. . . .

Durnford, his useless arm tucked into the special insert tailored into his tunic, strode behind the lines of his Basutos waiting in volleying position, their rifles resting on the ground over the edge of the *donga*. He was looking anxiously backwards, every few paces or so, to the centre of the camp, waiting for the supply of ammunition Vereker was supposed to have guaranteed. His one hope was that it would arrive before the Zulus charged again. The buzz from more than 20,000 throats filled the valley like an infinity of wasps. His Basutos were affected deeply, and Durnford understood their feelings. Suddenly he shouted, 'Let them buzz! We'll make them buzz too! Make your bullets buzz-z-z, boys. Wait ... set your sights at two hundred yards ... when they come make every bullet count....'

The tension on one of the triggers had apparently passed the point of restraint, and a random shot rang out. 'No hold it, hold it!'

Then the buzzing transformed into a huge simultaneous roar, an incredible effect of voices in unison, considering the distance over which it issued. The cry transformed into '*U-Su-Tu! U-Su-Tu!*'

The renewed south-east offensive which Durnford confronted formed at approximately 700 yards. Martini-Henrys could be effective at that distance, but not as perfectly effective as at a nearer one. Durnford reissued his order, 'Hold fire. Aim! ... Fire at two hundred yards.' One of the Basutos called out, suddenly pointing to the rear. Durnford turned, and, elated, saw Vereker and another of the Sikalis riding forward side by side each with a hand on the rope handles of a case of ammunition. Behind them came several more carrying ammunition boxes in the same way. At the front, the forward bow of the new Zulu line, screaming out its infectious 'Kill!' threat, had developed with the speed and power of a black tidal wave.

218

Eight miles to the south-east the naval attaché, Milne, trim bearded, his uniform and self unruffled by the heat of the early afternoon, rode down from the high point carrying his naval telescope. Colonel Crealock had come forward to meet him. Milne leapt from his horse, saluted and reported, 'I watched the camp, but I saw no one for twenty minutes, sir ... there is an atmospheric mist which obscures much ... but I would say that the tents have not been struck. I saw some bursts of smoke, possibly shell-fire. I believe I was able to distinguish that the cattle had been moved into the camp....'

He paused as Lieutenant Harford, who had an hour earlier gone off with Hamilton-Browne to bring support to the distant camp, now galloped into view and then forward to them. Out of breath, extremely excited, he reined his horse. His stutter, always present, was more pronounced than ever. 'The c ... c ... ccamp is under attack from a l .. l .. llarge force of Z .. Z ..Zulus....'

Crealock tried to calm him down and asked him from where he received his intelligence. A rather unclear story poured out of a courier having been intercepted by Commander Hamilton-Browne. Colonel Pulleine, said this messenger, was desperately requiring help. Hamilton-Browne was having difficulty getting his natives to continue forward once they had heard that there was a major attack by Zulus on the camp. Just at that point they were joined by Colonel Harness, who was still bringing forward artillery after a late morning departure from Isandhlwana. He thereupon decided to join with Hamilton-Browne, turning the gun carriages about for a return to aid in the defence of the camp.

Harford was not certain what overall credence Crealock gave to his report, but he did note that the man frowned at the information that Harness was acting against specific orders in turning the artillery about. Crealock mused over the problem. Finally, still reflect-

219

ing, he waved his hand southward. 'I see. . . . Lieutenant Harford, ride after Lord Chelmsford and acquaint him with the same intelligence you just passed on to me . . . but. . . .'

Harford, who in his excitement had already started away, stopped at Crealock's raised voice. '. . . control your passions, Mr Harford. Control your passions. A professional soldier must remain cool and thoughtful in times of stress.'

Harford nodded and visibly showed that he was in control of his feelings. He then wheeled his horse and rode in the direction Crealock had indicated, to find His Lordship. When Harford was gone Crealock turned to the naval attaché, Milne. 'Did your telescope bear out that fellow's assertions?'

Milne, as carefully and as neatly as his beard was trimmed and his uniform was hung, stated, 'At this distance, sir, the telescope, though powerful, is limited in its powers of discernment. The only supporting evidence I can give you, was a possibility that the smoke I detected was from the firing of artillery shells.'

Crealock thought about it for a time. 'There are a number of circumstances I can imagine where artillery would be used, short of a large-scale attack upon the camp.' He beckoned a nearby officer with the rank of Captain, who rode forward, and saluted. Crealock spoke with quiet authority. 'Ride after Colonel Harness and order him – and his guns – to return to his orginal route, south-east. He must adhere to Lord Chelmsford's orders, until they are countermanded from an authorized source.'

The Captain wheeled and rode rapidly to the west and north to prevent Harness from bringing his artillery back to Isandhlwana.

26

When Bayele had reached the edge of the plateau exhausted, battered, and intensely conscious of the ache produced by two days of starvation clutching at his middle, he crawled between some rocks where he could rest and watch the progress of events which were now certain to follow. If he could wait here long enough, without being discovered by one of the mounted patrols, he would be able to fulfil his dream of participating in the assault against the Redcoat invaders. At first, he thought it would be necessary to continue to struggle across the plateau in a north-easterly direction and then mount the slope beyond which was the ravine where the main army was waiting. But by the time he had reached this hiding place he could see the patrols led by Roberts and Raw, and when they passed him by, then vanished further up the slope, he realized that there was some chance that they might discover the position of the main army. If so, Bayele thought, they would be intercepted and never be able to report their discovery. Off to his right, which was to the west, coming up onto the plateau itself, he saw for the third time the well-dressed precise-riding black troops under the command of the large powerful black rider and the yellow-haired British officer who had twice already posed such threat to Bayele's purpose. But not this time, not where he was hidden now, unless they were very lucky.

The plateau they had to patrol was very wide, and Bayele was very well hidden, brown-skinned against brown earth, and surrounded by rocks and boulders where horses could not be ridden. His body ached from the blows it had received, and the rope burns on his arms and legs where he had struggled to free himself of bondage brought even sharper pains. His fatigue was such that there were times when his eyes closed, but even this was not particularly unsafe. In fact, the fitful napping seemed to bring some strength back into his tired muscles. When, below, he had seen the one-armed chief and his mounted Basutos ride far out to the east, he experienced the elation of knowing that once more these foolish soldiers were weakening their defensive possibilities by spreading themselves across the countryside. The one-armed chief and his black riders would be brought down in an instant by the left horn when the attack started.

Further to the left he had seen the small group of blue-clad white soldiers with a troop of native foot soldiers, clearly an escort for the peculiar, short, stubby cylindrical objects which looked like some type of strange gun, but which were drawn on wheels by mules instead of by horses as the large guns were. This group had branched off from the mounted troops who were led by the one-armed warrior chief, and had positioned themselves a mile further to Bayele's left, also pointing their unusual weapons upwards towards the plateau.

It was evident to Bayele from the general positioning of the guns, the direction taken by the largest section of mounted troops, and the area being covered by the patrols, that the present defenders of the camp now, at last, realized that the true threat would be coming from the north. Yet, this very morning the larger group of soldiers had split the defences by moving south-east. Clearly the morning leavers were misled by the information which he and his now dead companions had passed on to them and which would have been confirmed by their sighting of the decoy army. Well, it was too late for them all now. Their realization had been too long coming.

He heard the shooting start and then saw the retreat of the patrol that had ridden up into invisibility towards the crest of the mountain. It was evident that there had been mutual discovery. These then were the first shots of the battle already begun. Within moments Bayele's deductions were confirmed by the first appearance of the huge circle of warriors who followed up from the ravine and spread out right and left in their faultless ranks along the inner edge of the plateau. From that position they would still not be seen by the men in the camp, but at the pace they were moving they soon would arrive here on the outer edge of the plateau where Bayele waited. They would appear here and strike terror in the hearts of the paltry few thousand of defenders and it was here Bayele waited to join them in the attack.

But the first contact with the foes occurred far to the east and south of him, when the left horn encountered the mounted Basuto troops led by the one-armed chief. Bayele recognized the brown and white shields of the *inGobamakhosi*, his own youthful regiment. He was proud that they were amongst the first to be in battle action. He yearned to be with them, fighting alongside the men he knew best. But then to his right he saw the yellow-haired officer and the black scouts ride back over the edge of the plateau to return to the centre of the camp, and not too long after came the marching companies of Redcoats to defend the area beyond the north of the camp. He watched this battle develop also and saw the awful effects of the withering fire-power as many guns spoke at one time, so that the charges of the Zulu attackers were slowed down by the mounting heap of their own dead over which they had to climb. This was a sight that was terrible to behold ... and he had a vision of the great mourning which would engulf the *Kraals* of Zululand after this war.

The *Impi* which arrived here at the position where Bayele was hidden on the plateau, just above the big guns which were pulled on their wheels by horses, was the *inDlu-yengwe*, commanded by the renowned Usibebu. Bayele knew the name of Usibebu, as did all other Zulus. As a relatively young man, Usibebu had thrown in his lot with Cetshwayo during the Great King's struggle for ascension to the Zulu throne against his contender brother. Even now, these seven years later, Usibebu was only in his early thirties but a man of great importance and of indepedent will. He had been the leader of the peace party in the higher councils of Cetshwayo; he believed that agreeing to the ultimatums of the British, however galling, was worth the avoidance of this war. When the British came to know Zulu ways, they would trust them, Usibebu said. But Usibebu and those who had agreed with him lost out to the ones who wanted the military showdown, and having been thus voted down and finally completely overriden by the royal decision, Usibebu took command of his fierce and loyal *inDlu-yengwe* regiment and placed it and himself at the service of the Great King.

It was to this fiery, brave and intelligent premier *inDuna* that Bayele was now led, to report of his experiences and his observations. The sharp featured, hawk-eyed, youthful looking *inDuna* probed with many questions. Clearly he was interested in the possibility of attacking the large guns to capture them. Bayele was able to report that he had seen the guns swing their muzzles to the south-east to train against his own regiment who were attacking the one-armed chief in that sector. The big guns were taking a dreadful toll of Zulu lives and were demoralizing those who had to fight among its range of explosives. But Bayele had noted that the guns only fired when the white soldiers had pulled the rope and then ran to one side as the fire shells blasted out towards their destructive goals. Usibebu was very pleased with the knowledge. He immediately set up runners to tell the young warriors of the *inGabamakhosi* to take cover whenever they saw the soldiers who fired the big guns run to one side. Thus the fire demons were tamed. And indeed this tactical response to the large weapons the Zulus had never before experienced was to reduce their effectiveness to acceptable limits.

Chief Usibebu decided that this was time to launch the attack against the Native Corps defending these guns, especially now that they were not pointed in the direction from which the attack would be launched. And, if Bayele were up to it, he was welcome to join this attack. He could carry the shield of the regiment and become an honorary member on the spot. Bayele was proud of this appointment by so great an *inDuna*, who stood next to the Great King himself in his councils and in his decisions.

The Natal Kaffirs, whose runners had failed to return with ammunition for their pathetically few guns, gaped when they saw the great wave of Usibebu's attackers rise and start forward. Their officers rode behind the terrorized men, shouting and cursing, trying to prevent them from breaking. But this battle was lost before it was started. Many of the men immediately tore away the red insignia they had been given to distinguish them as British soldiers, casting the tattered bits of cloth aside as they ran in whatever direction might carry them away from this terrible arena of death and slaughter. Of course, *real* British soldiers did not run away from battle (except when defeat was beyond doubt). On the other hand, a Royal Artillery unit had a special mission – to preserve its big guns at all costs. Lives of soldiers were labelled 'dispensable', but the shining metal fabrications, with their removable frontal pieces called limbers, were another matter. They were rare and costly and it was a point of great pride that their capture be prevented whatever the human cost. Therefore, when the first charge scattered the forward defenders of the guns, Stuart Smith was left with no alternative. He withdrew his sword and shouted to the gun crews, 'Limber up! Limber up! Save the guns!'

Desperately the gun crews attached the limbers to the gun carriages and with frantic speed the horses were harnessed into their traces. Down the slope from the plateau the Zulu lines boiled, closer. The horses struggled but had hardly moved before the front line of the Zulus arrived. The gun crews started fighting, stabbing with bayonets, shooting when they could get off shots, dying and killing. The men in the limber boxes flailed the horses to make them strain harder until the wheels took hold, then moved. Here was transportation out of hell! The fleeing native defenders tried to grab the traces in an effort to mount the carriages – one lone way, possibly, to escape the deadly warriors. But the crews used their bayonets to beat and, finally, stab them off.

The forward Zulus arrived. Every weapon that was at hand was used – bayonets, spears, hunting knives. Some of the defenders were dragged off the carriages by Zulus. Some of those who were trying to mount the carriages were dragged off by those behind them who wanted to take their places. The carriages had built up speed. The most swift-footed of the Zulus were running alongside, and *assegais* plunged into the backs of those who thought they could get away faster by mounting the gun carriages. The fire of the gun crews on the limber seats was directed particularly against those Zulus who were attempting to *assegai* the animals. The guns began to outdistance the pursuers. Rocking like armoured sulkies, they raced back towards the camp, the heavy wheels flinging off the clutching hands of the Zulus, the horses riding down and crushing intervening bodies, the huge wheels jolting over fallen dead and dying bodies, bloodying the earth with crushed flesh and fragmented bones.

Within 100 yards of reaching the eastern defence line manned by the Imperial troops at the camp centre, the wheels of one of the gun carriages crossed with the wheels of the other. Axles locked. Both carriages slewed violently, throwing off several of the men, then together whipped to a stop. The gun crews leapt to the ground struggling to separate the locked axles. A hundred yards away, CSM Williams was repositioning a squad, including Private Williams, on the inner camp defence line when he saw the danger to the interlocked artillery pieces. The pursuing Zulus were catching up rapidly and could not be brought under fire without imperilling the artillery crews.

CSM Williams made an immediate decision. He waved his arm for a forward charge, calling out, 'Save the guns...! Save the guns...! He ran, followed by his squad of Redcoats, including Private Williams. They reached the stalled guns immediately and started to help the artillery crews struggling to free the wheels. No time. The Zulus converged.

The Redcoat squad, responding to CSM Williams's shout, left the wheels to engage the Zulus, first shooting and then, with no time to re-load, bringing up their bayonets against the spears. Private Williams was confused by the mêlée, but jerked his gun to his shoulder as a Zulu charged him. To his considerable surprise it went off and he saw a large bloody hole appear on the powerful black chest of his attacker; the man fell. The private immediately wanted to tell CSM Williams what he had done, turned to see the Sergeant bayonet a Zulu by parrying the *assegai* thrust, then with great ferocity thrusting the blade through the centre of the black warrior's body so that it protruded by several inches at the other side before he withdrew it to allow the dead enemy to fall to the ground.

Private Williams felt he had to congratulate his stalwart leader, and shouted out 'Sarn't'. This call caught the

CSM's attention just as two more Zulus appeared along-side. Private Williams realized he should not have distracted the Sergeant as he saw the Zulus thrust together. CSM Williams sagged to the ground. The two Zulus, intent upon getting at the guns, didn't bother to take the added measures that were necessary to finish off the fallen man. Instantly, Private Williams was down on his knees alongside his Sergeant trying to pick him up. The battle for the guns swirled about them. Private Williams was crying, begging, 'Come on, Sarn't! I'll help you ... up....'

But shocked white as he was, dying, CSM Williams recognized the danger of any assistance whatsoever from this particular source. That would be the end of all chance of succour. As Private Williams struggled to raise him, CSM Williams pleaded with what little strength of voice he had, 'No ... no ... please don't.'

But Private Williams was not to be deterred from his responsibility. And somehow he raised CSM Williams to his feet and there, holding him erect, he spoke his last words, 'Don't worry, Sarn't, I'll take care of everything....' Possibly CSM Williams, certainly not Private Williams, saw the single *assegai* thrust that penetrated both their bodies, so that they fell and died together in an instant, pinned together, a Siamese twin corpse named Williams.

Just beyond them more Redcoats died to give the guns time to have their carriages unlocked and the attempt to save them to go on. Somehow the locked wheels were separated, and soon the rocketing wheels of the limbered guns were moving at speed, the horses once more galloping towards the defence lines at the centre of the camp.

But there was no longer a simple avenue to safety at the end of which lay a defended refuge for beleaguered men, for frightened beasts, or for the polished guns of the Fifth Brigade of Her Majesty's Royal Artillery. Another swarm of Zulus, running with deft purpose, shouting their war cries in shattering unison, had broken through from the north, so that the Redcoats at the centre had to turn from the guns to defend their own backs. There would be no more protection behind these defence lines. The men on the limber boxes steered the horses southward. It was all too much for the animals – the flailing of the gun crews trying to get them moving, maddened shouting from every quarter, the wild running of the Zulus, and the closeness of the crashing volleys. The horses whinnied in fear, reared in their traces and then, crazed by the discordant violence, careered forward, their hooves pounding as they accelerated south, crossing through the lower camp centre, the heavy destructive wheels and the swerving big guns dragging down tents, overturning hot cauldrons which still boiled violently over the fires of the field-kitchen. Some men thus met death by scalding; the scything guns crushed others and the charioteer artillery men themselves were flung from untenable perches to the rocky ground, some to be mangled immediately under the furious great wheels, the other mortally hurt by the sheer violence of their falls or else quickly caught by the pursuing Zulus whose *assegais* flashed out death so rapidly there was hardly a pause in their pursuit of the fleeing gun carriages.

Vereker's white servant, Harding, saw that the camp was falling. He ran into the tent to gather his master's effects, having decided that his services to the young honourable could best be performed away from this destructive maelstrom, though precisely where he had not yet a way of knowing. He packed as much and as quickly as he could into a case, then from his pocket extracted a tiny, elegant pistol with which he intended to defend himself. He raised the weapon, held it before him, then stepped outside of the tent squinting his eyes to avoid seeing too much of the danger. He should have looked. There was hardly time for even horror to register on his

face for he had stepped directly into the path of a careering gun carriage. Harding was knocked down, fell under
the horse's hooves, and if there was any life left in him
after that, it was crushed completely away by the over-
weighted wheels. His master's belongings flew from his
hand and scattered on the bloodied earth. Vereker's cut-
glass claret bottle shattered, the ivory-tipped swagger
stick broke cleanly into two pieces, and the good paper
from his silver-edged writing kit, linen-based and of a
most excellent watermark, fell under the wheels and was
ruined beyond further use.

Stuart Smith and the few remaining artillery men still
clinging to their precarious pitching gun carriages had
broken through the south-west corner of the camp and
for a desperate hopeful moment it looked as though they
might continue on the path which had brought them to
this site, on to Rorke's Drift.

The guns could be saved!

But from behind the west side of Isandhlwana the front
tip of the right Zulu horn appeared, crossed the Rorke's
Drift track to obliterate the possibility of such retreat.
The chariot guns attempted a hard veer to the left, on to
the nearly precipitous course to the south. The abrupt
turn was too much for the rear gun carriage. It keeled up,
then over, and crashed against a rock, overturning in
entirety. The men who were on it were hurled to the
ground. Some of them never did rise to their feet again,
and those who did were in the next instant executed by
the black, exultant avengers, now converging from both
sides. And whilst Stuart Smith looked back at this dismaying scene his own plunging horses detected the cliff
edge that fell away into ravine in front of them. Only
when their hooves dug into the rock surface trying to
prevent the inevitable, did the huge, black bombardier
react, tugging at the reins as if this could stop the forty-
foot sheer plunge into rocks falling to torrential waters.
The irrevocable Newtonian laws of momentum would

not be flaunted – the weight of the carriage and of the dense metallic mass of the gleaming bright gun barrel forced the animals forward, over the ravine edge, into unsupported space. Men dropped from the falling gun carriage like soft fruits from a shaken tree.

A many-branched tree that grew out of the cliff face broke the fall of the giant black bombardier who had clung on to the carriage, although most of the others died instantly on the rocks where they fell. He crashed through the branches of the cliff tree, then fell through to the stony-bouldered shore below, on to his back. He was still conscious, just long enough to register in his awareness the amazing sight of two horses dangling in their traces on opposite sides of the bole of the tree which had caught and held the gun carriage. The animals were suspended above him, kicking frantically in their traces, whinnying their desperation. And he saw Zulus clamber up from the bottom of the gorge, hanging on to the rocks and the roots until they were under the horses and were able to *assegai* them, stabbing them in the belly, ending their fears and their lives.

The Zulus cut through the leather straps that held the horses. The dead animals fell away. Then that gun which the bombardier, alone among men, had been able to raise single-handedly free from its carriage, which he had polished unceasingly for the months before this dire moment, crashed downward to become the prize of war of these other black men who had forced it on to this, its last path. The injured bombardier, dazed, tried to rise. At this moment one of the Zulus who was tugging at the captured gun quite casually stepped away from it and stabbed his uniformed black brother, who had fought on the wrong side, to death.

A grizzled Zulu *inDuna* appeared at the top of the cliff and called down. The men in the gorge, tugging their shiny metal prize, raised their spears exultantly. They had captured the mightiest weapon which these vaunted

British soldiers, who were masters of the forces of fire and steel, were able to bring against them. What greater victory could there be?

27

Vereker with his, as yet, essentially intact Sikali troop had a decision to make; but of *sensible* choices he judged there were nil. He had been leading his troop to support the north defenders but ordered a halt when he saw the defences around the artillery positions at the north-east collapse. He had seen the start of the gruesome, ungainly chariot race of the great guns, the fighting between the crews and the fleeing native forces, their near capture by the Zulus and their final escape towards the centre of the camp. Should he reverse and ride to their aid? But while he considered the unlikely possibility of catching up with, let alone protecting, these madly careering vehicles, a tumultuous shout came from his left. He and his riders reacted in time to see the Zulu attackers flood through the gap opened by the fleeing Natal Native contingent, who should never had been posted to defend that vital sector in the first place. Their supply runners had come back with no ammunition. They had neither the inner resolve not exterior weaponery to make a stand. They fled, and the roaring Zulu lines were all in a moment given the opening to attack the back of the north defenders under Cavaye and Mostyn.

Vereker's useful options suffered immediate further reduction. His northward skirmish would now be merely an act of ineffectual bravado, and could be suicidal. Vereker returned his glance southward again. He saw the big guns continuing their flight to the south-west and now, following, also fleeing, native elements streaming south of the camp towards the ravine that terminated that rocky slope. The flight of the refugees was being protected on the east flank by the continuing defence of Durnford and his Basutos. At the camp's centre the square formations of the Imperial companies of the First of the Twenty-fourth, although ragged and penetrated in some spots, still held the semblance of defensible positions. These men would neither break nor run, nor would their officers command them to do so while there was the least vestige of sensible struggle. Earlier there had been more ammunition at the centre than elsewhere, but now the weakness of the volleys indicated that here, too, that same critical lack was developing. One probability for making a useful contribution, Vereker saw, was to once more add his forces to Durnford's The increasing attempt to escape along the path to the south-west could be delayed by supporting Durnford's action, which was keeping the flight path open and the south-east horn from closing.

Durnford and his Basutos re-mounted, then raced from the Big Donga to take up positions closer to the camp. Durnford knew that this would be the last point of possible retreat. He would make the stand 500 yards behind the *donga* at what would be the south-east corner of the encampment, if the encampment still had sufficient formation left to determine its south-east corner. There had been a dramatic increase of refugee traffic from the battle following the lone path to possible escape. And that path would remain open only so long as Durnford prevented the left horn from closing forward at will. As he led his men back for this last stand, as it seemed it must be, he became aware that young Vereker was riding hard from the north, leading his Sikali to this new position. Reinforcement seemed welcome, but yet not of vital importance. Durnford found himself in a strangely uplifted frame of mind, excited, energized, and all his orders flowed easily to his tongue; his men continued to rally to his shouts, and find strength where there should be none, and courage to face death when that came.

What was it amidst all this agony and death and destruction that lifted his spirits now? There was a terrible wrongness all about, but not within him — why? Was it not a strange and awful contradiction which he felt with the edges of his being. There were far more potent forces within him than the exercise of mere mental control with which one practised leadership in war. Something had given him a feeling of incredible power: he was certain that he could make each man under his command surpass himself; that he, Durnford, had it within himself to make even the Zulus themselves exceed their own spirit in the act of defeating him, as now they surely must.

Here now arriving were the incredible Sikali Horsemen, his own recruits, with William Vereker, that remarkably suitable youth, leading them. Behind them ran a squad of some forty Redcoats who had been running southward, but had veered to Durnford, determined to make a stand when they saw a commander under whom they could place themselves.

The advance Zulu line emerged from the *donga* which Durnford and his men had just departed. They formed up to run the gauntlet-distance of death by rifle-fire, to engage the one-armed *inDuna's* men in their new position; but for a significant while the Zulu commanders withheld the next charge while they measured the positon taken up by the remaining defenders under the exultant madman that the one-armed *inDuna* had become. There were still sounds of the defence in its last stages from the north sector. There were important pockets of resistance amongst the crumbling centre. And hence in this southeast sector, as the Zulus came past the abandoned *donga*, the *inDunas* considered how they would attack this flimsy but persistent force before them, only half of it still mounted, but now being reinforced by a number of foot soldiers who wore red coats, and also by the mounted well-uniformed black men, whose numbers had only been slightly decimated throughout their wide-ranging actions.

Vereker and Kambula arrived with the Sikali to place them at Durnford's service.

'How do you wish us to dispose ourselves, sir?' Vereker asked. He clearly saw the illumination which was transforming Durnford's personality. He felt completely confident that Durnford would give the most precise and suitable expression of what needed to be done at this difficult moment. It was strange, thought Vereker, that so short a time ago he had expressed to Lord Chelmsford the commonly felt doubt about what faith or trust one might invest in the leadership of this man. Now, in this embodiment of Hell, that his leadership was along a path to certain death didn't seem relevant. Here was the man who would tell them what to do, where, and when – and, finally, how to die. That he was the man was beyond any doubt.

'Lieutenant....' Durnford then turned his head to include Sergeant Kambula, who was alongside Vereker, 'Sergeant, I will use your help only briefly. When I command you or alternatively, should I fall before I can issue a command ... you are ordered to take what is left of your company and use every means you have to survive. Make for Helpmakker where there are reinforcements, although I still doubt that the Zulus will follow across the Buffalo in force. Now, mark, these are your orders....'

The two men listened with their fullest attention, though their eyes continued to take measure of the Zulu formations 500 yards to the front, visibly readying for their next assault.

Durnford talked with swift clarity and compelling certitude. First he stated the opinion that hope of withstanding defeat could no longer be said to exist. It was appropriate, therefore, that the saving of lives now become the prime consideration; however, capitulation and headlong flight for individual salvation would be counter-productive, inevitably ensuring the maximum of slaughter. The only chance of some of them escaping was that others delay the pursuit. Even then, only those who were mounted and retained their mounts could have reasonable hopes of survival.

Accordingly, he, Durnford, with the Redcoat reinforcements and other foot elements, would keep this south-east attack at bay for as long as possible to protect the south refugee route behind them. The Colonel's immediate concern was the rapid extension of the south-east horn by the continual arrival of Zulu reinforcements. Its steady growth would soon enable it to circle south of Durnford's new defence line, to threaten it from the rear and simultaneously cut off the refugees path.

He suggested that Vereker and Kambula with their Sikali skirmish south to engage the Zulu charge at its extended tip, riding hard to prevent any flanking threat, using maximum fire-power to delay its advance. Durnford's troops would maintain a holding position with careful use of whatever fire-power they had and, when that became futile, would fall back again. This last retreat would be a tactical fall-back to encourage the Zulus facing the Sikali to sortie north to get to the encampment by the less dangerous opening thus offered them. Having contributed to diverting the encirclement, the Sikali could depart knowing there was nothing else useful they could do. Therefore, let them gallop west and south themselves to the escape route to the ravine. If they succeeded in reaching the river, and then were successful in crossing the river torrents, Durnford recommended that they use the ammunition left to them to cover any other refugees attempting the crossing. But in due course the ammunition would be exhausted and opposition of all sorts would be of no avail. Then let them all, and this was his final command, make full effort to escape Zululand, to ride to Helpmaaker and there ally themselves with the last-resort defences of Natal, should that course be necessary. Durnford paused. Vereker and Kambula sat silently on their mounts. Their instructions were complete and their job, they knew, was to carry them out exactly.

'And may God go with you,' said Durnford quietly.

'No, my Colonel,' said Kambula, 'Let the Good Jesus stay here with you.'

Durnford looked at this man, the son of another who had died for him at Bush Pass seven years before. This one he had justed ordered to live. For Vereker there were no words, though he felt the need to hold out his hand and create some contact between them. At this moment the Zulu cries of 'U-Su-Tu' reached their loudest. All thought fled as the final charge against the south-east defence was launched.

The Sikali horsemen whirled southward, whooped out their own battle cries, spurred to carry out their defence as Durnford commanded.

The final defence occurred as Durnford had predicted. Vereker and the Sikali harried the south end, making it falter under a dashing, elusive attack and its accurate firing from saddle. In spite of the intensity of their own engagement, Vereker kept watch on Durnford's action. He saw the foot-soldiers end their racing retreat to kneel in a long ranging line, turning to face the upper arc of the attackers. The *inDuna* on the hillside thrust his spear forward, the mass 'U-Su-Tu' cries for the blood of their enemy rang from the 5000 throats as the thundering attack converged forward.

On Durnford's shouted command of 'Fire!' there was a thunderous volley at 200 yards. Many Zulus fell but the others continued forward without pause, and it was clear that another organized volley could not take place before they were upon the defenders. Durnford shouted, 'Reload! ...Fire at will!' and the last stages of the defence were initiated. The men on foot fired until there was no option but to stand and meet the *assegais* with their bayonets. Durnford stood with his sword and, such was the demonic account that he gave of himself as death flashed about him, that the group of Zulus who first encountered him fell back to reconsider how this divinely maddened one-armed man would be dealt with. The Sikali Horse troops continued to fire and fell back on their own section, but only to avoid direct engagement as they had been commanded.

Then came Durnford's shout for his own planned last fall-back. His men fled inward. As he had predicted, the Zulus facing the Sikali ran north to take advantage of the gap this action created. Vereker shouted his final order, and obediently the Sikali Horsemen and the mounted Basutos who had come with them wheeled so that they need no longer watch the death throes of the men who stood with Durnford. They rode toward the ravine and its possibilities of escape. Only Vereker held his position until he saw Durnford inundated by the last forward surge of the Zulus which swallowed all visible evidence of those who had participated in Durnford's last stand. Only then did Vereker rein his horse about.

His men were already disappearing as their horses fought for footing along the steep downward path into the ravine. Vereker kicked Dandy forward. After a few moments the declivity steepened. Suddenly Dandy's front hooves slipped off the edge of an unbalanced rock, and tumbled to his side. Vereker was thrown. Dazed for a moment by the force of the fall on the rock surface, he was aware that the horse had scrambled to its feet and, in alarm, bolted on downward. Vereker was horseless and the Zulus from behind were advancing. He calculated his chances for what they were, but his mind hazed. He tried to raise himself to flee, but the blow to his head had a more pernicious effect than he had imagined. When he was halfway up, he paused, wavered, and crashed back to the ground again, unconscious.

28

At the centre of the camp, Henry Pulleine tallied his
losses. He looked to the north, saw a fresh Zulu line
forming up well to the south of the *donga* which was
supposed to have been the holding line for Mostyn and
Cavaye's companies. He had to presume they were gone
and that his beleaguered Imperial companies holding at
the centre of the camp would now have to bear the added
weight of direct assault from the bull's head and loins, as
well as the frontal eastern assault and the closing end of
the horns from the south-east and ultimately the south-
west. At the south-east there seemed to be some fragmen-
tary defence from Durnford's men. He used binoculars,
but there was no sight whatsoever of his one-armed
senior officer. He noted that some of the irregular and
native mounted elements were making their way towards
the river via the rocky ravine he knew lay in that direc-
tionl With only the defenders of the camp centre to supply, the ammunition trickle was now being maintained.
But each assault of the Zulu warriors, unending in their
determination, seemingly unfearful of the sure death for
so very many of them, had created irreparable breaches
in the lines.

He stood in front of his tent, sword in hand, calculat-
ing their chances when the north charge was finally
launched. He concluded that continuing the defence after
that would have a negligible effect. He noted Lieutenants
Coghill and Melvill on their excited, shying horses,

themselves sweated, black with gunsmoke, shouting commands at the Redcoat defenders, using their pistols and swords with quite excellent results. Good chaps, he thought, and damn shame. Why hadn't His Lordship responded to the urgent messages he had sent? There must have been at least three in a row he could remember, he was sure now. These lads deserve some support. If only some of the artillery units with which poor Stuart Smith had claimed he could win the battle, had been returned, or some of those companies that Chelmsford had taken with him. He wouldn't be in this predicament, this predicament of making a final decision. The point was, one didn't flee a going battle, if there was any chance at all, and even then one did one's best.

But there were some things also one must not leave undone. For instance, one didn't let the damn enemy capture big armament if one can possibly help it; at all costs, one didn't let the regimental colours fall into the hands of a bunch of damned killers. This might be the end of a sizable section of the regiment, for the moment, but there was always future regimental history to consider. Yes, the moment was very near at hand. The line at the north was gathering; once again the warriors were increasing the noisy beat of their shields, shouting out the war cries that would propel them into battle on the command from the wise, grey *inDunas* who were directing their action.

Pulleine decided. He stepped quickly into his tent and re-emerged, carrying the Queen's colour of the First Battalion in its old leather case. There was fighting all around him as he emerged, Zulus stabbing in duels with bayoneteers, redhot guns which had jammed now being used as clubs to defend the soldiers who still had effective weapons they could reload and fire. He moved as quickly as he could to Melvill; both of the young officers looked at him, not understanding what he was doing here on his feet looking up at them, trying to get their attention

242

through the noise of the battle.

'Gentlemen, I would be grateful if you would carry the colours to safety.'

An objection formed itself on Melvill's lips, but he followed Pulleine's gaze northward and saw the sweep of the Zulu centre bear down towards them. To acknowledge the need to leave with the colours at this point was to acknowledge that they would be abandoning those who remained to the certain and dire fate which had already taken so many of the camp. There were shouts and screams of frenzy and pain, and the two mounted officers turned their heads to see the lines in front of them crumble further, and more and fiercer hand-to-hand develop. Melvill reached down from his saddle, and received the case at the end where the staff protruded. He placed it across the saddle, and then he and Coghill shook hands with Pulleine. Melvill raised himself in the stirrups and shouted out as loudly as he could, 'Save the colours! Save the colours!'

Coghill raised himself in a similar fashion and echoed Melvill's shout. There was the briefest pause as the Redcoats took in the implication of what they were hearing. Then there was a loud cheering response, 'Save the colours! Save the colours!' The defenders redoubled their work and Coghill and Melvill spurred on, breaking through a gap in the south end of the square, heading for the opening towards the ravine still being defended by the remnants of Durnford's group.

From the steps of the supply wagon Boy-Pullen watched the two officers ride away carrying the colours. He was still helping Quartermaster Bloomfield drag out the ammunition boxes and serve the ammunition to the runners who still had to dally longer than they should.

'They went away with the regimental colours, Quartermaster,' Boy-Pullen's voice was weak, apprehensive.

Bloomfield's answer was characteristically hearty, 'We got seventy thousand bullets here, boy, and there aren't that many Zulus left, are there?' He winked at Boy-Pullen. 'We're not goners yet, son. Now you stay along and help me, understand.' Boy-Pullen did as he was told, but he didn't feel at all well, nor even reassured.

After Melvill and Coghill had disappeared in the rocks to the south, Pulleine returned to his tent. Inside he sat at his writing table, taking his pistol out of its holster and laying it alongside some sheets of paper. He seized a quill and started to write. He hadn't time to dispatch a letter to his wife before they'd left the last position *en route* to Isandhlwana. If there was any chance whatsoever that he could give her some reassurances about how he felt about this moment, about this end ... he forced himself to put the words correctly in his mind ... he would feel a good deal more content. But then he broke off the writing, signed quickly as the exterior sounds confirmed his own prediction that when the north assault reached the Imperial lines, the defence would end. He must join his men ... but even before he could rise, the flap of his tent was pulled roughly aside.

What he saw was quite astonishing to him. He was certain that this was the young man who had been his captive the night before. The stalwart young Zulu warrior had his *assegai* lifted into thrust position. Pulleine was able to snatch up his pistol and fire. He saw blood form on the young man's cheek. Bayele felt the sting, touched his cheek and saw the blood. He saw the officer's gun point more precisely. He lunged forward and stabbed at the officer just as the gun fired a second time. The officer slumped across the papers on his desk, dead.

Bayele looked down at his own body to see if the second bullet had injured him, but there was no evidence that such had happened. He didn't understand why this was so, but he was quite ready to accept that it hadn't. He noted the bottle of ink on the dead officer's desk. He picked it up and sniffed it, wondering if it was something pleasant to drink, like the strong fiery alcoholic liquid which he knew was called gin. But the ink exuded an unpleasant smell. He turned it upside down and poured it on to the partly turned-up face of the dead man. He saw the man's cheek turn black, bluish-black, as if he were turning into a black man. This amused Bayele and he poured the rest of the ink over the man's face. He examined the pen and he picked up the pistol, which he tucked under the antelope hide waistband of his breach clout, and then he examined some of the other strange and finely wrought objects in this domain, where, for the moment, he was master. Then some other warriors looked into the tent and indicated that they were going to run on to the south to chase the soldiers who had escaped in that direction. Bayele stabbed at Pulleine's mid-section, releasing his warrior's spirit, then ran out of the tent carrying the mementoes which were his prizes.

He ran swiftly southward down the slope, towards the ravine that crossed at the bottom of the plain. Bayele had been a part of the opening fray of this war, and he wanted to see it to its victorious conclusion. The Redcoat soldiers who were running and riding away, he wanted to make sure, would not run too far. There was still justice, Zulu justice to be done. The Great King would expect this from his warriors and they expected it equally from themselves.

Inside the tent, Pulleine looked a bit as if he had fallen asleep while writing a letter, his head cradled on his arm; the letter was still intact, signed with his final love for his wife to whom he had always written so regularly. But the preternatural stillness, the awkward thrust of his arm across the desk, the blood that stained his red jacket into patchier darker red, and the ink that Bayele had poured across his blond features in a grotesque blue-black stain were evidence that this was the irreversible sleep so abundant here this day under the peak of Isandhlwana.

245

The charge from the north, which had carried Bayele through the crumbling lines, had also engulfed the particular ammunition supply wagon where Quartermaster Bloomfield and bugler Boy-Pullen had been working desperately to open the intractable boxes, trying to meet the endless requirements of those trying to stay alive for a few minutes longer. Other of the wagons had already been set afire with brands of firewood which some of the attackers had conveniently found in the cooking fires that had been scattered by the passage of the gun carriages.

Boy-Pullen did not want to look outside when he heard the Zulus arrive, and hardly looked up when a desperate Redcoat defending himself with his bayonet entered the rear of the wagon in his retreat from three Zulus lunging at him with their stabbing spears. Bloomfield dragged out his pistol, trying to centre it on a target. Boy-Pullen ducked below the stack of cartridge boxes. But the Zulus dispatching the Redcoat came no further into the wagon; this was not out of shyness, but because almost at the same instant some of their enterprising fellow warriors had applied the burning fire brands to the canvas of the wagon on its outside. There was a quick upward *whoosh!* of flame and heat, and in the next moment an inferno of burning canvas. The Zulus were forced to back out quickly as gouts of the burning material fell inward. Bloomfield, inhaling this super-heated atmosphere of smoke, choked almost instantly and fell to the floor clutching his throat. Bending low, hysterically fearful, Boy-Pullen streaked for his life to the back of the wagon. Burning, choking, he emerged. Perhaps there was a fraction of second of horror in his eyes as he saw the *assegai* that was to spit him, then impale him into the wood stanchion of the wagon rear. It had lunged out at the same moment that he thought he might be free. Cartridges from the cases in the burning wagon were already exploding in violent staccato cacophony. Pinned through his body to the wagon, the young Bugler boy's uniform and body started to burn as he joined his Quartermaster in this final fiery conflagration.

After this there was no significant defence left anywhere in the area of the encampment. More and more of the Zulus were streaming towards the ravine where the few refugees had fled. In the camp itself, large hordes of the attackers were looking for the booty that in some small measure would signify the vastness of their victory. If movement among the many there fallen was discovered, a spear thrust terminated it. In most cases the release was merciful. Wagons and tents still cracked fiercely, in some cases, but in others the burning was already dying out. A down-draught of air from the mountains made the burnings fierce and brief. The long shadow of the sun that was descending behind the Isandhlwana peak already began to reduce the grotesque clarity within the two-mile-square area of carnage and death. The air was rapidly growing colder, and it would not be long before the naked-chested warriors who roamed, turning over bodies and searching through the contents of the fallen tents, would begin to feel it. But at this moment the heat of battle was still with them.

29

Coghill and Melvill were desperately fighting to control
their horses as they scrambled down a most hazardous
rocky declivity. Twice, using swords and pistols, they
had fought their way through groups of Zulus who had
launched onslaughts. Everywhere the Redcoats or Native
soldiers who were on foot were being overtaken. And
whatever account they managed to give for themselves in
their last efforts to survive, they were dispatched relent-
lessly and without exception. But the young officers had a
single mission – to save the regimental colours. Somehow, if this happened, an illogical equation would be able
to be drawn in the future whereby the loss of the Imperial
forces would not be considered total. The colours, the
precious colours would have been saved.

The river torrent at the bottom of the grade was still
another fearsome challenge. Where to cross? But there
was not time to choose among equally dangerous possibilities. Behind them a rattle of stones brought their
heads about – rushing full tilt down the slope they saw
the pursuing party of Zulus. These paused not at all
when Coghill and Melvill emptied their handguns at
them. The young officers reined about, drove their reluctant animals into the torrent. Hardly one step into the
swirling water and there was no more footing. Saving the
colours became a matter of sink or swim. The two young
officers clung to saddles as the horses swam, heads lifted
against the pulsing torrential water. Melvill made far

shore first, started up the embankment. Behind him, Coghill's horse found hooves-purchase on the river bottom. Coghill climbed on to the saddle, but the horse shied even as his master half raised himself in the stirrup. Coghill was thrown on to a sharp rock; he grimaced in anguish and when he tried to find footing, discovered that his right leg just couldn't support him. Melvill came back quickly to the shore to give his friend a hand out of the rapid waters. Coghill found all movement unbearbly painful. Melvill struggled with him, then suddenly shouted in pain, grabbing his own arm. In fact, they were being fired at by three advancing Zulus using captured rifles. The wounded men waited helplessly.

But then Kambula's riders, who had crossed tactically, appeared downriver. They quickly skirmished upriver along the embankment to engage the Zulus who were firing at Melvill and Coghill. There was an exchange of fire, but suddenly a downpouring of more attackers leapt among the Sikali. Men were being dragged from their horses, and in spite of the superb control of the riders, the animals began to buck and whinny at the fury of the onslaught. No more defence was possible. Melvill and Coghill were cut off by a small army. Kambula had to lead those remaining up the far bank in the sole direction of escape whilst this was still possible. Coghill and Melvill, now alone, both hurt badly; they clung together, dragging each other up the embankment. They reached the horses and somehow each managed to fall across his saddle, but the Zulus were upon them. They and their horses were quickly brought down even as the animals attempted to scramble up the embankment. When they and their animals were dead one of the Zulus picked up the regimental colours, tore it from its standard and waved it aloft.

The squad of Zulus ran in formation looking for other

fugitives, the one man running in front of them bearing the regimental colours of Her Majesty's Twenty-fourth Foot.

Nearly 2000 men had remained on the lower slopes of Isandhlwana that morning when Lord Chelmsford had departed them. Only a few dozens, the fortunate few able to retain horses for the most part, were to survive.

Vereker had managed to fall into a space between two boulders that provided him unexpected concealment. It was even possible that the most dangerous thing he did was to revive minutes later and attempt to move. He was half risen before he even realized where he was and what was going on. But as recollection broke through his daze, he started taking account of his position. First he turned his head in an arc covering the north view from west to east, and he saw instantly that coherent defence had everywhere ceased. There were pockets of firing and of movement here and there, but many of these terminated even as he watched. He saw the hordes of Zulus foraging, searching the area for booty. Some were even attempting to move the great wagons. There was more purposeful movement to his immediate right and left. He was able to recognize that the *inDunas* who were still actively commanding the search contingents were directing them into paths of pursuit towards the ravine. He realized too that he had no choice but to move forward immediately. He removed his hands from the rock supporting him, and promptly started to sink to one knee again, eyes glazing as he panted to fill his lungs with air. He waited for the onslaught of dizziness to subside. He pressed his hand to his head and became aware of an intensely painful area at his temple, recognized the fact that his helmet was missing and that his hair was thickly wet with blood still oozing from what felt like a rather nasty jagged head wound.

A hundred yards in front of him he saw the two Boer volunteers controlling their horses with difficultly down the precipitous rock-strewn slope which led to the bottom of the ravine. If only he could rise and call them. But they were being pursued themselves, and they disappeared quickly downhill. It was immediately evident that his single chance at survival was to get himself on horseback. He noted a few riderless animals, but all at distances that made trying to reach them impractical.

Yet every moment that he remained where he was would increase his chance of being detected, whatever the security of this small area of concealment. Peering over the edge of the rock he saw a tiny flash of red colour from behind another group of boulders just forty or fifty yards to the south, along the pathway he would have to follow. That wasn't – there *was* another soldier there, trying as he was to stay alive, hoping for some succour to mitigate against the inevitable. Vereker wished him luck.

Indeed, it was the red sleeve of Private Store's tunic that Vereker had seen momentarily. That young man's quite marvellous aptitude for survival had continued to work for him all the way from the north defence, through the centre of the camp where death could have occurred many times in any one minute, and now down here more than a mile and a half from his starting position, within sight almost of the river across which lay his sole chance of safety. But how to get to it, and across it, and through the marauding Zulus who were already there and waiting in many locations? He too was searching for a free horse, although as an infantry man his experience of riding was very limited. He tilted the bottle of gin his Corporal's coin had purchased for him from an optimistic mate. He held the bottle up steeply, for this was the end of it, but he was grateful for the minor warming comfort that it brought.

Then his chance came! As he stared steadily at one of the riderless horses that had been grazing at a distance too far for him to chance, it raised its head in a whinny, for no good reason at all, then trotted forward in the direction of Private Store's boulder. For a moment it looked as if the beast would come directly to the rock where he waited. Store had no way of knowing that fifty yards above him towards the battlefield a young blond subaltern was hoping that the same horse would veer a bit more northward. The horse, however, accommodated neither of the two concealed men to the extent that each wished. But it did end up reasonably close to where Store had stretched himself out flat on the ground behind his less concealing rocks. It was now or never. He raised himself to a sprinter's crouch and, holding on to his rifle, the last piece of military impedimenta he had not yet discarded, launched himself forward. But only when he was well and truly exposed, completely committed to his course of action, the horse took one frightened look at the figure sprinting at it, reared, then bolted. Store cursed and lunged, touched the flying reins only to feel them slip through his fingers.

He was instantly aware that Zulus who had been running on a path parallel to his down towards the ravine stopped running as they saw him. They cut across from their path of chase to the suddenly revealed quarry. He had landed belly down after his flying leap. He sat up to bring his rifle forward to his shoulder. But he also knew that he had only one round of ammunition in it, already loaded. He had been saving that for an eventuality, and this was undoubtedly an eventuality, multiplied by twenty-five or thirty; for this was the number of Zulus who were charging towards him. Store still felt that he had the power for making a decision. He could at least pick the man he was going to kill.

'Make it a good one, Store, ... it's your last.' He searched among the advancing Zulus for the target that most appealed to him. But then he noted that 200 yards behind them stood a pair of *inDunas* who had been directing the encircling movement of the horns. He was able to make out the grey head of the one he felt was acting with the greatest authority. Store very carefully aimed and fired his last round just before the marauding party reached him. The *inDuna* fell from his perch on the hillside and rolled inertly down the hill, ending his descent in a lifeless sprawl. By the time he had absorbed this satisfying bit of information he was in no position whatsoever to defend himself against the simultaneous strokes of the *assegais* that plunged into him, taking his life also.

Neither did Store realize that he had made a contribution to the chances of an officer, Vereker, who used the distraction of the most forward party of Zulus going for Store to take a chance of his own. In a low crouch he managed to reach one of the aimlessly moving riderless horses. He seized its reins, and then after a groggy moment of steadying himself, he dragged himself across the saddle and finally managed to sit upright in it. But then to his surprise, apparently from nowhere, ran two of the uniformed Basutos from Durnford's own mounted infantry. They cut directly into his path. They moved forward pointing to the horse and to Vereker and speaking rapidly in their own tongue. Vereker stared, realized that he was being told something quite urgently. The words were similar to the Zulu language, that he knew, but these were spoken in a strange accent and with such a tumble of varying inflections that he could extract only a minimum sense from them. One of the Basutos was badly wounded and he was the one that was speaking most excitedly. Vereker shook his head, showing his perplexity.

253

'What are you saying old boy? What about this horse?' He turned his head to the fitter of the two black men, 'What's he saying?' And then he repeated the question immediately in Zulu.

The second Basuto answered him firmly, in English, pointing at the animal on which Vereker sat. 'His horse. He say you on *his* horse'.

Verker stared at the two men for a moment. He looked beyond them and noted also that Zulus were converging from several directions; the remaining moments for doing anything sensible were few indeed. On the other hand, what could he do in the face of the information he had been given?

'I see ...,' Vereker said slowly, 'it's *his* is it?' The second Basuto nodded seriously.

Vereker pensively slid off the horse back onto the ground. 'Didn't realise old chap, dreadfully sorry.' Watching the closing Zulus he helped the wounded man on to the saddle. The second Basuto lost his aplomb as the Zulus coverged within yards and he clambered desperately on to the back of the saddle. The forward man spurred and the horse managed to gallop with the tandem riders, plunging down the slope beyond the grasp of the Zulus who tried to close in on it. Vereker watched the Basutos go for a moment, then stooped down to pick up a handy-sized rock, wondering if somehow or other he could defend himself. He wasn't even aware of the group of warriors who had closed in behind him while he waited for the likely forward onslaught. But, if he had been able to turn, it is quite possible that he would have recognized that one of the *assegais* that extinguished his life – a substance of greatly diminished value to him these days, in any event, was held in the black-knuckled grasp of the young Zulu whom he had held prisoner until this very morning of his last day.

As far as Bayele was concerned, the justice in his final

254

act of battle for his King was truly perfect, a consummation of devotion to the great spirits who had made the Zulus, the Children of Heaven.

30

The information that had been reaching His Lordship had not been particularly clear. It was, however, of persistent enough nature to suggest that there was, possibly, something quite seriously wrong at the encampment he had left at Isandhlwana. That there were forces of Zulus in considerable numbers in the direction of the Nqutu plateau seemed now to be undeniable, although he had earlier thought that this was most unlikely. Considering the choices he had at hand, he had come to the decision that it was advisable to rejoin his separated forces, and that the most direct way of seeing this done was for him to take his own column back to the encampment. Then, he had decided, if the defenders were in more serious trouble than he thought was probable, he would be there at the right place at the right time to save the situation.

He had sent orders forward to stop Hamilton-Browne's advance to the encampment so that a cohesive and a fully implemented force, including Hamilton-Browne's natives, could meet whatever problems there were there, in a united fashion, under a single command, his own. The companies he commanded, his own staff, the elements of artillery under Harness which had been intercepted, Chelmsford's own pipers, Crealock and Harford, and the Seventeenth Lancers who made such an imposing escort moved at a measured pace towards the west and slightly north from whence they had departed not that long ago.

The trader, Fannin, rode toward the shadow of the peak of Isandhlwana, his head hanging down. He was more than half-paralysed with the continuous flow of alcohol he had been imbibing since the time he had decided he would be safer back at the encampment than hanging on with Hamilton-Browne and his recalcitrant native soldiers in the middle of no-man's land between two large Imperial armies. The horse was plodding forward by instinct rather than under the direction of its stupefied master drooped semi-conscious in his saddle, eyes more closed than open, unaware of his surroundings. The weary horse carried Fannin through the strewn boulders at the far south-east of the battlefield and outlying evidence of devastation. The horse plodded on.

A party of Zulus searching in fading light moved amongst their victims, not heeding the approaching rider. For no good reason, particularly, the fat man raised his head, looked about to see where he was. A disturbing aspect of the vision before him managed to penetrate through the fog of his inebriation. He sat blinking, jaw sagging, trying to cope with the details.

What he saw before him, only by yards, was the bared back of a Zulu warrior bent over a prostrate red-coated figure, attempting to roll it face up. Fannin didn't realize there was anything wrong in this until it was evident that what the Zulu was after was the rifle upon which the soldier had fallen. When the Zulu had untrapped the rifle he dropped the corpse, revealing it for what it was. The precise meaning of the incident still evaded the plump trader, but it was evident that he did not in the least approve of what the Zulu was doing. Swaying, trying to focus, he raised a peremptory finger and, thick-lipped, started to scold the man, saying 'I say ... there, you. . . .'

The Zulu looked up, saw Fannin, raised his newly acquired rifle and squeezed the trigger. The bullet threw up dirt at the feet of Fannin's horse, which promptly reared, whinnying in terror, whereupon the Zulu fired a second time. Miraculously Fannin held on and when the horse returned its four feet to the ground he was already pointed in the opposite direction, and galloping away. Clinging to the neck of the out-of-control beast Fannin was nonetheless able to twist about to get a more comprehensive view of where he had been. The only moving figures were Zulus. A group of them appeared, chased after the horse, brandishing their spears and laughing, but not really making a serious attempt to bring down the panic runaway. Their King had told them they could distinguish between civilians and soldiers by the red tunics that the white soldiers would be wearing. These warriors merely enjoyed the terror of the fat white man on a horse, and tried to increase it with their shouts and their fleet pursuit; for a moment it looked as if they would catch him up, horse or not. Other Zulu groups, stripping other red-coated corpses, taking command of the weapons and articles of clothing, looked up to see the fleeing rider but did no more than get on with their more rewarding effort. Fannin could see that when the bodies of the fallen Redcoats were stripped the abdomens were stabbed open.

A mile and a half south-east of the outer limits of the battlefield Fannin appeared as a small riding figure charging towards the returning army led by Chelmsford. Signal was given, halting the column, but shortly after, when it was discerned who it was who rode towards them the march forward was continued. Harford had spurred ahead during the brief halt and, some hundreds of yards in advance of the main contingent, could be seen intercepting the fat man's path. Fannin had reined in and was talking excitedly, pointing his finger back towards the camp. There was a change in Harford's demeanour as the message was conveyed, and brought instant concern to Lord Chelmsford's features. He rode directly to the two men, stopped and looked questioningly at Harford; but, characteristically strangled by his severe stutter when emotion beset him, the tumble of words Harford wanted to say refused to issue from his throat. Fannin, his face and mouth slack with fear and the undissipated effects of the alcohol he had consumed, finally supplied the information. 'The camp is fell, my Lord. . . .' He snuffed in and swallowed. '. . . in the hands of the Zulu . . . I saw them all dead . . . dead my Lord. . . .'

Crealock intervened to protect his master from the absurdity of so obscene a remark from this grotesque figure of a man. He spoke sharply to an adjutant, 'Remove this man, he impairs our progress. . . .'

But Chelmsford was transfixed, staring and not doubting in the least.

He spoke to Crealock, not even turning his head, and without pomposity or attempt at command. His voice was low. '. . . No . . . this man would not say what was not so . . . not now, not here. . . .'

Crealock stared. The appalling truth which Chelmsford saw so quickly now struck him with its full force, and the same realization came to all the others within hearing distance. Crealock stared and whispered, 'Fallen . . . ?'

Fannin, in his grossness, didn't have the discretion to recognize the impact his words had had. He had to go on, 'There is not a scrap of fighing left, Your Honour. Just the Zulus everywhere, stripping the dead. I only got away by the mercy of God and . . . ,' he was compelled to finish his utterly gross lie, '. . . and by the use of my pistol . . .'

But Chelmsford hadn't even heard the words, nor was he conscious of the stares of Crealock and all the others, who could do no more than wait for his response. Chelmsford was listening only to his own internal voice, the words that were forming in his mind that he would have to know when the time came for him to have an answer. Were these blurred faces before him inquisitors for whom he need provide an understanding of what his role was in this unbearable tragedy? The voice in his head was saying, '... I would venture to remark that my orders to Lieutenant-Colonel Pulleine and Colonel Durnford regarding the defence of the camp were distinct. The number of soldiers I left behind, six full companies of fine Imperial troops, giving a fire rate of four rifles per yard, was sufficient in my opinion to hold off the entire Zulu army....'

Had he actually spoken these words? or were they only an echo of a future event? He tried to look more clearly at the faces of the mounted men who were waiting for him to speak. Crealock saw that he would have to fill the vacuum. He spoke precisely, even a bit sharply, 'The Infantry will be here in twenty minutes, My Lord.'

Chelmsford's eyes focused, and Crealock could see him run back over in his mind the words that had just been spoken. The delay before they made sense was visible. But Crealock had given Chelmsford the clue he needed to respond to the men who waited for his leadership.

'Yes, we will wait for the Infantry, here, and when they arrive,' his eyes turned to the darkening peak so very close now, 'we will skirmish forward in a defensive position. We will be preceded by mounted scouts to assure that we are not walking into a trap. On arrival at the battlefield area, we will *laager* intensively for the duration of the night, and at first light take account of the situation as it stands there. Arrange guard rosters on full alert at all sectors.'

He nodded curtly to the commander of his escort who understood such signals from His Lordship. The escort commander responded immediately by ordering his men to circle forward and take defensive positions. The command was passed to other sections and the general 'stand to' was maintained as the company waited in position where it had halted.

Young Harford, his mobile features showing the depth to which he was disturbed, looked at Chelmsford, and then squinted his eyes into the sunshine of the west sun almost behind the Isandhlwana peak. He was trembling, and he could not maintain his silence. He spoke in utter disbelief, his agonized stutter impeding almost every word that issued from his throat.

'Y . . . yo . . . you . . . wait for the i . . i . . infantry, m . . m . . m . . my Lor-Lord?'

And with this, he reined his horse about, his intentions evident. Crealock spoke sharply, quickly, to stop him. 'And so will you also, Lieutenant Harford!'

Harford stuttered again in his all-consuming anger, 'So will I n . . n . . n . . not . . !' He kicked the flanks of his horse and it spurred forward towards the increasingly shadowed mountain.

Crealock, white with anger, shouted out, 'Arrest that Officer. . . .!

'*Arrest that officer!*'

Members of Chelmsford's escort who had moved ahead attempted to seize Harford's horse, to intercept his forward movement. But his momentum was too great and he easily veered aside and beyond them. Crealock continued his angry shouting, and might have given some chase himself if Chelmsford had not reached across to his military secretary's horse and plucked him at his sleeve.

'Calmly now, Crealock, calmly. . . .'

Crealock turned, surprised at the mildness of his commander's tone.

Chelmsford continued to speak, 'Calmly now, Crealock . . . there is disaster enough here and perhaps young Harford will bring us useful information.'

For once, all of his emotions appeared on Crealock's face. He was stunned. . . . What were the resources of self-containment that His Lordship had within himself to confront such vast tragedy with such equanimity? He listened in further amazement to His Lordship now

261

speaking in the same mild tone to the commander of his Lancer escort.

'Take a troop of ten, follow Mr Harford. Be alert for ambush, and take no risks. Return in the event of emergency and report your observations. Persuade the young man to do likewise.'

The designated troop galloped forward, watched by those who remained. Crealock, covertly studying his master whose expression was still ringed with a discernibly beatific smile, became aware that the man he knew so well and served so long was outwardly unruffled because most of his attention was given to some curious inner voice that none but he could hear.

And indeed this was the case. The habit of a lifetime was now coming into play to serve its owner's greatest need. He had always, ever, been able to give good account for himself in trying situations, because of this ability to plan the best words from the moment when the need for an account arose. Indeed, it was possible that General Lord Chelmsford heard himself speaking to an imaginary tribunal, before a vast array of important, inquiring people who were waiting to hear what he had to say about this most urgent matter, '... earlier reports from reconnaissance, carried out in the direction from which the enemy in fact eventually did advance, fully justified my moving eastward from the mountain of Isandhlwana....' For one terrible moment His Lordship felt panic in his mind. How would the word 'eastward' be interpreted. Could it mean both *north*-east and *south*-east at the same time? No of course it could not, this would all have to be said differently. Yes, differently.... but the men about him observed only that His Lordship was displaying remarkable self-control in the face of possible disaster of gigantic proportions, already suffered, with another impending, of possibly even greater dimensions. If one column had fallen, why not another? And if that, why not all of Natal? Night was well on its way before the foot companies arrived so that they might move, and the last of the day had vanished completely when His Lordship commanded the halt about a mile south-east of the fallen camp.

Norris-Newman, 'Noggs', was seething with more incredulity than he had ever felt in a lifelong career of exposure to fell chance and wilful violence.

Could it be true? – asked the newsman: two regiments, armed representatives of Her Majesty, including six superb companies of Imperial Redcoats, supported by artillery and even new-fangled rockets, a considerable body of cavalry effectives, (which even if not regular artillery were competent native riders) and several contingents of irregulars and volunteers representing sons of Natal colonists – all these exterminated? Yes! – that was what was said, *exterminated!* Wiped out for ever, by naked savages whose armour was only a shield of peculiar toughness but completely penetrable to rifle bullets, and a weapon made of a sharp blade of iron, bound to hardwood stick, *and*, unmitigated willingness to serve their King and their nation with extraordinary fervour and limitless courage. If the story were true, what a telling it would make! That he should be here, approaching the actual site of such an enormously tragic and unlikely event must be fateful. He didn't dare approach Chelmsford, nor for that matter any of the lower-echelon officers, with his usual questions or probes for information. They couldn't know, no more than he, if they were going to meet the same fate as the comrades with whom they worked and lived and invaded and from whom they had been separated for only a part of one day.

The newsman 'Noggs' had to count himself lucky that he was here at all, moving with these men to observe historic drama beyond expectation. Norris-Newman, as a man, shared with all the other men present the frightened

263

horror of too suddenly seeing torn, mutilated, lifeless versions of men he may have spoken with not that many hours ago. He had to judge what his own response would be to an unseemly question from a news reporter, from anyone, at a time such as this. Of course, he knew the answer, and so he held himself back from carrying out his job in the way to which he was accustomed. There were throbbing pressures at his temples which he had never before experienced. But he rode closely enough behind Lord Chelmsford to observe and remember what he could for future telling of what the most important figure on this evolving landscape would do under these dire circumstances.

His reporter's experience of detecting true states of feeling behind uttered words, however well those words and the postures of the speakers were calculated to conceal the emotions, or intentions, that generated them, had told him instantly all that Chelmsford had successfully kept from the men he led. He read the terror and confusion where an outward mien of calm and control had shown. Noggs tried to think of adequate words which could possibly describe the exploding inner world of a man who a few hours earlier thought he was stepping at last on to the rainbow of success, to find instead that he was plunging into the sulphurous bowels of an endlessly deep hell. The reporter thought it remarkable that this man found resources to issue commands of any kind, even as simple and as useless as the one to wait, at a moment of such possibly urgent need for the infantry to advance. And now here they were, picking their way with utmost caution through an unrevealing night, approaching a destiny unknown and horrors unfaceable.

31

The outline of the peak was clear against a star-filled sky. There were shapes of wagons, or so it seemed, but there was no sound. If there were Zulus here, once again they were achieving remarkable quietude and wraith-like invisibility in vast numbers. Chelmsford had ordered one company to deploy forward to a hill which it would be advantageous to hold if there were lurking foes. This short charge to occupy the hill was preceded by four thunderous volleys, the effect of which could not be known. There was no response, and then the men charged forward. There was more shooting, clearly from British rifles, and then some sound of cheering. A hill had been taken, but against no opposition. The enemy, which Noggs strongly suspected was not to be found on this site at all, had made no stand.

What a pathetic victory for so great a General, thought the reporter. Shall I write of this one? And how will all my readers, and, indeed, the whole of the nation, and the peoples of Europe, and Disraeli, and the men who sit at Westminster, and Her Majesty herself take this news? A wave of pity for this Lord General who commanded blind charges into the unresisting night, against ghosts departed, filled him. Poor man, he thought, poor man. But then in the next instant he was chiding himself, because in his feeling for what Chelmsford would do, based on his reporter's insight, he knew that this man was capable of subtly but surely reconstructing the true history of these terrible events. Whether or not he would be successful was another matter. There had already been words uttered, of finding early evidence that his orders for the defence of the camp had been violated ... blatently so, was the inference.

As they had approached from the east of the camp there had been some alarming signs – fallen bodies of the units that had served under Durnford, which in fact marked the four-mile outer edge of his defensive retreat back to the camp. But hadn't Chelmsford's orders been to maintain the defence *within* the camp? Had such an order been given to Durnford in particular? If so, he had disobeyed it. From miles out! Wasn't Durnford senior officer – senior to Pulleine – and that being so, should he not have taken command of the camp and, at the same time, taken over the orders passed by His Lordship to Pulleine, which were, to be sure, to hold the defence *within* the camp?

Then suddenly there was movement ahead in the darkness! Near-naked, dark figures appeared, and instantly shots rang out. Two of the figures fell before terrorized voices of the others declaimed who they were. Now soldiers ran forward, and it developed that these were by no means an attacking sortie of Zulus, but only a pitiful handful of their own NNC who had been hiding in a ditch in quaking fear through the entire day until just now when, hearing the sounds of their own army, they finally moved forward to find safety. And now one of them was dead, and another seriously wounded. Noggs's despair was bottomless; how could he ever tell these things?

The bivouac was called. In the dark, the army of the living lay down to sleep with the army of the dead. Although at a considerable distance from the main camp where the real carnage would only be revealed when the sun rose again, even here at edges of the battle were many bodies. Some were mutilated, some limbless, some white and some black, the white mostly stripped of clothing, boots and arms ... horses and mules sprawled in their death with the spears that ended their lives protruding from their bloated bellies ... spilled boxes and sacks, supplies, overturned wagons and everywhere the corpses of men, macabre, gruesome even in the blackness. The utterly tired men slept next to those who had fallen in the forward defence positions or during their last desperate and unsuccessful attempts to save their lives by fleeing.

Chelmsford himself, and senior officers he had detailed to assist him, moved among the front lines of the halted column, cautioning the men not to sleep, to stay alert against the possibility of attack from the *Impis* who had not yet revealed themselves. But men who were as tired and as depleted as these were, who had slept so little for three nights, now had no means of staying awake, and no concern or threat could keep them from closing their eyes. But if they turned and moved restlessly they might indeed wake suddenly to find themselves in near embrace with a dead man they had known as a comrade.

These scenes etched themselves in the reporter's mind and their telling would require no notes. He was not under Chelmsford's command, he decided, so that if the Imperial forces were ordered to wait here (he knew that Chelmsford would never allow the morale of these troops to be tested by a daylight view of the main camp) he might never have the opportunity to move forward to see what there was unless he took the chance himself. He doubted Chelmsford's overweaning cautions about lurking enemies, but even firm evidence that Chelmsford might be right about the imminence of attack, were of no consequence compared to his obligation to one day report what lay ahead. There was no possibility that he would be observed in this darkness flaunting Chelmsford's orders to halt. He slipped forward silently, using the silhouette of the hump-back peak against the night sky to guide him.

Noggs moved through the night to the centre of the camp. Though it was difficult to see he could well picture the tableau of destruction from the shadowy forms that covered the ground. He looked up to the sound of drunken singing from Zulu voices. But these were few and scattered. At another instant he felt a sudden draining of strength from the shock of an exploding gun. But it was a single shot, fired at random, and was followed by a second one further away. He came to a burnt-out wagon full of unopened ammunition boxes, and he grimaced and closed his eyes when he saw the charred body of the perky bugler boy known as Boy-Pullen; face charred but recognizable, swinging upside down with his body cut open. But all the postures of death were ugly and unbearable to look at in detail, and here on this plain they seemed endless. There were some spots of light further up on the mountain range. These were undoubtedly camp fires of Zulus who hadn't parted yet, he was certain. But the main force had left, to where he did not know.

At least, Noggs mused, this would test to its fullest Chelmsford's and Frere's theory of the Zulu intention of invasion. With this enormous victory to start them, with the complete shattering of the second column, what was there to prevent them now from crossing the Buffalo and carrying the war into Natal? The answer in short was, nothing at all. The reporter couldn't rule out the possibility, but somehow he doubted that it would happen. And if it hadn't happened, if there was no invasion, then how futile, indeed, was this war of supposed containment, this invasion to stop a counter-invasion that was never meant to be.

Noggs was surprised at his own stamina. He should have been much more tired, much less capable of moving through the night along these rocky slopes and steep inclines. He had noticed, in the past few days of travel, that some of the surplus of flesh which had weighed him down on arrival was beginning to vanish. The nattiness of his clothing, of course, had diminished greatly. He was becoming increasingly aware of the personal uncleanliness which beset his body, and he wondered at the fortitude of the soldiers who, with far fewer amenities, could march endlessly and then fight under such conditions. They were remarkable men, and the officers were remarkable in their way, too. He found it difficult to fathom the meaning of lives that made them impervious to these conditions, and willing and eager, indeed, to find glory in combat for what often seemed ill-defined purposes.

Noggs had been moving further west and slightly south so that he passed the edge of the lower slopes of Isandhlwana. He realized that he was on the trail to Rorke's Drift, and that if he continued in this direction that twenty or so miles further along he would be back where he started. He paused to stare at a curious redness in the sky. Could this be the beginning of morning so soon? No, of course not, and it would be a ridiculous sun that rose in the west, wouldn't it? He turned and hurried back to the area of the bivouac.

When he arrived it didn't take him long to discover the figure of Chelmsford, still pacing, still peering forward into the blackness. Norris-Newman sensed that it was no longer inappropriate to approach the General. He did so, and Chelmsford paused in his pacing to look at the reporter with mild curiosity, and with none of his usual antagonism.

'Excuse me, my Lord. Something I must convey to you ... I walked a little way along the track to Rorke's Drift....'

Chelmsford waited impassively for the reporter to finish what he was saying. Evidently Creaiock had become aware that his senior was being accosted by the reporter, and he skirmished forward defensively in case his services were required.

Noggs continued his speech, 'The rise in the ground prevents you seeing from here, sir, but the sky above Rorke's Drift, just at the horizon, is red with fire.... I would venture to say they were under attack.'

Chelmsford simply stared at him. From the high slope of Isandhlwana came the eerie distant drunken singing again, and there were laughs and shouts that were unquestionably Zulu. Again a single rifle shot cracked out and echoed between the hills. Crealock spoke, his voice hoarse with the tiredness of the late night.

'Your orders, My Lord?' He waited but there was no reply for him either, so he went on, 'Do we move back to the Drift, My Lord?'

Now Chelmsford turned on him sharply and spoke with a sudden harshness. 'I repeat my orders, Crealock: do you understand, we do not move until first light. Before first light – hold until then! Those are my orders.'

Crealock assented with a nod of his head, uncomfortably, saluted and then moved away.

Noggs felt that he knew how to provoke conversation with Chelmsford. He would give the man a lead and see where he would take it, and accordingly he said, 'I have taken the occasion to walk a distance forward into the camp. If you will permit me, sir, may I say that I would deduce from the disposition of the bodies of the Basutos under Colonel Durnford's command.... It seems also that he was joined by a company of Redcoats at the very end....' His voice tailed off at the sight of the curious evolution of expression on Chelmsford's face. The Lord General was staring at the reporter, not as if he were a talking human being, but as if to some instrument which could somehow record words. He wanted Noggs to record and remember what he was saying. He wanted Noggs to know that whatever he would say in the future, and however he would say it, in this moment he would speak an absolute truth.

'We have spoken of Durnford's judgement in battle. We have spoken of his tendency to act impulsively and without due and prior consideration of consequences. This time his stupidity has cost me my career – I stare on ruin. That man, without malice and, I daresay, with considerable aplomb and with the courage that you have frequently noted, has consigned me, his commander, to ruin. I will spend the rest of my life decorating social functions....!'

He paused for a long time, while Noggs absorbed the full meaning of what had been said. Then Chelmsford raised his eyes to the mass of black mountain that would for a long time mark the enormous graveyard beneath it. He continued to speak as if he were addressing a tribunal, or standing in the House of Lords and accounting for himself for what happened.

'... when I ordered Colonel Durnford to the support of Colonel Pulleine,' he said with almost formal rigidity, 'I refrained deliberately from sending any fresh instruction which might only have confused an already confused situation....' He went on in the same tone of voice, with enormous precision detailing how Colonel Durnford lost the battle of Isandhiwana. He did not fault the man for lack of courage, for ability to lead, for resourcefulness – only for the one absolute, that he had neglected to follow the orders which would have secured the encampment from its defeat. Its terrible, total defeat.

32

Who precisely brought the news to Pietermaritzburg cannot be known, but it probably first arrived as a rumour, which was disbelieved, regarded as wholly untenable, probably carried by some of the Native Corps who had broken away, deserted and escaped across the rapids of the Buffalo in Fugitive's Ravine before the Zulus closed that avenue. Even word-of-mouth news carried by men on well-prodded horses wouldn't have arrived until the second day after the debacle, and some of the white mounted survivors didn't reach Pietermaritzburg to give more reliable confirmation until two full nights after the event, that is, on Thursday, 24 January 1879. The preceding rumours had already created some sense of panic, but probably more incredulity. Verification, however, was to increase. The following morning the correspondent of the *Standard*, Noggs, arrived, and the full scope of the slaughter became known. Not only were the Imperial companies and their officers lost, but also several hundred European volunteers – sons of the colonists of Natal, many from Pietermaritzburg itself, their own.

The grief of the personal loss touched all, but the knowledge that the community had been left defenceless by the failure of the Imperial troops was harbinger of terror. The full triumph of the Zulu could be consummated at any moment. Moving with their known, unmatchable swiftness they could come in their ravening thousands, into the unprotected heart of the royal colony.

The simplest calculation showed that the attack was at hand, and indeed, overdue. Barricades were thrown around the principal buildings, loopholes were made in walls of churches and places of business, and civilians were supplied with weapons and ammunition.

The roads entering the capital from its inland side started to fill with refugees fleeing from the interior, their panic heightened by the sight of the crude preparations for defence already taking place in this city which they had presumed to be their refuge. Wagons were filled with personal possessions, but in some cases whole families arrived walking, bearing what they could, children and oldsters together. The new arrivals were harrassed with questions: Had they seen any invaders? What was the news from the disaster area? And when, amongst them, some of the refugee soldiers began to appear, each became a target of more probing questions, indeed harangues about why *they* survived when so many others had died? At the other end of the town another refugee line out of Pietermaritzburg to the coast had already started. But these too would find when they reached Durban at the sea that there was not a person in all of Natal who didn't share the alarm, or who didn't view the ocean's edge as yet a further barrier to escape. The vision of the *Impis* of Cetshwayo fulfilling their mission of destruction and revenge, when earlier it had been contemplated only as a possibility, and against which a sturdy defence could be mounted, had gripped the imagination of the whole of the Royal Colony of Natal. But in Pietermaritzburg it had become imminent reality. Anxious crowds milled around the High Commissioner's mansion day and night, kept from invading the actual grounds only by armed guards. Further news and reliable information were at a premium. And Sir Henry Bartle Frere was himself still seeking enough detail to issue a placatory statement that could quell the passions of fear that immobilized his capital.

Lord Chelmsford and his escort rode in four days after the battle, and it was immediately learned that he had called for a Court of Inquiry to gather and analyse evidence that would determine the reasons for the loss of the camp. Frere agreed with His Lordship that it might be a good idea that they meet for an advance review of such testimony as might be given to the tribunal, and also to evaluate events. The High Commissioner agreed that this meeting take place informally, but immediately, that is, on the very night of Chelmsford's arrival.

Lieutenant Harford, who since his show of resistance to His Lordship had found himself in somewhat more favour than otherwise, had been sent to collect CSM Simeon Kambula from the newly established capital HQ. Kambula, who as one of the few men who had actually participated in the battle and escaped was sought for interview at the Governor's mansion that evening. They rode together through the densely packed crowds, skirting the barricades, and pushing themselves through the refugee lines until they were forced to dismount and walk their horses through the crowds to the entrance of the mansion. They were admitted by the Redcoat sentries, but none the less had to push their way through still others whose business was considered valid enough to have been granted admission, even thus far, and who were crowding the verandah of the mansion. The two soldiers were directed along the covered porch to the guarded entrance of the morning room, through the windows of which they could see Lord Chelmsford, Frere, Crealock and other members of the senior officer staff listening to His Lordship speak. The guards at the door, expecting them, admitted them forthwith. They eased themselves into the room, their presence noted only with glances as the others present, seated, listened to what His Lordship was saying.

'... Colonel Durnford, hearing my orders to Colonel Pulleine, would know that he must obey them exactly as

274

if they had been given to Colonel Durnford himself, directly....' Chelmsford's glance flicked briefly to the new entrants, but he continued speaking. '... none the less, it was evident from the disposition of their slain bodies that Colonel Durnford had taken the majority of his command away from the encampment, not to defend against the enemy, as I had ordered, *but to engage it*, an action which had every appearance of a military adventure, at odds with the clearest orders to the contrary.'

Chelmsford paused. He was looking past Harford and Kambula who were standing awkwardly just inside the door that led from the morning room. Outside on the verandah had appeared the gaunt, purple-robed figure of Bishop Colenso, accompanied by his daughter Fanny. Others in the room followed the glance of His Lordship and even young Harford assayed a glance backward as the loud and demanding voice of the Bishop of Natal was heard through the glass. It was clear that he was being forcibly prevented from making an entrance into the morning room, and that the commotion that he and his daughter were making was creating a considerable disturbance. The fact that the *Impis* of Cetshwayo had still not appeared on this side of the Buffalo River, even these four days from their overwhelming victory, had given substance to the Bishop of Natal's contention that invasion had *not* been planned by the Zulus. And the name of 'Colonel Durnford' could be detected in the shrill and angry interpolations from Miss Colenso.

The guards were, however, firm in their restraint. Chelmsford returned his attention to the matters taking place inside the room. He and Frere exchanged momentary glances, and Frere nodded that they continue and ignore the exterior disturbance which was already subsiding in view of the force with which it was being restrained.

'I believe we should take this opportunity,' said Chelmsford to Crealock alongside him, 'to question the

Sergeant-Major and to permit him to return to his command as soon as convenient.' Chelmsford had, on arrival, re-established his HQ – less a batallion or two – on the Pietermaritzburg site from which they had departed for glorious invasion only days before.

Crealock nodded and cleared his throat. Kambula stood rigidly erect, conscious of the fact that he was in the presence of very senior officers. His personal handsomeness and the excellence of his outfitting, which miraculously had been maintained at a high level throughout the action, gave him a military bearing which impressed his audience, and reduced considerably their usual condescension to their black-skinned colleagues. Crealock adjusted his iron-rimmed glasses, glanced down at a paper and, without looking at Kambula, cleared his throat again, saying 'Sergeant, you and members of your troop, alone of Colonel Durnford's command, survived the battle of Isandhlwana, so to speak. . . .'

Kambula stood at the strictest of attention, not knowing how this proclamation from Colonel Crealock was going to end, but none the less restraining himself from protesting, as he felt impelled to do, that he had left the battlefield only under direct orders from Colonel Durnford. Nor was that the end of his participation in the battle. He had lined the Edendale contingent of the Sikali Horse on the far side of the raging Buffalo in Fugitive's Ravine, having made that bank under the greatest of hazards, and kept them actively defending the crossing until it was impossible to carry out that task any longer. Nor did he feel in his deepest self that he should be required to defend what he and his men had done before this particular group of non-combatants. If they wanted his *opinion*, he would say that he wasn't satisfied at all with the wisdom which had led to the departure from the camp prior to the battle, leaving such wide and unmangeable gaps in its defences. And he believed that there had been insufficient scouting of the Nqutu plateau, from whence the main Zulu attack ultimately generated. Had his own men not been restricted in the area of their search?

And he had other grievances, too, to pin on some of these who questioned him here, although he knew not yet why he was being questioned. Kambula had been raised by his father Elijah at the mission station at Edendale, raised as a Christian, and educated in the ways of the colonists. He believed that he and his men, who were raised and trained as he was at the mission, had long ago earned full membership into the society which had modelled their behaviour and beliefs. He knew that the white Christians outside of the mission itself did not share this view, not most of them at any rate, but he didn't mind the burden of having to prove his point from time to time. He and his kind were late entrants to modern society, he admitted, and he accepted that in some ways he had still to earn its acceptance, and to prove his ability to participate in it on an equal footing, to be judged on equal intrinsic abilities. He didn't say that this was a just demand from that society, but he accepted it.

Certainly, by the standards which he had been taught to accept, he and his riders were several steps upward on the ladder, well above the Natal Kaffirs and even of the Natal Native Corps. He yielded to no man or group of men in matters or religious devotion to the white God Jesus Christ, who was, he believed intensely, to be the God of all men. But when, *en route* to the battle at Isandhlwana, he carried a message of complaint from his own men, who required further recognition of their equality with the white troops beyond Colonel Durnford's issuing them Martini-Henry rifles, his requests that they not share the kitchens and inferior diet of the other native troops was rejected. It had been wrong that he was turned down in this request. The foolishness that inspired the rejection was the same kind of foolishness that compounded all the oversights and mistakes which

277

he felt had led to the ignominious defeat. At least the Zulus proved that blackness of skin was not an indicator of inferiority at war. The discipline which had been inculcated in him, and the knowledge that there were fine men amongst white people who accepted his equality and the equality of his other riders – yes, there was even that fine young officer Vereker as well as Colonel Durnford, dead but remembered with passion, whom he could number among these – made it possible for him to accept the rebuffs and crude attitudes which so often stung his towering pride. These high placed men examining him had limited right to judge Colonel Durnford, or himself.

But, of course, he spoke none of this as Crealock continued with what he was saying; indeed it all occured in his mind as an instantaneous blur of passion that arose from having reviewed these matters many times before. He knew where his loyalties lay, and why, and why they would continue to do so. That some of these men did not deserve them was not an issue to him, at this time. And he would give them their due for their grand station even if, in this case, it was not supported by achievement.

Crealock was saying, '... our evidence, which is deduced from the disposition of the casualties on the portion of the battlefield where we were able in the short time to observe it, was that Colonel Durnford rode eastwards from the encampment, that is, eastward and curving up northward toward the edge of the Nqutu plateau, taking his units as much as four miles from the centre of the camp. We understand from other inquiries that you were a witness to this departure....'

Kambula waited. He hadn't been asked a direct question as yet, but after a moment he decided that the upward inflection on the end of Crealock's sentence was indeed a proper inquiry. Kambula nodded his head slightly, maintaining his erectness and said, 'Yes, sir, Colonel Durnford did that.' Now Chelmsford intruded, cocking one of his combed-out, white-tipped eyebrows, 'Did you ride out with him, Sergeant?'

Kambula shook his head negatively, 'No, sir, he asked me to stay behind, and stay with the young Lieutenant and Colonel Pulleine.... The reason Colonel Durnford went up...'

Crealock cut in quickly, and speaking very precisely. 'We are asking you the question as to whether or not you saw him leave the camp. In fact, we are asking if you saw him vanish from sight with his column. Away?'

Kambula immediately realized the question of the distance was urgent. That is, it was urgent for the purpose of this inquiry. He also knew that Durnford did not believe that he was riding at a distance so great that he could not return rapidly should that requirement arise, as indeed it actually had. The fact that Durnford's Basutos were well deployed on horses and could return, carrying out defensive action as far as was needed back to the camp centre if required, was the tactically important fact. Kambula felt that the point in proceedings had been reached where this needed saying. Yet, he had been asked a specific question by Colonel Crealock and he had to answer it in the terms in which it was asked. He tried to phrase his words carefully, but his command of speech under these pressures was not what he wished it to be.

'... well ... yes ... he done that but ... because he know, he knew that if the Zulu were out there, they could attack....'

Crealock's intrusion was even sharper now. 'Gentlemen, I take it that we are not interested in the Sergeant's opinion, or in anyone's opinion, as to why Colonel Durnford flaunted clear and specific orders. The Sergeant has clearly testified to the salient fact, that the senior commanding officer at Isandhlwana, when attack was believed to be imminent, in fact when it *was* imminent, left his post....'

Kambula's outrage broke through in an instant, 'That

279

man, that Colonel did not run away, sir. I saw that man die. . . .'

'Sergeant!' Crealock's interjection bore all the authority of his position, and Kambula reacted to it with conditioned exactness. His heels clicked together, his head snapped back, and his body froze to full attention. 'Sir!'

Chelmsford surveyed the towering black man, and radiated kindness and sympathy and understanding. His voice was low and friendly and approving. 'Thank you most kindly for your information, Sergeant. That is all we require at the moment. . . .'

Kambula remained stony-faced for a brief moment, then saluted, pivoted and proceeded to the exit. Harford held the door open for him as he departed. When he was gone the officers all relaxed slightly. The High Commissioner, Sir Bartle Frere, with his cigar, sucked on it thoughtfully and cleared his throat, 'Ahem . . . Frederic. . . .'

Chelmsford waited for what Frere had to say. Chelmsford knew quite well by now what his own course of action would be. He had only conducted this war, however disastrous it was so far, but it was Frere who had required it, created it. Somehow he felt Sir Bartle's opportunity for redress would be less than his own. This war might still have other battles in it, battles Chelmsford could win with more men and more time to plan on the basis of lessons so cruelly learned. But Frere had his own specific concerns, very great ones, and what he was saying now was giving air to them: ' . . . from the viewpoint . . . that is, of holding a tribunal. That is, one which will be given proper credence in London, I am saying, do you think it would not be preferable to have eyewitness testimony from persons of . . . say, officer rank. . . .?'

Chelmsford turned and looked bitterly at this man who had asked for a war, but had proved himself less able to provide all the sinews and forces that war required and would require. It was at this moment that Frere realized

Chelmsford was no longer his ally.

Very carefully, His Lordship enunciated his reply. 'Sir, we do not have such choice...!' Frere visibly recoiled from the intensity of the glare with which Chelmsford transfixed him, as he went on, 'To this moment we have counted less than *forty* survivors of near two thousand men – and you ask me to select them by *rank*?'

Outside, Sergeant Kambula thrust his way through the crowd, descended the steps from the verandah to find his mount and return to the new HQ His Lordship had established back here in Pietermaritzburg, eighty miles south from the crossing at the Buffalo River.

Many of the Zulu *Impis* which fought at Isandhlwana were disbanded now and returning to their *Kraals*, but the King's own *Impis* were returning to the royal *Kraal* at Ulundi, even as Harford stood just inside the doorway of the morning room of the High Commissioner's mansion listening to the officers discuss what had happened at Isandhlwana. The word was repeated and repeated: Isandhlwana. I-sand-hl-wana. . . . How did it happen – at Isandhlwana? What went wrong – at Isandhlwana? Who was to blame – at Isandhlwana? What will future history tell – of Isandhlwana? Which was to say, what would *their* history tell of what happened on that day? It would tell of errors and mistakes and poor decision, as to who was to blame and who was not, or what was to blame and what was not; but would it speak of the will, of the discipline and the organization, of the strength, of the bravery, of the national devotion that had made it possible for bare human flesh armed only with shield and spear to stand up against the continuous, withering blast of metal and gun-powder from the armoury of a mighty force of the mightiest Empire the world had then yet known?

On the rocky slopes beneath Isandhlwana the silent

devastation and countless remnants of death on the ruined terrain would remain for a long time. Eighty miles to the north the marching song of the King's own *Impis* grew louder, drew closer. They had departed on a night and were returning once again just before the break of another Zulu dawn. They were returning to hear from their Great King how they, in their courage, had resisted the great force from the north, so sure of its civilized ability, so certain it could crush the custom and nation-hood of the people it did not know – but instead, was crushed itself!

And it was to be many thousands of miles to that north that a most eminent man who lived there, Disraeli, Chief *inDuna* of the white Queen of the whole world, would put a perplexing question to the consuls of that Great Queen: '*Who*, tell me *who*, are these Zulus? Who are these remarkable people, who defeat our Generals, who convert our Bishops, and who on this day have put an end to a great dynasty?'

The army returned to the royal *Kraal* with exquisite timing, just as night ended and dawn redness tinted the eastern horizon. The marching song chanted by the returning victorious men throbbed with exultant power. To match the magnificence of that sound required the bursting brilliance of the sun that now thundered over the horizon on this memorable dawn in Zulu history, which celebrated the victory at Isandhlwana. The King of the Zulus emerged to welcome the return of his armies. The victors raised their shields and their *assegais* in massed salute to their true King.

'*Zu! Zu ... u ... u! Bay–ed–e!*' One voice, one people.

These: these are the Zulus, Mr Disraeli.

Appendix

Mlaba-Laba is played with great skill and rapidity by its Zulu practitioners.

In the more primitive areas, a diagram of three nestled squares is scratched on to the earth; playing pieces consist of stones or pebbles of opposing colours. The pieces are called 'cattle' (such as 'the brown cattle' and 'the black cattle'). In urban areas, although the pieces are still called 'cattle', the board is very often chalked on any convenient carton top, and the playing pieces very often soft-drink bottle tops.

Boards are of several designs depending on the regions where *Mlaba-laba* is played. The one introduced here is the most advanced and leads to the most interesting and strategically precise play. The game is structurally the same as a medieval European game called Nine-man Morris. Presumably it was introduced into Central East Africa several centuries ago by the first European missionaries; then, within the tribes, evolved into this challenging, more rigorous, and more complex Zulu twelve-man version. As a devotee of games and recreational maths, I determined to learn the game from the tribal Zulu cast employed on my film *Zulu*. Soon the European cast followed suit, and its popularity on the location set suggested to me that the many readers of *Zulu Dawn* might find it worth learning.

Two players each start with a set of twelve playing pieces in the form of counters of two opposing colours.

The object of the game is to capture all of the opponents counters. There are three phases of play and capture.

Capture Phase 1 ('Placing out')

Pieces are played out alternately by the two opponents, each piece being placed at one or another point on the board, designated by the intersection of any two lines. There are twenty-five such possible placings, numbered on the diagram, 1 to 25.

Each player attempts to place a piece on his turn so that he can get three in one line, as in noughts and Crosses (i.e. Tic Tac Toe), while at the same time, if possible, preventing the opposing player from doing so. Each time a player manages to get three counters in a line he is entitled to remove any one of his opponent's pieces. (See note below and diagram for exception.)*

Capture Phase 2 ('Sliding')

At the end of the 'placing out' phase, depending on the number of captures, one or more points are unoccupied by pieces. Play is continued by sliding a counter from one point of intersection to any unoccupied adjacent point, connected by a line.

The intent of this 'sliding' play is the same as the preceding, that is, still to get three of one's own counters on to one line, or to block the opponent from doing so. Each time three-in-a-line is achieved, any one of the opponent's pieces can be removed. By this procedure, the board is gradually emptied of the pieces, either to the

* The exception noted above is as follows:
All counters placed three-in-a-line are hits, except those which originate at the centre points of the second concentric square, that is, Points 5, 15, 11 and 21. Thus the following combinations are *not* hits:

5, 8, 13	15, 14, 13
21, 18, 13	11, 12, 13

All other combinations of three-in-a-line are hits.

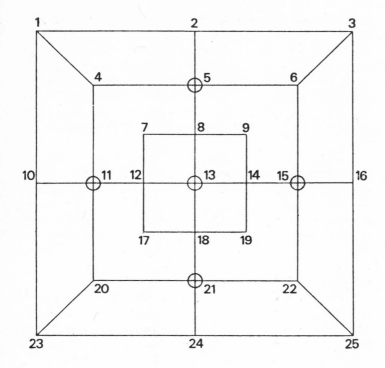

point when one of the players concedes defeat, or until his pieces are reduced below the number of three (so that it is no longer possible for this player to continue to arrange his own pieces in three-piece winning combinations).

Capture Phase 3 ('Jumping')
Although the losing player may resign when it is obvious that his pieces are going at a much faster rate than his opponent's, he has one more course of play when his pieces are reduced to exactly three. When he has only

three pieces left, he is no longer restricted in movement to sliding a piece from one point to an adjacent one. He is now permitted on his move to hop a chosen one of his pieces from one intersecting point to any other, either to block his opponent or to complete a three-in-a-line for himself to implement another capture. (Naturally, when a player 'captures', the selection for capture is a piece which will weaken the chances of the opponent to develop a three-in-a-row winning position.)

A successful placing or a sliding of three counters on to one line (that is, three linearly connected points) is called a 'hit'. Every time a player makes a hit, he is allowed to remove any one of his opponent's pieces from the board. If there is a possible hit position that could be achieved on a player's move, he must make it when his opponent points it out, but if there are several 'hit' positions possible, then the player himself decides which one he wishes to take.

It is also possible to make a 'double hit', that is, form two three-in-a-rows by the single placement of a piece. The reward for a double hit is the removal of any two of the opponent's pieces. For example, per diagram, if a player has his pieces at positions 10, 11, 13 and 14, and if he also has a piece at 7 or 17, then, on his play, by sliding 7 or 17 into vacant position 12, the one piece simultaneously completes two hits: that is, 10, 11, 12 and 12, 13, 14. Another example of this would be if a player has his counters on positions 10 and 23, and also on 2 and 3, and at 4. If position 1 is not occupied, then he can move from 4 to 1, and the counter moved on to 1 simultaneously completes hit 1, 2, 3 and hit 1, 10, 23.

Strategy note

The above are the rules of the game, and make no attempt to instruct in the tactical and strategical considerations of play. However, it should be noted that the first part of play, that is the part concerned with the placing down of the pieces until each player exhausts the twelve he starts with, should be primarily concerned with the placing of pieces in position where mobility for making hits during the second or sliding phase of the play is the main consideration. Although it is possible to win pieces during the initial placing-down phase, one must be careful, in so doing, not to cramp one's position for later successful play. If no hits are made during the placing-down phase, there is one point unoccupied, which forces the first 'slide' move of the Starting Player. Starting alternates at each game.